VOW

BETHANY-KRIS

Published by Bethany-Kris

www.bethanykris.com

ISBN 13: 978-1-988197-74-6

Cover Art © Mignon Mykel

Editor: Elizabeth Peters

For anyone who has ever loved the right person for the wrong reasons.

CONTENTS

ONE

The cold grip of a late February wind clutched at Andino Marcello's throat even as he tried to flip the collar of his jacket higher to keep it out. Nothing worked—nothing ever worked to keep out that kind of cold in this fucking city.

They still had another month of this shit to go, too. Winter wasn't going to let up until it had ravaged New York with one cold blast after another, even if it was the last day of February.

Usually, he didn't mind the weather as much as he did this winter. He could ignore the cold, and get lost in work, or something else. This year was not shaking out to be quite the same. So was his fucking life lately.

A giant dumpster fire.

A lot like his mood, too.

Andino grunted at the enforcer who held open the restaurant door for him to slip inside. On another day, he might have given the man a nod or thanks. Not to-fucking-day. All he wanted to do was get this goddamn meeting over with, and go home.

He wasn't even planning to *work*.

Andino was acutely aware of the eyes that fell on him as he entered the business. Men from his family, and men from another neighboring New York Cosa Nostra. Although, where the Marcello family *hated* the Calabrese organization, they tolerated the Donati crime family.

It probably helped that Dante had finally accepted the fact his daughter was going to be with Cross Donati whether her father liked it or not. Andino gave it less than six months before his cousin married the cocky Donati fucker—everybody got to have their happily ever after.

Except him, apparently.

He was still alone.

Haven still wasn't his.

And all for what?

Andino glanced around the restaurant, and the men waiting on him to come in and take a seat, so they could begin this meeting. Apparently, he gave her up for this.

This life.

His family.

The legacy.

Duty.

1

He didn't want to be bitter about it, but that was difficult. Harder than he expected it to be, frankly. The problem was—nobody gave a damn, and he couldn't find it in himself to let them know how he felt.

Not yet, anyway.

No man in this life wanted the people around him to know he was struggling emotionally, or with something silly like *love*. Or the loss of it, for that matter. It was a simple weakness for someone to pick at, or hone in on. Andino wasn't in the business of showcasing his weaknesses like badges of honor for someone else to use as fucking target practice. He was still intended to be the boss.

The boss couldn't *be* emotional.

Or so he was told.

Besides, they had bigger problems to deal with at the moment than his feelings. Too many issues to name. Every single one started and ended with the fucking Calabrese family, and the fact John had killed their boss.

Surprise, surprise.

It was a mess waiting to happen.

Why was anyone *shocked?*

"The roads are terrible," Andino grumbled under his breath as he took a seat beside his quiet uncle. Dante hadn't *asked*, but the quirking of the man's eyebrow was enough for him to silently ask, *Where the fuck were you?* "The storm picked up."

"Should make for a fun drive home," his father said across the table.

Andino shrugged. "That's February for you."

He didn't miss the look that passed between his father, and his other uncle, Lucian. Andino had been in a mood for days, and it wasn't about to change anytime soon. He couldn't fucking shake it, no matter how hard he tried. He was grateful that, for the most part, the men around him who knew him well chose not to ask.

That made shit easier.

On him, at least.

"Shall we get started?" Dante asked.

Andino nodded. "Yeah, let's start."

"We need to figure out a way to handle the Calabrese," his uncle said. "We *all* need to come to some agreement that will clean up this mess— preferably in a peaceful manner."

"Their violence is escalating," Giovanni added.

"They're directly targeting Capos, or their crews," Lucian said.

Andino sighed, and scrubbed a hand down his face. They all offered this information as though he didn't know it to begin with. Like he'd had his fucking head shoved under sand for the last while, and pretended that he didn't know what was happening out on the streets.

He was the *underboss*.

He got the calls.

He handled the Capos.

"I know what's going on," Andino snapped. "And I'm aware that we need to figure something out to handle the fucking Calabrese."

Dante shifted in his chair, and said, "Other people in this restaurant are *not* aware." With that statement, his uncle gave a nod in Cross Donati's direction, adding, "Or at least, he doesn't know the latest details. He's the boss of another organization in this city—this growing war between our family and the Calabrese could indirectly disrupt his business and organization."

Shit.

Yeah.

Andino needed to get back on his game, and fast. "All attempts to reach out to the Calabrese, and settle this by less violent means has been shut down at every turn."

"Then, what do they want?" Cross Donati asked.

Wasn't it obvious?

"A problem."

Dante chuckled dryly. "That, and to one-up the Marcellos. They've always had a hard nut for that, yeah?"

A quiet agreement passed over the men sitting at various tables. There were more Marcello men in the business than Donati men. It looked like Cross had only brought a select few to the meeting.

"Do you have an opinion?" Dante asked the man. "Anything you would like to add?"

Cross folded his arms over his chest, and relaxed in the chair. "Attention in this business is always a bad thing when it comes to officials, and I can't say that I like how many times I've seen the New York crime families' names on *Breaking News* banners lately."

Andino cringed.

That was accurate.

"Us either," Dante agreed.

"Continuing this feud with the Calabrese will only bring more attention our way," Cross said. "And I say *our way* because all three of the New York families know that when one organization gets attention, the other two get the same gift just by definition of association. A lot has happened over the last year—none of us, or our organizations—can afford that kind of attention right now. We need to keep the officials *out*. At least, that's my take."

Dante didn't disagree.

Andino couldn't, either.

"The problem with that," Lucian murmured, staring straight at Dante as though no one else in the business mattered to him, "is that it means we

3

somehow *bend* to the Calabrese, or whatever demands they decide to make when they get around to it. Is that what the Marcellos are willing to do, now—cower to a family that killed my blood?"

Dante didn't even blink. "If it means keeping our family safe, then yes."

"And what if that leaves us exposed—weak?"

"It won't. It makes us smart."

Lucian let out a dark noise under his breath, but turned to stone when he stared out the window to his left without another opinion to share. Andino sympathized with both of his uncles' positions. He knew why Lucian felt the way he did, and why Dante—as the boss, and the one who needed to make the hardest choices to keep everyone safe even when pride was a factor—refused to give his brother what the man wanted.

Nothing in this life was easy.

It couldn't be.

"We have to protect our family," Dante repeated.

Only this time, he said it to Andino.

Like he needed another reminder.

Look at all he sacrificed for his family.

For his *duty*.

He didn't need to be reminded.

• • •

Andino's Lexus crawled behind the heavy traffic. Brooklyn was good for that—like almost every *other* part of the fucking city. That wasn't really what had him on edge, though. This small part of Brooklyn was the only area where the Calabrese organization had territory. They kept a stronghold over it for years.

Which was, sort of, Andino's whole point of being there today.

Just because one family held territory in the city didn't mean other families couldn't … work, so to speak, in the same area. Or rather, own legitimate businesses. A Marcello Capo had long since owned a club down in this part of Brooklyn. The man had never before had problems with the Calabrese, or the fact he was in their territory.

Until now.

The Capo assured he could—and would—handle it, but Andino decided to take a trip his way to check in, and make sure the man was fine. That was the job of the family underboss, after all. That, and Andino did actually like this particular Capo.

Still, being in this part of Brooklyn just had a tendency to make Andino nervous for a multitude of reasons, what with the Calabrese being in a fit like they were. Those bastards didn't even think before they jumped the gun, lately.

Violence was all too common.

Andino's eyes swept the streets as he passed, and the businesses he knew for a fact belonged, or were attached in some way, to the Calabrese family. Sure, they wouldn't be able to see through the dark tint of his Lexus' windows, but that didn't mean anything. His car was well known, and so was the fucking driver inside. No one but him drove his car.

He didn't trust the Calabrese bastards with an *inch*.

Not now.

So yeah, he kept his eyes peeled even as he drove through streets that, only a few months ago, he wouldn't have thought twice about getting out to walk down. Things were not the same, now, and shit had most definitely changed.

Not for the better, either.

Business was dangerous.

Andino reached over, and pressed the button on the stereo, saying, "Call Terrance."

The call rang through the speakers, and the Capo in question picked up on the third ring. "*Ciao.*"

"I'm making a drive over to the club. You around today?"

Terrance sighed, and Andino heard the rustle of papers in the background of the call. "Define busy, boss."

"Too busy to have a chat with me?"

Andino already knew the answer to the question before the Capo even answered. It was simple, and the rules of their life were clear. When the actual boss of the organization wasn't out and about, the underboss was the next best thing.

No shunning a boss.

It wouldn't end well.

"I'll make time," Terrance said. "What did you want to discuss?"

"The Calabrese."

The man made a disgruntled sound. "Listen, it's nothing I can't handle."

"So, they *have* been overstepping their bounds with your place."

"Is it overstepping if I'm in their territory?"

"Are you causing problems?" Andino returned.

Terrance chuckled dryly. "Do I ever cause problems?"

"No."

And he didn't.

Terrance was good like that. All he really gave a fuck about was making money, and paying his tribute every month on time. He cared about bottom lines, and profits. He made sure to keep his head down, and his business as clean as possible.

If there was ever a Marcello Capo that Andino figured the Calabrese would leave the fuck alone, it should be Terrance. The man wasn't even *trying* to get in between the problems happening amongst the two organizations. Sure, his loyalties lied solely with the Marcellos, but he wasn't going out of his way to antagonize, either.

Andino needed to get this shit figured out, and soon.

"I'll be over in about twenty minutes," Andino said, "and we'll figure it out. Traffic is a bitch today."

"It always is in Brooklyn. See you when you get here, then."

A quick goodbye later, and Andino hung up the call. Beside him in the passenger seat, Snaps chuffed as he sat up a little straighter, and glanced out the window. Usually the pup liked sprawling out across the back seat when they drove, but today, he wanted to be up front. Andino didn't care either way—whatever made the dog happy.

"What are you getting excited for over there?" he asked.

Snaps passed him a look with those big, dark eyes of his. His stubby tail wagged as the traffic crawled along. For no particular reason, the dog became progressively more excited the more the traffic moved.

"What?" Andino asked.

Snaps let out one loud *woof.* He turned his big body in one circle on the seat—although with his size, he slipped on his paws a bit—and stared out the window. His head kept moving back between looking out the window, and staring at Andino.

It took Andino a second to realize where exactly they were, and what had his dog so excited. He didn't know if every dog was like his, or if Snaps was just a special fucking case, but the animal always seemed to recognize wherever they were going when they drove. He remembered who lived or stayed where, and if those were people he liked.

Snaps barked again as they came to a red light, and Andino pulled to a stop. He hadn't turned his blinker on to turn right, but he looked down that way anyway. He knew why Snaps was alerting, and what the dog was excited for.

It'd been a while since he came down this way.

Too long, maybe.

Just looking down that street made his fucking heart clench, and his chest became tighter with every breath. It physically hurt to look that way, and *wonder* ...

"We're not going to Haven's club," Andino muttered.

The light was still red.

Snaps still looked out the window, and when Andino refused to give his dog any attention, he actually put his paws up *and dragged them against the window.*

"*Snaps!*"

The dog just did it again.

Jesus.

"We've got no reason to go down there. The place isn't even open right now. Who knows if she's there? We're not going."

Andino wasn't sure if he was telling his dog these things, or *himself.* Seemed there was a part of him that needed those little details played on repeat, too. Like his goddamn heart.

Life truly was a bitch.

A mean one.

Snaps whined loudly when the light turned green. Andino *fully intended* to just drive straight, but his body was suddenly on autopilot. He was cutting the wheel to the right, and cutting off the guy next to him before he could think better of it. He was a good few car lengths down the street that Haven's club was on before he even realized what he was doing.

He wouldn't stop.

He wasn't going to see her.

He'd made his choice—he'd done what was asked of him because he didn't have a choice, and this was what had needed to happen. And really, keeping her out of his life … away from the mess that had become his fucking life, was the better choice. This was better for *her.*

Even if it fucking sucked for him.

That's what mattered.

That didn't mean she never crossed his mind. Because she did. Every single fucking day, and every night before he laid his head down on the pillow to go to bed. Haven was the first and last thing on his mind, no matter what he tried to do *not* to think about her.

It was like he couldn't control it, or something.

It was just as much torture to him as it was *bliss.* He still loved her— that was never going to change, regardless of the rest.

Of that, he was most sure.

Too bad it didn't make a difference.

Andino slowed to a crawl on the quiet street as he neared Haven's club. This road wasn't as busy as the main road, and he barely even noticed the cars passing him on the other side as he drove by *Safe Haven.*

The club was quiet—dark windows, and signs turned off. There were a few cars in the parking lot closest to the building. Likely the managers, but not Haven's car that she rarely ever used anyway. She had always seemed to prefer cabs, anyway.

A *big* part of him wanted to stop.

Just to see.

Just to *check*.

He had to force himself to keep driving. She wouldn't be happy if he showed up there, anyway. Andino had no doubt of that, and he didn't want to shove his way back into her life just to fucking hurt her again.

Hadn't he hurt her enough?

Andino figured so.

Snaps all but clambered over the seats like he was a puppy on new legs again. He landed in Andino's lap with a heavy *thud*, and stuck his nose against the glass. That only made Andino feel even worse because the dog didn't understand. He couldn't explain it in a way that Snaps would comprehend that … Haven was gone.

At least, to them.

Snaps had been a bit of a distraction that forced Andino to hold the steering wheel tighter, and look out the windshield. Not so much so that he didn't notice the sign on the side of the club, though.

FOR SALE, it read.

Andino did a double-take just to see it again. To be sure he hadn't missed it, or read it wrong. He hadn't, apparently.

Safe Haven was up for sale.

Well, *fuck*.

• • •

Terrance threw back his fourth shot of whiskey since Andino had walked into the man's quiet club. The place wasn't open—not until well after dark, anyway—but this was where the Capo did the majority of his business. At least, in the daytime. Like a lot of them.

"And even your crew is getting shit?" Andino asked.

The Capo nodded, and set his glass down to the bar with a loud clink. "Yeah, 'cause this is where they come to check in, and shit. The Calabrese know who all of them are. Some of them were followed … nothing happened there. Just to scare 'em, I think."

"And the others?"

Terrance let out a sigh, and scrubbed a hand over his face. "Two Calabrese enforcers beat the hell out of the guy who looks after my guys on the streets. I guess they got in to a verbal thing on the corner, and they followed him home. That was the first real aggressive act. After that, they started showing up here."

Andino's brow lifted, and even he needed to take a drink for that one. *Damn*. It seemed like the Calabrese were really starting to grow a pair of balls. Then again, with their father dead, there was no one to hold the

Calabrese brothers in line, so to speak. Kev Calabrese had taken over for his father, as far as Andino knew … he'd always been a fucking shit.

Not that the younger brother, Darren, was much better.

"They just come here, take a seat, and make themselves known," Terrance said. "Flexing their fucking muscles, you know?"

"But it's uncomfortable."

And *rude*.

"Very uncomfortable," Terrance agreed. "I can't afford to be having official attention on my club. You know how much money and product I move through here. I've had to cut that down a bit since all this started up just in case an incident *does* happen, and the police get called in. I don't need the fucking cops digging through this club, and finding all the stuff I have hidden in the back rooms."

Yeah, none of them needed that.

The bigger problem was the fact now the Calabrese were starting to cause issues for *business*. Not just the Marcellos on the street, or in a personal way, but actual business. That meant money was being lost, and no man was going to take that lying down.

Certainly not Dante.

Nor Andino.

It needed to end.

"This will be fixed soon," Andino assured.

Terrance nodded, and reached for the whiskey bottle again. "Hope so—I'm too old for a fucking street war. Not sure I got it in me, you know, even if it is those goddamn snakes."

Andino chuckled, and smacked the man on the back as he stood from the barstool. "You're barely over forty. You're *fine*."

"Says you. This life ages you." Terrance passed Snaps, who'd been quietly watching them from beneath a table, a look. "Like dog years, or something."

Wasn't that the fucking truth?

"I'll pass all this along to Dante."

The Capo agreed, and that was that. Andino said his goodbyes, finished the last bit of his *one* glass of whiskey, and whistled for Snaps to follow him out of the club. Andino was no sooner out into the cold March air and had the club's front door closed behind him than the bullets started flying.

Andino didn't even see the color of the car because he didn't notice it coming.

Snaps was the one who took him to the ground as bullets peppered the red brick of the building behind him, and pinged off the metal door. Andino barely managed to catch himself what with Snaps' jaw clamped tightly around his fucking wrist.

9

The smart part of his brain that still seemed to work at a bad time remembered to cover his head, but the pain in his shoulder made the action torture. His arm screamed in pain, but he didn't dare lift his head.

The bullets kept flying.

His Lexus' alarm went off.

Glass shattered somewhere.

He didn't even wonder *who* had done this, or why they would target him. He bet those bastards knew he was around the second he drove onto their territory just like the Marcellos always knew when someone was in their areas.

Fucking Calabrese.

TWO

Haven Murphy's hardest lesson had finally been learned. Or, that was her feelings. It wasn't a lesson she had been willing to learn, or even wanted to, for that matter.

It just happened.

It just *was*.

She'd always thought that the things that didn't challenge her in life wouldn't change her for the better—it was the motto she had tried to live by for years. In a way, she still believed it to be true, but she also knew that those changes from all the challenges she faced weren't necessarily good, either.

Sometimes, they just hurt. Sometimes, they left tear stains on pillows. Sometimes, it left her empty.

And oh, so alone.

Haven was never more aware of that feeling than when she walked through her empty house. One of the few things she had held so close to heart because of the pride she felt for it. It was hers—she bought it, and kept it up. She lived and loved here. She had *grown* as a person here. And now, she was getting rid of it.

If only she could find a buyer.

She passed a stack of boxes that needed to be taped up in the hallway. Full of pictures she'd pulled down from the walls, and a few knickknacks that needed to be wrapped in paper before they too could be put in a storage container.

Who knew if she would get back to them?

Or *when?*

It wasn't like she really needed all this stuff for her move. So, instead of paying an arm and a leg to have it all sent to where she was going, she opted to put it all in storage for the time being. Or maybe that was just her way of thinking ... *there's still a chance you'll come back here someday.*

That's what her heart kept saying. Her mind screamed, *no way*. She was ready to go. Ready to leave.

New York could keep its fucking memories, and all the pain. She would be fine and happy to finally get rid of those tear-stained pillows, and restless nights. Maybe if she had a little more distance between her and New York, then her heart and memories would let go of all the things that weren't ever supposed to be hers in the first place.

Maybe it would let go of *him.*

Andino Marcello.

Haven sighed, and shook off the heavy feeling. The longer she stood there staring at those boxes, the worse her mood would get. She couldn't afford for that to happen—not right now, anyway.

She was still responsible.

Still *smart*.

This was all for the best.

The only things she hadn't packed up or taken apart when it came to furniture, were the things she still might need to use. Some dishes, her bed, and the kitchen set. Even her television had been taken to storage last week, along with all her books.

She had been hoping for a quick sale, really. The house was priced reasonably on the market, and it was in good shape. Not *too* old, all things considered. She'd done a hell of a lot of upgrades since she moved in, and brought it up to spec.

It should have sold quickly.

So far, there'd not been an offer.

The realtor came around the corner of the hallway, exiting from the kitchen. In his tailored suit with not a speck of dirt to be seen, and his hair slicked back, Haven thought the man seemed more suited to be sitting behind a desk somewhere.

She didn't *assume* it, though.

Not anymore.

Andino had taught her not to assume anything about anyone that she crossed paths with in her lifetime. Nothing good came from underestimating who or *what* someone was underneath their nice clothes, and charming smile.

All that meant was you wouldn't even see them coming for your heart, and you'd miss it entirely when they broke it to pieces except when you *felt* it.

And God knew ...

God knew Haven felt it all over now.

Funny how that worked.

That lesson she learned ... it'd been simple. One person could change your life, and not necessarily for the better. It only took one single soul to rip away yours, and keep it forever. One moment in time could put you on the same path as someone else, and there you would be, entirely ruined.

You didn't get to choose.

Love didn't work that way.

This was not the lesson Haven wanted to learn.

Not yet, anyway.

"You're still firm on the price?" the man asked.

Haven folded her arms over her chest. "Any less, and I'll be losing out. I'm not doing that."

"It'll sell quicker if you drop it even ten grand."

No, she needed the money.

She wasn't telling him that, though.

"The market is tough right now on starter homes, which you know—"

"Is basically what this is, yeah," Haven said. "I know, but that's my bottom line. It's the number I want, give or take a thousand."

The realtor nodded. "How's your mom, by the way?"

Haven hid the way the frown threatened to dance over her lips. She was doing pretty good with this whole holding herself together thing, even if the only thing she wanted to do was hide away from the rest of the world.

She was too strong for that shit.

Nothing was taking her down now.

"Good—started her first round of chemo last week," Haven said.

"Praying for her."

"Thanks."

She wished—*fuck*, she wished so badly—that her parents would have told her the truth about her mother's health when she had come to visit. Instead, they'd simply chosen to focus on the fact that Haven was there, and the time they spent together. They didn't think to mention to her at all that her mother had just gotten news only a few days before her arrival that the cancer had come back, and it was more aggressive than ever.

They didn't want Haven to move to Florida to help. They wanted her to keep living her life, and handling her own business. *It's your life, and your time*, they kept telling her. She didn't care about any of that. She had years yet to go; her mom might only have a few months if the chemo didn't work.

Nothing here mattered to Haven anymore. All it took was a single man to upend her entire fucking life, and remind her that she wasn't good enough for him to *choose her* ... and that told her all she needed to know, frankly.

She didn't need to be here at all.

She didn't care if she was.

Haven walked the realtor to the front door to say goodbye. The man plucked up a toy from the floor—a doll Haven must have missed in her effort to pick up things that had fallen to the wayside while she packed. It was one of those dolls that Maria loved the most with the big heads, funny colored hair, and huge eyes.

"You have a niece, or something?" the man asked. "I didn't think you had kids."

"I don't," Haven replied, taking the doll from the man. "It was my roommate's daughter's toy. She left it behind."

Like everything else in her life now, something else was gone, too.

Valeria and Maria.

Haven remembered the night she'd come home *vividly*, and her friend was gone. No note, no nothing. Valeria had taken only a few things, and left almost *everything* behind. Haven tried calling her friend's phone, but got no response.

Valeria had said once she might go, and she wouldn't say a thing. Haven accepted that was what happened because maybe Val felt it was time to move on, or she was scared that her past was going to catch up to her again.

Who knew?

Haven didn't.

Nobody thought to tell her.

Nobody thought to worry about her.

This was her fucking life now.

• • •

Jackson pushed off his seat on the bar the moment Haven came into the club for the meeting. She could already see how the girls who danced and served or worked behind the bar glanced her way with a wary stare—unsure of what was happening.

That was her fault, she supposed.

Haven hadn't really told them *anything*.

Maybe she hadn't been ready to.

And then, the realtor showed up at the club a couple of hours before opening a few days earlier, took pictures of the inside and outside, and slapped the *FOR SALE* sign on the front. There was no hiding what was going to happen. Her employees had questions, and Haven was here to try and answer them as best she could.

Without getting too personal.

Hopefully.

Nothing was ever that simple.

"Sorry I'm late," Haven said, walking across the floor. "Traffic was horrible."

Jackson nodded, and took the coat and purse Haven handed over before sitting the items on the bar top. "Everybody is here, and waiting. So, no worries."

Yeah.

No worries.

That was a fucking joke.

Haven didn't expect that her girls were going to be happy about the things she had to say, but she was prepared for their anger. That was something. Something was better than nothing at all.

Taking a seat on one of the barstools, Haven turned to face the waiting girls who had scattered themselves in various seats around the club. She didn't even bother to wait for anyone to ask her questions, she simply started talking.

Better to get it all out, then to try and explain while people asked questions, she supposed.

"As you may have noticed—or heard, if you weren't working that night—there was a realtor who came in to take pictures of the club, and I am sure many of you have noticed the sign out front. The club was put on the market the day after the realtor came here."

One of the girls opened her mouth to speak, but Haven lifted a hand to quiet her, saying, "Let me finish, please. Selling Safe Haven is the very last thing I ever wanted to do—this club is where I grew up, even if it did look a little bit different then than how it does now. Point is, I love this place, and it's as much my home as it is yours in ways. But that's the thing about life, right. We don't always get what we want, and sometimes, things are just out of our control."

Haven glanced down at her hands, but kept speaking. "I am *not* selling the club because it's failing. I am not selling it because I'm tired, or because I don't want it anymore. I am selling it because I have other *important* responsibilities to take care of, and I won't be here anymore to handle this business. And I don't want to manage it from afar—I don't want to hope that whoever I let manage the club doesn't run it to the ground with me still attached to it, regardless of how far away I am while it happens.

"My mother is sick," Haven said, refusing to go into more details in that regard, "and so, I need to be where I am needed. I know you may feel like I am leaving you all hanging, or that I don't care about what happens to you after I leave, but that's not the case. The details of the sale will be clear to the buyer—the club is to remain as it is, with the same name, and the same business. You will all still have employment as long as you continue to act like the employees *I* hired. Jackson will remain here, too, because this is what he loves doing. But beyond that, there is nothing more I can do. And I am sorry. Any questions?"

Haven waited a minute, and then two. The girls were quiet, but she expected that. She figured they were trying to absorb the information she gave them, and how they wanted to deal with it, or respond.

They were all adults.

Sure, this felt like a little family at times. She looked out for the girls, just like the security, and even Jackson. They looked out for her, too. This club was her happy place, in a way. And she hated to give it up ... but what choice did she have?

For her mom, she needed to go.

For *herself*, she needed time.

15

"I hope your mom gets well soon," one of the girls finally said.

Haven found the one in question, and smiled. "Yeah, me, too."

Slowly, the same sort of condolences trickled in. A few of the ladies had questions, and Haven tried to answer them all as best she could. The meeting lasted maybe an hour or so, and then once everyone was satisfied, she said her goodbyes.

Today was her day off.

One of the very few.

Every single time she left the club now, she got the strangest feeling in her chest. It was as though a heavy weight came to sit there, and make itself at home. Like her mind and body's way of reminding her over and over again that she was saying goodbye.

And soon, that goodbye would be permanent.

Unlike her house, she didn't expect Safe Haven to stay on the market long. Already, with only a few days being listed, she'd gotten three offers. All were lower than her sale price, but she knew what that meant. Someone else might bite at a quick sale, but if she chose to wait for the right one, her sale price was going to be well worth the effort and time.

She'd just stepped out of the club, and felt the cold air bite against her skin, when an ambulance blew down her street. Sirens raging, and lights blazing. Two cop cars followed right after.

Haven tightened her coat, and watched them go.

Her first thought was *Andino*, even though she had no reason to assume that. Yet, every time she saw one now … she thought of him. She did watch the news in her office, after all, and it seemed that organized crime in New York was getting a hell of a lot of attention.

Apparently, the streets were dangerous.

So yeah, she thought of him.

And right then, she just felt cold.

• • •

Haven dropped her bag to the floor beside the kitchen island, and kicked off her shoes right at the same spot. She didn't see the point in taking them off at the door anymore—even the fucking welcome mat was gone, now. Her gaze drifted between the bottle of whiskey she'd left on the counter from the night before, or the instant coffee jar tucked into the corner beside the electric kettle and the fridge.

A good shot of whiskey was needed after an evening like the one she just had. Not that the employees at her club had been bad, or even awful about the sale. They *hadn't*. Far from it, really. Although sad with the fact *she* would no longer be their boss, they were understanding of her position and why she chose to do what she did.

Not that she was surprised.

It was all just stressful anyway.

This whole thing was the very definition of *stress*.

She opted for the coffee instead of the whiskey. She planned on calling her father after she filled her empty stomach, and she didn't think he would appreciate hearing her sloshed. It wasn't like he needed more things to worry about what with her mother being sick again, and all.

Once Haven had her steaming coffee in hand, she sipped from the drink as she fiddled with the knobs on the small radio in her kitchen to bring in the station she liked the most. Since she'd put the television into storage, the radio was the only thing keeping her sane during the quiet moments at night.

Music was good for the soul. The closer to the brain, the better. As far as she was concerned, anyway.

A song she didn't like that much blasted through the speakers once she tuned into the station. Turning down the volume just a bit, Haven tried to focus on drinking her coffee, and letting go of the tension weighing down her shoulders. Very little worked lately to do that, and this was no goddamn exception.

Unfortunately.

It was only when the host came back on the radio station to announce the upcoming songs did Haven break out of her zone, and turn the radio back up. She listened to a few of the commercials—loans for cheap interest, and car salesmen with promises of great deals. She almost tuned the noise out until the host started discussing the news for the day.

Different things that happened in the city.

A major pileup on an exit ramp had caused the terrible traffic in Brooklyn—not that Haven could say she was surprised. A robbery in Hell's Kitchen had ended with a shop owner shooting the would-be thief. A drive-by shooting in Brooklyn—

Haven's head snapped to the side as the details of the drive-by in Brooklyn started coming through the speakers; the location of the shooting hadn't been all that far from her club, which was what surprised her the most. She liked her location *because* it wasn't a violent neighborhood. Drive-bys were not at all common.

The host spoke in a monotone which told her that he was likely reading from a paper, and not from memory. He wasn't a news reporter or journalist, after all.

"One gunshot injury was reported at the scene," the reporter said. "The victim, according to police, is in fair condition, and is being treated at the trauma center in Brooklyn. The victim was identified by police as Andino Marcello—they believe the drive-by to be related to the infamous Marcello family, and not a random event."

Haven blinked.

She heard his name, that he was *okay*, and yet … it still felt like an echoing whisper humming through her mind all the same. An echo of fucking pain, and of fear. For him, and for herself. For her *heart*.

It took her far too long to realize, at the same time, that the police seemed to have no issue with outing Andino's name to the public as the victim involved in the shooting. Not to mention, adding his family and their history into the mix like it should be used as an add-on to the fact he was shot.

Like that was the only reason *why*.

It was shocking.

And *infuriating*.

Haven's anger was only a backdrop, though.

Her fear was far more present.

THREE

"Stop hovering," Andino snapped.

His mother didn't stop, though. She barely even gave him one of her *looks* for his tone, actually. Guilt compounded in his chest even as she quietly moved to fix the pillow on his bed that he wasn't even using, for Christ's sake.

All she wanted to do was love him, and help. All he could do was act like a spoiled little shit.

Andino was quick to grab his mother's hand before she could move away from his bedside. With a little tug, she turned her attention on him. There, he saw the fear she'd been hiding with her silence and gaze turned away from him. There, he saw her pain.

"I'm sorry, Ma," he said.

Kim pressed her lips together into a thin line, and nodded. "It's okay."

"It's *not* okay. I'm just ... edgy."

He hated hospitals with a passion. Every memory he had of hospitals were *bad ones*. No Marcello came to a hospital for good things ... a baby hadn't been born into their family for *years*.

His recent memories of hospitals were not ones he cared to remember. Like the time his cousin tried to kill herself, and his entire family spent the night in hard, plastic chairs waiting for word on her condition. Or back when he broke his wrist as a kid, and the doctor told his father he'd given Andino something for the pain, but actually *hadn't* before he reset the bone. Gio had not been happy about that—someone died for it, he imagined. Andino never thought to ask, really.

It didn't matter.

Hospitals meant bad things.

Usually death.

Today was not an exception to the rule except for the fact Andino hadn't died. He had been shot, though, and the burning that was constantly radiating from his upper arm was enough of a reminder of just how close he had come to losing his life today on a quiet Brooklyn street.

And he *knew* .... knew without a doubt and without needing to ask ... that his mother was even more aware of just how close he'd come today than even he was. He'd been there; he'd taken the bullet graze that left a jagged chunk taken out of his arm. *Him.*

But she was also his ma.

"You're supposed to be *safe*," Kim whispered.

"I know, Ma," he replied. There was nothing else he could tell her that would make this any easier. No apologies he could make, not that it was really his fault. She was still going to worry, and fret. It was what mothers did. And when it was a mother of a made man? Andino suspected that only made it worse. "I'm sorry I scared you."

Kim's hand came up to pat Andino's cheek with a light touch. He was acutely aware that the reverberation of her palm against his face made his arm sting even worse, but he held back the flinch. He didn't want her to think for even a second that she was causing him pain. That would only make her worry worse, and the guilt would start.

No one needed that.

"I knew what this life meant," she told him, "and what could happen. Of course, I knew. I don't know anything different, my boy."

Andino frowned. "It's okay, Ma."

Kim nodded. "It's not, but it is what it is. I just … you're my only child. Don't make me bury you, Andino. Parents shouldn't have to bury their babies."

He blinked.

He was a grown man, and yet, still his mother thought of him as her *baby*. He wasn't quite sure what to do with that.

Instead, he simply said, "You won't bury me, Ma. I promise."

Andino did his best to keep his word when he gave it for something. Being who he was in the life that he led, sometimes his word was the only thing he really had at the end of the day. Not that any of that mattered, either. This was his mother … not just *someone*. His word to her held even more importance.

Kim smiled. "Enough of this, huh?" She patted his cheek again, and that pain flared. Still, he held back from showing his discomfort. It was the very least he could do at the moment. "Do you want something? A drink, or your phone?"

Andino knew that he simply needed to make his mother busy. If she was busy, and had her mind focused on something other than him, then she would be just fine for a while. She needed to fret and worry, but she also needed something to do while she did it.

Not so hard to figure out.

"Water would be great," he said.

Kim nodded. "But not from the machine, right?"

"Bottled, yeah."

"Okay. I'll be back."

His mother slipped out of the room with a soft smile over her shoulder, but she didn't bother to close the door behind her. Andino was grateful. It allowed him to listen to the conversation filtering out from the hallway that was happening between his uncles, and his father. He was quite aware that a good portion of the Marcello family had showed up to the hospital as soon as they got word about what happened.

So was their way.

No one had been allowed back to his room, though. Not that Andino was in the mood for guests, to be honest. The pain was making him snappy, and more irritated than normal. He was seriously starting to regret refusing pain medication.

And the stitches were pulling like a bitch in his arm.

Fuck.

"We need to do something to end this," he heard Dante say out in the hallway. "This cannot happen again. Who will be next? And will the next shot be the one that kills?"

"Or," Andino's father said sharply, "we could fucking answer them back."

Lucian grunted under his breath. A quiet sign that he agreed with what Giovanni said, but didn't verbally voice the opinion.

Dante sighed heavily. "And then what, Gio? It continues. The violence escalates. More people get drawn into the mess. We start keeping a body count. Men get buried. Wives and children are left *alone* and without. That is *not* our way."

"Our way is also not to allow a rival family to step out of bounds like they did today with my son!"

"That's the only reason why you're reacting this way is because it's Andino."

"I would have said the same thing if it was Catherine, Michel, or any one of Lucian's four kids. And you fucking *know* it."

"But that's not thinking clearly—it's thinking with emotions."

Gio made a dark noise, saying, "And I am allowed to have them."

"You get to keep your son today," Dante returned, "but the next man might not be as lucky. Is that the choice you want me to make? Vengeance for yours at the sake of someone else's? We talk about sacrifice and the duty we have to one another in this family, so let's have that conversation again."

"No fucking need. Not right now, anyway."

Andino wondered what had made his father back down, but he didn't have to consider for long. Soon enough, two plain-clothed detectives were darkening his doorway. He didn't have to see their fucking badges to know who they were. He swore cops all walked the same, looked the same, and smelled exactly the fucking same to him.

So was his damn life.

Avoiding these fuckers.

Behind the detectives stood the doctor in his white lab coat wearing a frown, and just behind the doctor were his father, and his uncles.

Apparently, his quiet, empty room was about to get a hell of a lot louder, and crowded.

Fun.

"I have no comment to make," Andino told the detectives before they could even introduce themselves. "I don't know who shot at me, and I don't even remember the make of the car."

"We're sure," the taller of the two men said dryly. "Still, indulge us."

"Call my lawyer. We'll set up a meeting. In the meantime ..." Andino turned his gaze on the doctor. "Get my papers to sign—I'm leaving."

The doctor pushed past the detectives. "I don't think that's a good idea."

"Did I ask what you thought, though?"

Because he was pretty sure he hadn't.

And he was not staying there one more minute.

• • •

"I don't *like* Dante's decision," Andino told his father, "but he is right."

Giovanni made that same angry, disgusted noise he'd been making all fucking night. "Had that been—"

"I know, had it been one of his kids, this conversation might be very different. It also might be exactly the same. He's ready to step down, and let me take the seat. Do you really think he wants to do that *during* a war with a rival family?"

"Stop moving," his cousin muttered.

Andino flinched when the needle Michel was using to fix his busted stitches went through a particularly sensitive part of his injury. "*Fuck*, be careful."

"I am. You keep moving. And for the record, my father could have easily started a war for me with the Irish in Detroit, but what did he do? If anyone needs a reminder ..."

Andino passed a look at his own father.

Giovanni rolled his eyes. "I'm not saying Dante doesn't have the right *idea.*"

"No, you're saying you don't like it," Michel replied. "We all hear you."

The needle poked again.

"*Fuck, Michel, I swear—*"

"Stop acting like a baby," his cousin bitched. "You get shot, then you get stitches. And had you just stayed at the hospital long enough for the blood to start to clot around the first fucking set, you wouldn't need to have me here putting these ones in."

Jesus Christ.

Andino loved his cousin. Sure, he did. Michel, John, and Andino had all grown up together. Like three thieves, in a way. He didn't get to see his cousin nearly as often as he liked because Michel was in the midst of doing his residency as a trauma surgeon, and the man's wife was trying to make it as a partner in a major Manhattan law firm. Michel was busy, and so was Andino. Their paths didn't cross a lot.

Still, he loved him.

And right now, he wanted to *kill* him.

"They tore because he picked up Snaps as soon as he got home," Gio said, tattling on him like a fucking baby. "The dog was in a fit, and Andino couldn't have that."

"Shut up."

"Really?" Michel asked, glancing up from his work to dead stare Andino right in the face. "That dog is eighty pounds at least."

"Ninety-two, and he's very healthy. Thank you very fucking much."

"You can't pick up anything more than fifteen pounds until these stitches heal."

"Well, that's going to be impossible."

Michel let out a long, slow sigh. "How many times do you want me to come here and put these fucking stitches in, Andi?"

He snapped his jaw shut in an effort to keep quiet. "*Fine.*"

Michel rolled his eyes, and went back to his work. Andino went back to talking to his father in an effort to keep his mind off the pain in his arm that intensified with every slip of the needle through his skin.

"They *have* to answer for what they do," Gio said. "We can't allow the Calabrese family to go unchecked when they act against us."

"And we will," Andino replied quietly.

"By making *peace?*"

"For now," Andino replied. "For now, yes."

His father gave him a look, and then Michel. "What are you—"

"It's not important right now."

And it wasn't.

His plans would have to wait. Because he did have plans, and while he understood his uncle's position regarding the Calabrese, and that protecting their family from more violence was what would be in their best interests … he also agreed with his father more.

Andino would never bow to the fucking Calabrese.

Not after what they did to John.

Now *this*, too?

No way.

Once his cousin had gotten Andino all stitched up, and he walked his father and Michel to the door, all he wanted to do was relax for the evening.

Michel pulled a small baggie from his inner pocket, and handed it over. Inside were pills. Michel only shrugged when Andino gave him an inquisitive look.

"No driving when you take one. Vicodin. For *pain*. Don't be a fucking hero."

Andino laughed. "Can I take it with whiskey?"

Michel glanced over at Gio as if to say, *What the fuck do I do with him, huh?*

"I can't say yes to that," Michel settled on saying.

"But you didn't say no, either."

"Because what is the point?"

His cousin's and father's laughter followed them out of the house. Andino was quick to lock the door behind them, and go back to the kitchen. Snaps was still in his spot in front of his food bowls, and his dark eyes watched Andino as he moved around the space to get a shot of whiskey ready before he pulled one of those pills out.

He wasn't one for meds. He could handle pain. But his agitation level was already so high that he figured, what the hell? Something to take the edge off for the night would be *perfect*.

He'd just popped the pill, and swallowed a shot of burning whiskey when a knock echoed through his quiet house. Snaps still hadn't moved from his spot; the dog always alerted with a loud bark to the fact someone was approaching his house, and right then he kept staring at Andino.

Except ... his tail was wagging.

Andino should have known then.

The dog only chose to not alert when it was *her*.

He didn't waste time as he practically ran from the kitchen back to the front of the house. He didn't even move the shades to look out the window before pulling the door open.

And there she stood.

Skinny jeans molded to shapely, long legs.

Hair thrown up in a messy bun.

A black trench coat.

Blue eyes on him.

Like the storm or the sea.

Fire and ice, he thought.

"Haven," Andino murmured.

Behind her waiting at the end of the walkway, he could see the enforcer that had been posted at his house. Still fucking standing there. A precaution, his father said. No doubt, given the man was looking right at them, the fact she was there would somehow get back to his family.

Andino didn't care.

She was there. She shouldn't be, but she was.

More than anything, he wanted that. He also knew he should let this woman go. Turn her away, and get her the hell away from him as fast as fucking possible. He'd finally gotten her away from the mess that was him and his life, and she should stay gone. It would be better for her in the end.

He shouldn't invite her in.

He shouldn't keep hurting her.

"Do you want to come in?" he asked.

Famous last words …

FOUR

Do you want to come in?

Six words.

Six simple words.

On the surface, they seemed innocent and not at all problematic. They shouldn't be the kind of words that made Haven's chest constrict painfully, or her heart race out of control. They were not *those* kinds of words.

And yet, they were.

They were exactly those kinds of words.

Andino swung an arm wide, and took one step backward as if to open his place to her, and silently invite her in alongside his words. She would have responded right away, but she was a little struck at simply *staring* at this man.

That hard, square-cut of his jaw. The stubble dusting his cheeks. The way his lips curved slightly at the edges like he *might* be happy, but he wasn't willing to share it with a true smile. The greens of his eyes. A naked, expansive chest unmarked by ink or scars, and a railroad path of abs that led down to the pair of slacks he wore unbuttoned and resting low on his hips.

All of him, really.

Still tall.

Still broad shouldered.

Still terribly handsome.

Haven hadn't thought anything would change. Why would it? Other than how she felt inside, and in her heart, very little changed about her since the last time she saw him. Still, looking at him then was like seeing him for the first time.

It was overwhelming.

Very much so.

"Well?" Andino asked quietly. "Do you want to come in?"

She should have said no, and stepped back. She should have given him the truth—she'd only come here to check in on him, and make sure he was okay after what she heard on the radio that evening. Nothing more, and nothing less.

She cared.

He'd proven he didn't care at all.

Well, she'd gotten her answer. She could see he was fine, and that was enough to quell the panic that had lingered high in the back of her throat like vomit threatening to spill ever since she heard what happened.

It should be enough.

It wasn't even close to it.

Haven stepped into the house, and closed the door behind her. She didn't miss the way the enforcer at the end of the walkway looked her over, but was quick to turn his back when she shut him out with the door. Spinning back around to face Andino, ready to explain why she was there, and that she couldn't stay for long, something stopped her.

She finally saw it, then.

The injury—large and jagged—on his arm. Red, and sore. It looked horribly painful, and the stitches seemed to be barely holding it together.

Andino didn't miss the way Haven flinched. "It's not bad. Looks worse than it is, I swear."

"How did that happen?"

She knew; she wanted to know if he would tell her the truth. Whatever they had been was already dominated by lies he told, and the omissions he chose to keep away from her. Had he learned his lesson, or not?

"Had a run in today. Somebody else's gun got a little too excited about seeing me."

Haven blinked.

Sure, he left details out. He still told her the basics of the truth that she knew.

She didn't know what did it—maybe his blasé tone, or the fact that his injury made her hurt for him. It could have simply been that she was there *with* him after doing her very best to avoid him at all costs, and move the hell on.

Whatever it was that shot through her like a jolt of nostalgia, pain, and ... love, too ... it sent her forward without any warning. Haven didn't think about it; she wrapped her arms around Andino's neck, and found *peace* the second she was in his arms. It took him less than a second to react, and enclose her in his embrace.

Things were good for a second.

Good for them.

All the bad shit went away, and the pain dissipated. The rest of the world blinked out like it didn't exist at all, and she could pretend things were fine. She liked it here in his arms; nothing else had to matter. She could lose herself in his warmth, and hard lines. Breathe in his scent like it was the only air she was ever going to need.

Why couldn't they stay like this?

She wanted that.

Reality was a quick bitch, though. It was always waiting right around the corner to drag Haven back to hell kicking and fucking screaming, regardless of what she wanted. This time, reality came with a squeeze around her heart that hurt like nothing else because ... no, they couldn't stay this way, and she was still the same woman he'd discarded not too long ago.

Andino seemed to sense her sudden shift in thoughts, or maybe it was the way she tensed in his arms. Either way, he loosened his hold enough to allow Haven to step just far enough out of his arms' reach. The distance gave her some clarity, but it wasn't very much. Not nearly enough.

"That looks like it hurts," she said, gesturing to his injury.

It was the only thing she could think to say.

"The Vicodin with whiskey chaser is starting to kick in, actually," Andino muttered, glancing down at his arm. "Small fucking miracles."

Haven laughed, but it came out strained, and probably a little too bitter. She couldn't even control the rush of emotions that swept over her, never mind the anger that was still ever-present no matter what her stupid heart wanted.

She couldn't escape this feeling.

She didn't *want* to feel like this at all.

"Why are you here?" Andino asked.

She looked back at him, and shook her head. "I heard what happened."

"I'm fine."

Clearly.

He just completely missed the point.

Her anger swelled again. "You don't get it, do you?"

"Get what?"

"That I give a shit about you, I guess? I actually *care*, Andino. I wanted to make sure you were okay, but since the hospital said you voluntarily checked yourself out, that wasn't good enough for me. I *had to know*. So, here I am. I don't know. It's pointless, right? I shouldn't be here anyway."

Haven was glad she voiced that thought—she *shouldn't* be here. It wasn't a matter of wanting to be, but a matter of what was best for her. Of course, she wanted to be here. That didn't mean it was good for her.

Before she could overthink anymore than she already was, Haven turned to leave with a quiet, "Sorry, Andino. I'm glad you're okay."

She didn't even get the chance to grab the doorknob. She didn't see him coming for her until his hand was locked around her arm, and he'd spun her back around fast enough to make the room spin in her vision. Her gaze cleared in just enough time to see the emotion darkening his features before he closed all distance between them, and kissed her.

There was no hesitance in his kiss, and no wariness. Like he knew the moment his lips touched hers, she was going to respond just how he wanted her to. His mouth moved over hers in such a familiar way that she couldn't help herself but kiss him back. A deep, aching kiss that left her lips tingling, and her body weaker than ever.

He could own her with a kiss.

He took her rationale away.

Worries, anger, and control … all gone.

All he needed was a fucking *kiss*.

There was a part of her that wanted to step back from him, and reevaluate. She knew that was the smart part of her brain whispering through the haze of nostalgia and need. It was the slip of his hand curving around the back of her neck to pull her impossibly closer that silenced the little voice.

Haven reached back for him—her hands slipping over his naked chest to get more of his skin on hers. His tongue teased hers; a silent promise if there ever was one. She always thought he kissed a lot like he fucked. Deep, and fast, and a little wild. Like he couldn't get enough, but he was determined to get what he wanted, regardless.

And when he kissed her like *that*, then all of her ability to think clearly was quickly lost. *Like now.*

All she could focus on was him, and the way his hand tightened on her neck. His growing erection pressed against her body which only served to make her wet. She could already feel that dampness in her panties.

Andino pulled away from her mouth with a ragged breath. Those green eyes of his flashed with something dark and wild. "Upstairs, then?"

How simple that question was.

It should be an easy *no* from her.

Let this go.

Leave it alone.

Haven was still humming—still high from his kiss, and the promise of what was yet to come. Oh, she knew what would be *coming*. And that was a large part of the reason why she was quick to nod and say, "Yeah, upstairs."

Maybe if she gave it one last go—did this whole fucking dance with him one more time—she would be able to walk away. It'd be done; her need sated, even if her heart was still broken. She could feed the selfish part of her today, and mend the broken bits tomorrow.

That seemed like a good plan.

Stupid, but *good*.

Andino's hand pressed against her neck, and Haven moved at his urging. "Ladies first," he said.

She didn't need him to direct her through his house. She knew exactly where she was going, and what was going to happen once she got there. As she passed by the kitchen, a familiar pit bull came out to greet her in the hallway. Haven took a second to bend down, and say hello to Snaps. A thickness grew in her throat the longer she ran her fingertips through the dog's short coat.

"Hey, buddy," she whispered.

Snaps' stubby tail wagged hard. He licked the palm of her hand, and then pressed the very top of his head against her arm. His silent *hello*. She felt like it also sounded like, *I miss you*.

God, she missed him, too.

"You be good, huh?" she told him. "I'll give you a treat before I leave."

Because she would be leaving.

She simply didn't know when.

Andino cleared his throat, clearly not missing her statement to his dog. She didn't acknowledge his noise, instead saying a goodbye to Snaps before standing again. The dog didn't follow them upstairs, but that wasn't a surprise. Snaps was well trained, and knew to stay unless he was asked to follow.

Haven shivered when Andino's hand landed on the small of her back. He moved in close behind her as she stepped inside his room—just over the cusp of no return, she thought. His bed was still the same. Large, four-poster, with black sheets, and red pillows. She tipped her head to the side when his lips skimmed the back of her neck, and his hands drifted over her sides.

"I'm not supposed to be doing anything *strenuous*," Andino murmured against her skin. Well, damn. She hadn't even thought of that. "But I really don't give a fuck right now."

His teeth grazed her earlobe while his hands slipped around her front. One skipped beneath her shirt, and higher to cup her breast through the lace bralette she wore. He was quick to push the bralette down to get his thumb and forefinger on her nipple. His fingers tweaked the hardened bud until she felt a jolt of heat shoot straight down to her pussy.

His other unsnapped the button on her jeans, and dipped beneath the matching lace panties. The tight fit of his hand in her jeans made her hot—his fingers could barely move, yet he managed to stroke her just right. Enough to make her shake. And then he teased her with his fingertips stroking the seam of her sex before toying with her clit, too.

Soft, gentle strokes.

Not too much.

Not nearly enough.

"Do you know how wet you are right now?" he asked, those fingers of his teasing her pussy again. "Wet enough for me to bend you over, and have a fucking *feast*."

Jesus.

"Maybe you can do just that."

"You're mine for the night," he uttered.

Dark, and wicked.

His voice still made her wet.

It was kind of ridiculous.

"For the night," she agreed.

"Then strip."

The order came out sharp, and yet husky along the column of her neck. She was aching in all the right places. A small tremor worked its way over her body—the anticipation she felt making itself known.

"*Now*," Andino added.

He stepped away from her then, taking those teasing, talented hands with him. Haven felt the loss like a visceral sensation washing over her skin, but she was a little distracted considering he'd told her to do something, and she wanted more than anything to comply. She was quick to slip out of her jacket, jeans, and shirt. By the time she was down to her lace underwear set, Andino had perched himself on the edge of his bed.

"Come here," he said, tipping his head a bit to encourage her.

She walked across the room until she was standing in front of him. One of his hands came up to cup her thigh, and then stroke down over her smooth skin. His touch left a trail of heat behind.

"Still perfect," he murmured.

Haven let out a soft laugh. "You know, it'd be easier on me if you didn't say things like that."

There.

She said it.

Let him make of it what he wanted.

Andino glanced up to meet her gaze. "Is that what you want? Just to get fucked, and then get gone, girl? You don't want the rest?"

Oh, she *did*.

She wanted that more than anything.

Her heart just couldn't afford the cost.

"Yeah," Haven replied. "Just fuck me, and let me go, Andino."

He nodded.

That was all she got—not even a verbal agreement—before he reached for her. His mouth landed just below her navel at the same time his hands fisted into the waistband of her panties. He dragged the lace halfway down her thighs while his mouth kissed a slow path lower on her stomach.

"Just a taste," she heard him say. Her panties fell down her legs, then. "Open up for me."

She stepped out of those forgotten panties, and widened her stance. His mouth was already on her pussy before she could drag in her next breath. He hadn't lied about the *just a taste* thing. He teased her with his mouth and tongue just long enough to make her ready to beg.

And then he pulled away.

Andino tugged her into his lap; his hands grabbed her thighs with a rough touch, and fingertips that gripped hard enough to leave marks behind. And yet, she couldn't find it in herself to give a single fuck about it.

Not when he was spreading her wider.

Not when he was whispering in her ear.

"You want me to fuck you? You want my cock, baby?"

"*Yes.*"

Yes, yes, yes.

The answer was always going to be yes.

She fumbled with his pants to free his cock. Once she had his hard length in her hands, she took a moment to appreciate the weight and size of him as she stroked him slowly. All the while, that mouth of his was back on her throat—kissing, biting, and leaving behind more memories for her to feel even when she couldn't see them.

Every time she fisted his length, his hips jerked upward. His hands on her ass grasped tighter, and he pulled her hips into his groin. A low groan slipped from his lips, and skimmed over her skin even as she fitted him between her thighs.

That first inch of him was heaven. It was the bliss she missed the most, and a sensation she would happily die feeling. No one had ever fucked Haven quite like Andino did. No one filled her as full, or stretched her open like he did.

It was fucking delirious.

Or, that's how it made her.

"Take what you want, then," she heard him breathe against her chin when she tipped her head back. "Take it from me."

Being on top gave her back a sense of control, but his words only added to it. She controlled the pace, and how much of him she wanted to take. She decided when to make their fucking harder, and when to slow him down.

And still, all she wanted was everything.

All of it.

"Just *fuck me*," Haven muttered.

So, he did.

Hands firmly on her ass, and his mouth attacking hers. Thick cock bare, and making her ache with every deep thrust. She found stability tangling her fingers in his hair, and gasping for breath. But it was only an illusion. Even the control she thought he gave her had been an illusion.

He fucked her hard.

She begged for more.

He slowed them down.

Still, she didn't come. He wouldn't let her. Every time she came close enough, he pulled back until her body calmed, and then he went right back at it. Again, and again, and again. Until she felt like she was going to come apart at the damn seams. And she trembled on the edge until he was pounding into her again.

Until she was sobbing because her mind was a mess, and her body couldn't take anymore.

Please, please let me come.

It was all she could say.

It was only after he'd flipped her over, and fucked her hard enough to make her throat raw from screaming that he finally let her fly.

She broke apart all over again.

Fuck him for that, too.

• • •

"You're not going to say goodbye, then?" Andino asked.

Haven pulled on her jeans, and internally cursed herself for not getting up the second she heard his bathroom door click. Maybe it was fucking cowardly of her—oh, it most certainly was—but she figured slipping out of his place would be the easiest way to do this. Then, there would be no need for any awkward conversation.

Apparently, she hoped for too much.

Damn.

"Wasn't last night enough?" Haven asked. "I kind of thought it was."

Andino leaned against the doorway leading into the connected master bath. "I don't follow."

"Then, you're clueless."

"Don't be mean, Haven."

She let out a quiet laugh. "No, I suppose that's meant for you, right? You're the one between us who gets to make choices that hurts the other one. *You're* the one who does cruel things. It's entirely out of character for me to do something like that even if it is a reaction coming from my emotions. Yeah, I know. Don't worry."

He moved forward, but Haven put a hand out to stop him even as she zipped up her jeans with the other one. "Don't bother."

"You could have left last night."

"Why not stay for a good fuck?" she shot back. "At least then I'm getting something from this. It's done now. Count on that."

"Haven—"

The anger she'd been holding at bay—just long enough for him to fuck her until she couldn't think, and her body was a mindless blob of sensation—finally decided to come out to play. Last night had been too much, and all she wanted to do when they were done fucking was sleep off the overwhelming emotions and exhaustion.

She'd done that.

It was morning now, though.

She wasn't so tired, but she was still pretty damn emotional.

"Why?" she asked him.

Andino folded his arms over his chest. "Why, *what?*"

"Why did you do that to me? Why tell me you love me, and then leave me like that? Do you *know* how deep that cut me? How much it fucking hurts in *here?*" She made a fist with her hand, and pressed it against her chest overtop her racing heart. "I'm not something for you to use and discard, Andino. I am not a *toy*. And you don't get to treat me like one. So yeah, *why*. It's the least you can do. If you actually *love me*, then you can give me a proper answer."

He took a second, and then *two*.

"Except I can't love you," he finally said. Then, he corrected himself with, "*Don't* love you."

Haven straightened, and even through the stabbing pain making its way through her body, she hadn't missed his first statement. He stared at her like he was made of ice—cold, and unfeeling. Not really there at all. Burning her from feet away.

Still, she'd *heard it*.

The way his voice dipped, and his words forced their way out. Like he had to make himself say those things, and not that he actually meant them at all.

I can't love you.

She wanted to hate him.

Except she didn't.

"I see you're still a good liar," Haven said.

Andino glanced away with a hard-set jaw, and unfeeling eyes. "You should go."

Yeah, she definitely should.

Haven made quick work of pulling on the rest of her clothes, and avoided Andino's stare all the while. She made sure to keep her promise to Snaps, and get him a treat from the fridge where she knew Andino kept them stored. She didn't even look over her shoulder as she slipped out of the house. Looking back would have only caused her more pain, and she was trying her very best to let that go.

She needed to let him go.

"Hello," came a voice a few feet away.

Haven almost ran head-first into the chest of Andino's father.

Jesus Christ.

This morning couldn't get any worse!

Had Andino knew his father was coming over this morning? Because she really would have appreciated that heads up. She would have left far sooner than she had, actually, just to avoid this whole nonsense.

She met the man's gaze, and he quirked a brow high as his stare traveled from her, to the door she'd just closed. He said nothing for a long while, simply took in her appearance for long enough that a sense of awkwardness started to color up her cheeks with pink.

"Uh, hi," Haven said.

Way to go.

Giovanni smiled faintly. "You look like you had a long night."

Oh, God.

No, it could certainly get worse.

"Could we not?" she asked. "Because that would be great."

The man cleared his throat, and chuckled. "Sure."

"Thanks. Now, excuse me."

Haven stepped forward to pass the man on the steps, but Giovanni didn't move an inch. He stayed right where he was until she met his gaze again, and there was no way for her to hide the embarrassment on her cheeks.

The shame she felt ...

"I should give you a warning," the man said quietly, "about my son."

"I don't need one of those. Trust me."

Andino had shown her more than enough; she had all the warnings she needed about him to last her a goddamn lifetime.

Giovanni shook his head subtly. "Mmm, no. I mean, for a while, Haven ... you should be very careful about being seen with my son, and what you do with him. For *yourself*, but also for him. I know you don't understand or know about our life, and maybe that's for the better, but these are dangerous times for us. I worry that Andino doesn't see clearly enough where you are concerned to consider that. That maybe he's willing to allow ... well, that doesn't matter. This is about you, and not him. If *you* care for him, you'll listen to me. You'll be mindful, and careful."

Well, *fuck.*

That was the problem, wasn't it?

She did care.

Too much.

• • •

Haven's house was colder than she wanted it to be when she finally arrived home. Staying the night with Andino hadn't exactly been the plan, and now it kind of felt like the rising sun in the backdrop of her kitchen window was mocking her.

Well done, you fucked him again.

Maybe cold wasn't the right word for her place. Maybe empty would fit the bill better. And that was just as big of a problem as the cold thing, frankly.

She missed her friend.

Missed Maria, too.

She *really* missed Andino.

Was this going to be her life now?

The stupid girl who knew better, but kept going back for more until there was nothing left of her to take? Because that's how it felt, in a lot of ways. As though every time she and Andino crossed paths, she left a piece of herself with him, and he had yet to give those many pieces back to her.

He just kept them.

So yes, she was cold, empty, and entirely fucking alone.

She swore the faint ache between her thighs, and the hunger still burning brightly through her body was something else that was mocking her. Every step she took inside her home reminded her of the night before. Her skin still hummed from his touch, and how it left her higher than ever.

This wasn't fair.

Why did it have to be like this?

How could he look at her, say he didn't *love* her like he meant it, and just lie even though he knew it was killing her? How could she keep wanting him, and loving him when this was what he did?

How?

Haven was nursing her second cup of coffee, and feeling like the worst kind of shit when a knock echoed on her front door. She had every mind to ignore whoever the fuck it was, and stay right where she sat. The last thing she wanted to do was *move*.

Wallow some more.

Continue her pity party.

Not move.

When the persistent knocking continued, Haven finally got irritated enough to go answer the door. She practically tossed her cup into the sink, uncaring if the mug broke. She answered the door by flinging it open with a harsh, "What?"

The young man—he couldn't be more than twenty—on the other side of the door wore a white uniform with a flower logo printed on the breast pocket. He held out a bushel of mixed winter flowers.

"Miss … Haven Murphy?" the man asked quietly. "Sorry, but I was told to keep knocking until you answered."

Haven blinked. "Oh?"

"Yes. These are for you." He handed the flowers over, adding, "Have a great day."

Standing in the cold March air in her opened doorway, Haven stared at the flowers in her hand. Tucked in the very top of the bushel was a card with handwriting that wasn't familiar, but the name attached certainly was.

It simply read, *You're right. I am a terribly good liar.* —*Andino*

Because he did, she knew.

Loved her.

So, why did he have to hurt her?

Why play with her heart like this?

Why?

FIVE

Andino stepped out of his house, and eyed the quiet street. The sky was bright, and near cloudless. Despite the cold, it was a beautiful morning. The street looked peaceful, and Andino's presence on his doorstep hadn't changed that fact.

It wasn't that he expected something to happen the moment he left his place, considering enforcers had been posted at his door, and all that good shit, but still. He hadn't left the house since the shooting a few days earlier—doctor's orders. Well, and Dante's.

So, that first step felt ... cautious.

Yes, that was as good of a word as any.

He didn't for a second think the Calabrese brothers were stupid enough to attack him the very second he left his house for the first time, but it was hard to tell what those bastards were capable of sometimes. Hadn't they already proven that they were more than willing to kick a man when he was already down if that meant getting what they wanted?

Andino was not that stupid.

Fool me once, and all that nonsense.

He was not going to allow them to get one over on him a second time. He'd eat the barrel of his own gun first, and that wasn't even him being dramatic.

Snaps trailed close to Andino's side, but kept his nose to the ground. Apparently, even the dog wasn't going to leave anything to chance today.

So was his life.

"Come on, then," Andino said, pulling open the passenger door to a rental Mercedes. His fucking Lexus was still in the shop getting patched up. It'd taken ten bullets, and he didn't want the car back unless it was in *perfect* condition. Snaps gave the vehicle a look, clearly recognizing it wasn't the car he preferred. "Get in—we're leaving."

The dog huffed in that way of his—solemn and irritated at the same time—but was quick to follow the order, and jump inside the car. Andino closed the passenger door behind his pup, and then rounded the front to slide in the driver's side.

But not before giving the enforcer who was trailing him today a look. The guy had parked on the other side of the road, and given the cold March air, had stayed inside his running vehicle. Andino didn't blame him.

It wasn't long before Andino was on the road, and heading for the heart of the city. The faint sting in his arm kept him from getting too

38

comfortable every time he had to move the steering wheel even a fraction of an inch.

Fuck.

That bullet graze was not going to let up.

His phone chimed with a call just as he pulled onto a familiar block in upper Manhattan, but he didn't bother to pick it up even as the car's speakers told him who the caller was. His father. He'd see Gio in less than ten minutes, anyway. Surely, he could wait.

Andino pulled the Mercedes into a back alleyway, and parked. Snaps wasn't allowed inside restaurants, but certainly not businesses that didn't belong to Andino. Sure, this place was his uncle's, but that didn't make a difference to the health code, and inspectors. It only took one person making a goddamn complaint.

That just meant Andino had to be … careful.

With Snaps close to his side, Andino approached the back exit door of the business, and knocked twice with two knuckles. Quickly, the door was opened to showcase Lucian's enforcer who always kept watch at his post as long as his boss was working inside the private dining section of the business.

"Andino," the enforcer greeted.

Soon, the man would be calling him *boss*.

Andino had … sort of … resigned himself to that fact. He wasn't as fucking stuck in his feelings and emotions as he once had been about the whole thing. It might not have been what he would have chosen, but it was for the best.

And wasn't that what counted?

Apparently so.

"Your father and Lucian are in the private section," the man said.

Andino nodded, and stepped in the doorway. Snaps was quick to follow even when the enforcer gave the pup a look like he was going to say something. The man wisely chose to keep his mouth shut.

Going through the back was an easy way to keep Snaps from being seen. The hallway led past the offices, and into another section that allowed someone to go to the main floor, into the kitchen, or the private area. A patron never even saw someone coming in and out of the back.

Made for easy, clean business.

Lucian was smart like that—all his restaurants had this sort of design in the back.

It wasn't the first time the dog had been inside this particular business, but he did know it didn't belong to Andino. So when they entered the private section, Snaps was quick to sit his ass down next to the doorway just inside the room, and he didn't move even when Andino greeted his uncle and father.

"Starting without me?"

Gio grinned around the bite of waffle in his mouth. "We weren't sure how long it was going to take for you to drag your ass out of bed, son."

Lucian pointed a fork in his younger brother's direction. "Exactly that."

"Excuses."

Andino dropped into the chair beside his father, and didn't miss how Lucian was quick to press a button on the table. Less than a minute later, a server came in with fresh coffee, and a hot plate of breakfast food. She set it down in front of Andino with a smile before making her presence scarce.

"See, I didn't forget about you, *nipote*," Lucian said. "Eat first, business later."

Andino couldn't find it in himself to argue. Even though he'd gone several days being locked inside his house to rest after the shooting, and that meant he'd needed to let business slip a bit, this was a good way to start the day.

Food.

Family.

Business last.

Usually, business always came first.

The three ate in a comfortable silience. Snaps only left his position beside the door when Andino offered him two strips of bacon as a treat for behaving, but he was quick to go back to his spot once he had the meat.

It was only when Andino had finished his plate, and was sipping on the black coffee that his uncle decided to break the silence.

"We have a problem," his uncle said.

Gio was still working on his plate, so he said nothing. Andino, on the other hand, was all ears.

"We have a lot of problems," Andino returned, "so you're going to have to be more specific."

"John and Siena."

Shit.

Yeah, that.

Andino set his cup down, and scrubbed a hand down his face. "With the way things are right now, I don't see how the two of them can—"

"We made her a promise," Lucian interjected quietly. "She wants to be with my son, and he is happy with her. I don't give my word if I can't keep it."

"And you think I *do*?"

Lucian gave Andino a look that spoke volumes without actually needing to say anything at all. No, his uncle knew him well. Andino's word meant *the world*. If he gave it, then he kept it. That was the end of it.

But this ... this was fucking complicated.

All sorts of messy.

John was still in the psychiatric facility working on his shit, and Siena Calabrese was now locked away by her brothers. There were the beginnings of a street war echoing through the city between their family, and hers.

Nothing about this was *easy*.

"Dante wants a peaceful resolution," Giovanni said, finally finishing with his plate. He pushed the dish away as he glanced up, adding, "So, I don't know how that factors into the John and Siena thing, but not in any way that ends well for them, I imagine."

To say the least ...

"A peaceful resolution would be best," Andino agreed.

From the perspective of a boss, he understood the need. As a man who had been wronged by the Calabrese, and knew just how much damage they had already done, he figured burning them to the ground would be the better choice.

Yeah.

Not easy at all.

"She makes John happy," Lucian repeated.

"I'll keep my word," Andino replied.

A look passed between him and his uncle, silent and contemplative. An agreement without either of them actually saying a thing. Gio cleared his throat, and sat back in his chair to fold his arms over his chest, but he didn't add anything to the conversation.

"Dante intends to make peace," Lucian said.

"Well, he can try."

Andino didn't intend to let that happen; at least, not in the way his uncle wanted. There were things he would never bow to—the Calabrese was one of them.

His father frowned. "Dante might take that as—"

"Dante doesn't have to *know*," Andino said vaguely. "Not now, anyway."

Gio let out a sigh. "This is not how Marcellos work."

"If it isn't how we work," Andino countered, "then this breakfast never should have happened. You shouldn't have invited me here. And we shouldn't have agreed to move forward with our own plans in the first place. But here we are, and it needs to happen."

"It does," Lucian agreed.

No, Dante wouldn't like it. For now, Andino simply needed to worry about other things, and in the meantime, keep his uncle *happy*. When it was all said and done, what could Dante really do about Andino's plans for the Calabrese?

Nothing.

"All right," Lucian said, glancing at his phone. "I need to head out."

"You're going to see John, yeah?"

Lucian nodded. "I'm due a visit. Or at least, see Leonard. The man keeps me informed as much as he can."

"Say hello for me," Andino replied.

"I will."

It was only once Lucian was gone from the private room that Gio picked up his coffee cup, and took a sip. He turned his gaze on his son in that contemplative way again. Andino fully expected his father to ask about the Dante issue again, but the man surprised him.

And not in a good way.

"You're messing with Haven again," his father said. "You need to be careful."

Andino downed the rest of his coffee, and stood from the table. "How about you let me handle that, Dad."

"But *are* you?"

"Pardon?"

"Handling it, Andino. Are you?"

"In the way I want to."

For now.

It was the best he could offer.

· · ·

Andino held up a single finger and crooked it inward as Pink—one of his most trusted enforcers—darkened the doorway of his restaurant's office. He continued his conversation on the phone even as the enforcer stepped into the office, and closed the door behind him.

The man on the phone continued talking about numbers, offers, and price points. What he should do, and how he should do it.

"Listen, this is what I want," Andino said. "That's the offer I am willing to give on the place. They will *jump* at it."

"Yes," his lawyer—one of many, although this one was the one Andino used for the legal side of his businesses—said, "but you're offering twenty thousand above the asking price. *Why?* That doesn't make any sense."

"Because I want to win the bid."

"It's not worth the extra—"

"Did I say I cared about what it was *worth?*" Andino asked. "Because I am pretty sure that wasn't in the fucking details, Marty. Also, how much do I pay you again? Because I am starting to think it's too fucking much when you're this mouthy, and combative."

"Now, Andino—"

"I'm serious."

"You pay me enough to tell you when you're making a bad business decision."

Okay, that was fair. And it was also fair to say that Andino was more the type of businessman to talk someone's offer on a business, location, or building *down*, and not offer more. Which was probably why Marty was quick to point out how this wasn't the greatest idea.

Nonetheless, it needed to happen.

"Make the offer," Andino said, "*at the price I stated*. Got it?"

"Why do you want this place so badly?"

"Because I just do. And remember what else I told you, too."

Marty sighed, clearly frustrated. "Yeah, yeah—keep the deal tied up in paperwork and legalities for as long as I possibly can. Although, that seems fucking pointless too if you're so willing to offer more than the asking price because you want the business this badly."

He didn't want the business he was trying to buy at all. He just needed it not to sell to someone else. So were his ways.

Andino didn't intend to explain that to anyone. He never explained his motives before, and he wasn't going to start now for a fucking lawyer on his payroll.

"Just do what I fucking *said*," Andino snapped. "I have better things to do today than sit here and have a verbal sparring match with *you*. I pay you to do what I want, and not the other way around. Make sure to let me know as soon as the offer is accepted, too. Don't fuck around with me, Marty. You won't like what happens, I assure you."

There, his patience was gone.

Well, fuck it. At least he tried. That counted for something, right?

Andino hung up the phone with the lawyer without a goodbye. It was only then that Pink finally looked at his boss, and smiled.

"Rough day?" the enforcer asked.

Andino scowled. "Something like that. People regularly testing my fucking patience."

"What patience?"

"Exactly."

Pink laughed. "What did you need, boss?"

Finally.

Back to the business Andino *wanted* to do. Or rather, business that needed done as soon as possible.

"I need someone dead, actually," Andino said. "And I figured you're as good of a man as any to do the job."

Pink arched a brow. "Which man?"

"A Calabrese Capo, actually. The one Kev Calabrese always keeps close."

The enforcer whistled low under his breath. "*Damn.* I mean, next to Kev's own brother, you're striking out pretty close to the top there, boss."

"I'm not playing around anymore."

Dante might not want to respond for what the Calabrese did to Andino, but he was sure as hell going to respond. Then, and *only* then, would Andino try to make some kind of peace with the bastards like his uncle wanted.

Or, it was going to seem that way.

Andino was a damn good liar.

"Didn't the boss put out word that we weren't to antagonize the Calabrese, and we were to stay out of their way as much as possible until the rest of this was settled?" Pink asked. "Because something like this sounds like exactly the opposite of what he wants."

There was a method to Andino's madness even if it didn't seem clear, or he wasn't willing to give all the answers right away. This was how he worked, and he wasn't going to apologize for it, or explain himself.

"You'll do the hit, won't you?" Andino asked instead of responding to the man's statement.

"If you tell me to," the enforcer replied.

"I'm telling you to."

Pink relaxed in the chair a bit. "And when do you want me to follow this hit through, boss?"

"Tonight. Make a show of it. I don't want it to look like an accident. I want it to be *very* clear that it was intentional, and that it came from us."

"Us, as in ... the whole family, and not just you."

Andino smiled. "You can't let the snakes get away with even one bite or with the next one, they'll swallow you whole."

He couldn't help if his uncle disagreed.

That wasn't his problem.

• • •

Andino knew the very next minute after the hit had gone through on the Calabrese Capo because Pink was quick to call him. The enforcer knew how to follow directions, thankfully.

But even if Andino hadn't known ... had Pink decided to wait even ten more minutes before calling his boss, Andino still would have known the hit went through successfully because in their business, word like that was quick to make the rounds.

So fast, in fact, that before Andino even hung up the phone with Pink, Dante was already calling. His uncle barely said a word other than to spit out an order for Andino to get to the mansion right fucking now.

Somebody isn't happy.

That was putting it mildly.

Andino had been listening to his uncle rage for the last ten minutes. Well, ever since he arrived at his grandparents' mansion, anyway.

This was getting dull.

"What were you *thinking?*" Dante snarled.

How many times had he asked that now?

A few.

Funny thing was, Dante wasn't actually looking for a proper response. He just wanted to shout and rage at Andino because he hadn't followed the rules set out for him. It wasn't that his uncle actually cared about the *whys*. Those weren't important details.

"Well, *talk!*"

Andino gave his uncle a look. "Do you actually want me to this time? Because you've asked me that same question at least three times in five minutes, and haven't allowed me to explain, so—"

"Fucking *talk*, Andino!"

"I was never going to let that go unanswered," Andino said, shrugging his broad shoulders. "Not what they did to me. I will *not* have someone make an attempt on my life, and let it go. Peace, or no peace. They weren't willing to sit down with us at the table even when you didn't retaliate against them for coming after me—let's see what the Calabrese want to do now when they see we're not fucking around."

Dante scrubbed a hand down his jaw, and gritted his teeth. He shot a look in the direction of his brothers who were both seated, and quiet in the office. They knew better than to speak up. Gio, because he was of the same opinion as Andino, and Lucian, because he was just fucking smart.

Since his uncle had decided to keep quiet, Andino continued talking. He had the floor, after all. "They're snakes—we know this. They thought they had some kind of upper hand on us, and I just showed them how wrong they were by taking out one of their highest Capos, and Kev Calabrese's closest friend next to his brother. They're *not* stupid men. They know an honest to God street war with the Marcello family would not be in their best interests."

"He has a point," Lucian said. "And when we chose to not react against their actions, they only got worse. What might something like this change, Dante?"

"There was a point to what I wanted, brother."

Lucian nodded. "But was it the right choice to make?"

Dante glared, but quickly turned his attention back on Andino. "You were not given permission to make a hit like that; you were out of fucking line."

So be it.

"Are we finished here?" Andino asked.

Dante looked ready to blow his fucking top. He doubted his uncle thought that in all the people he could have chosen to take over after him, Andino would be the one to cause him this much trouble. He loved his uncle—respected the man more than anyone would ever know.

But Dante was stuck in a different time. He wanted different things for the Marcellos than what Andino knew the family and organization needed to thrive well into the future. Allowing a faction like the Calabrese to believe they had any kind of control or weight against their family would lead to nowhere good.

He understood why Dante wanted peace.

It was still wrong.

"We're done," Dante uttered through clenched teeth. "For now."

That was fine with Andino.

He only needed this to start the ball rolling elsewhere.

After all … this wasn't just for the Marcellos. This was for him, too. He was going to get what he wanted one way or the other. His uncle had given him the means and the motive when he said it would be the men sitting at the Commission who held him back from having Haven. It was the people there who would tell him no, and refuse him the woman he wanted the very most.

So, fine.

He'd make sure those who made up the Commission were people he chose to be there. That's all there was to it.

That was the rope Andino needed—some men might hang themselves with it when given the chance, but he wasn't that kind of man. He was the kind of man who didn't mind using that rope to hang someone else.

And if the Marcellos came out better for it, which they would, then he didn't see the problem. His uncle didn't need to know that, though.

That wasn't part of the plan.

Andino had just stepped out of the office while his uncle still muttered on behind him when his phone started to ring with a familiar tune. He grinned down at the name flashing on the screen.

Haven.

It took her long enough. He thought the note on the flowers was a nice touch … he just didn't think it would take her this long to call about them.

Because really, what else would she be calling for?

She constantly surprised him.

SIX

Haven eyed the bushel of flowers resting in the vase she had managed to find in one of the many boxes that she had yet to send to storage. Despite the confusion those stupid flowers made her feel every single time she even looked their way, she kept them on her table. Right in the very fucking middle.

They were the first thing she saw whenever she came into the kitchen, and the last thing she saw before she left. She watered them, fed them the plant food that had been shoved in with the stems, and even carefully pruned away any dead foliage lest it kill the healthy parts of the other flowers.

She *hated* them. She hated the beautiful flowers with their colorful, soft petals because they constantly reminded her of the man who gave them to her, and how cruel love truly was. Because they were something she wasn't willing to get rid of even if it would make her feel better to do exactly that, and then put them out of her mind … just like Andino. Because they caused her pain without meaning to, and she was not smart enough to put an end to that agony.

So yes, she hated them.

And yet, she took care of them, too.

It was not lost on Haven how fucking ironic it was that those flowers and the way she treated them with great love and care were a perfect mirror to her relationship with Andino. She treated their relationship the same way she treated these stupid ass flowers. With love and care. While he—like the stupid flowers—only gave her confusion and pain in return.

She tried her best to ignore the note that had been attached to the flowers. That only lasted a few short days, though, because like the flowers … she wasn't able to toss the note, or stop looking at it whenever she stepped foot in this damn kitchen.

How was she supposed to forget about something when she was constantly reminding herself of that very thing?

She tried to put it out of her mind.

And failed.

So, when trying to ignore the note and what it might mean failed, she regaled herself to *not* calling Andino about the note. It became her next task.

She failed at that, too.

Fuck her life.

"Ciao, mia bella donna."

Why did he have to sound like that?

All dark, smooth, and entirely bad for her health?

His voice alone was enough to get her heart pounding, and her chest tight. The sound of him calling her beautiful in Italian could make her wet between her thighs, and ready to run right back to him even if that was the very last thing she should do.

Oh, yeah.

Entirely bad for her health.

In more ways than one …

"Andino," Haven greeted civilly.

Somehow, she managed to keep her tone level. She thought she didn't sound stupid with her feelings just from the sound of his voice alone. She really fucking *sucked* at this whole thing, but it wasn't entirely her fault. It was *his*. He did this to her, and he kept doing it, too. She didn't want to be played with. Not her heart, her body, or her soul. She loved this man, but that didn't mean she had to allow him to keep hurting her, too.

That was Haven's hard limit.

It wasn't happening.

"What can I do for you today?" he asked.

Haven clenched her jaw, and passed the flowers another look. Not that those damn things were very far from her mind lately—*clearly*. It just irritated her so goddamn much that he could act as though nothing was wrong, and they were perfectly fine. That nothing had happened, and he hadn't watched her leave his house a few days earlier after telling her *he didn't love her*.

Like he didn't send her flowers that same day with this confusing fucking note!

"Do you care to tell me what that note means?" Haven said.

Andino made a low noise—sexy and husky at the same time. "Which note would that be, baby?"

"Don't call me that."

"Oh, you're in *that* kind of mood today."

Jesus.

Maybe calling him was a mistake. He seemed bound and determined to work every fucking nerve she had, and happily so.

"You know *exactly* which note I mean, Andino," Haven said, refusing to indulge the bait he offered. If they got in to that argument, then she knew there was no way in hell she would get the answers she wanted. "The one you sent along with these fucking *flowers*."

"Do you not like the flowers?"

He posed the question so genuinely that she wanted to laugh. Instead, she just let out a frustrated noise.

"Because if you prefer another type, Haven, just let me know, and I will have those sent to you tonight. Is that what you—"

Oh, my God!

"This isn't about the *flowers!*"

Andino made another one of those noises. "Then why are you yelling at me about them?"

Yep.

Every nerve—this man knew how to work them like a pro.

"The note—what does it mean?" she asked quietly.

There, she'd managed to gain back *some* semblance of control. How long it would last, however, was an entirely different story. Probably as long as it took Andino to start acting ... well, like himself, apparently.

"It means exactly what it said," Andino replied after a long pause. "That I am a terribly good liar, which means you were exactly right when you said that to me before you left my house. I am a good liar—I *lied*. And so, I felt the need to tell you exactly that."

"That you love me, you mean," she whispered. "You love me."

"I don't know how to *not* love you, Haven."

God, yeah.

That's what she wanted to hear.

That didn't mean she wanted to *know* it, too.

Those were two very different things. Like the different parts of her that kept warring back and forth day in and day fucking out about this man. Her heart and her soul knew exactly what they wanted—*Andino*. Her mind, on the other hand, was the part that kept screaming *no*, and *bad*, and *run, girl*.

Because him saying that—that he loved her—only left her feeling more pain and confusion than ever. He had made the choice. He had done this to them. She felt like rope being tugged in two entirely different directions. He had control of one end, and her mind had control of the other.

Healthy, and unhealthy.

Good, and bad.

What she wanted, or what she needed.

"You said it," she pointed out, not even bothering to hide the ache coloring her words as she spoke. "You said it—we're over. *Done*. You chose that, Andino, not me."

"I did say that."

"Then why are you doing this to me? You're playing a game with me, and I don't want to be played with. *I am not a toy!*"

She'd told him this before. She was going to keep saying it until he fucking *got it*. Her heart was not some bouncy rubber ball for him to play with when he was bored. He was not going to keep hurting her time and time again just because he fucking could.

49

Haven wasn't a masochist.

She didn't like pain.

"Please don't play games with me," she whispered. "Let me go, and let me move on, Andino. That's what I want."

"I can't do that. I want you too much to do that, Haven." Andino chuckled under his breath, adding, "And I think you want it to … otherwise, you wouldn't have called me today. You didn't need to call, woman. You could have thrown that note away, and forgot about me. You don't need answers to questions when you don't really give a fuck about them. So, what does that say about you? I don't think you want me to stop, or let you go. Do you?"

Well, then …

Fuck.

"You said we were done," she repeated.

So, shouldn't that be *it?* Shouldn't that end this? Shouldn't he let her walk away?

Haven felt so. Andino did not, apparently. She wished she could be surprised.

Without a hint of decipherable emotion in his tone, Andino replied, "And I lied. We're never going to be done, baby. Not now."

God.

She hated him too.

And yet she couldn't hate him at all. Not when she loved him.

• • •

"Are you ready for the good news?"

Haven looked up from the paperwork she had spread out on Safe Haven's bar to see Dale crossing the club's empty floor. In his hand, the realtor held a manilla file. On his face, a large, pleased smile.

She straightened on the barstool, and pushed the papers into a semi-organized pile that wouldn't be in their way during their conversation. Sunday happened to be the only day Safe Haven was closed, but despite the fact she could have done all her paperwork from home, Haven still found herself coming to the club.

For the memories, maybe.

Nostalgia.

She only had to peer around the empty place to know she was going to miss it once it was finally gone. The constant movement, and the people. All her hard work, and the decades of history that had walked on these floors.

Yeah, she'd miss it.

Her father, surprisingly, didn't have an issue with her selling the business. It was the fact she was going to upend her entire life and put it on hold that her father and mother took issue with. Even if her mom was sick.

"Tell me the good news," Haven said. "I need some lately."

To say the fucking least.

Her whole life was one giant mess after another, and nothing seemed to be changing about that any time soon. It all stemmed right back to Andino, too. She should just tell him to fuck on off to wherever the hell he came from, but a part of her didn't want to. Haven wasn't the type of woman to let a man play games with her head and heart, but here she was.

If only …

If only she could sell the club, and her house, then she would be free and clear to do whatever in the hell she wanted to do. Free to get far away from New York, and whatever strange hold Andino had on her. She couldn't think clearly when he was around, and she just needed … to get back to what made her, *her*.

Go back to the things that made her happy.

She'd *hoped* he could be the thing that made her happy, but Andino seemed to make a challenge out of proving Haven wrong every single chance he could. She had to start putting herself first—that much was clear—and stop allowing him to hurt her.

Simple as that.

Dale took a barstool next to Haven's, and threw the manilla folder to the bartop. He gestured at it with one finger, and a proud smile. "There's your good news right there. Take a look. Go on, and tell me what you think."

Haven quirked a brow, and reached for the file. Dragging it in front of her, she flipped it open, and did a quick scan of the paper on the first page. It was nothing more than a *very* large number scribbled on a white piece of paper.

Mind you, the number made Haven's eyes widen.

"Is this …"

"An offer for the club," Dale replied, his smile growing wider.

Oh, wow.

Haven blinked as she took in the number a second time. "That's a hell of a lot more than what I asked for."

Dale nodded. "I actually had two other offers come in the same day. One for a few thousand less than your asking price, and another for *exactly* the asking price. When I happened to mention that to the middleman for this offer, he was quick to say that he figured his offer would be the one you would be more interested in taking."

Haven cleared her throat; overwhelmed didn't begin to adequately describe what was running through her mind. "I can see why he thought that, yeah."

That extra money would do *wonders* for her mother's medical bills. Sure, her parents had insurance that covered a lot, but it only went so far. Haven had a savings that she didn't mind depleting for her parents—even if they argued or told her no—but having a bit of a safety net was always comforting.

Haven flipped through the papers in the folder, checking out the other details. It seemed the buyer didn't have an issue with the terms Haven put on the sale of the club like the name remaining the same, and the employees staying on as long as they were willing, and followed the rules as they always had.

"Who is the buyer?" she asked.

Dale reached over, and flipped back to a page Haven had quickly overlooked as it just had a business name, and details. Nothing that she found particularly useful.

"An investor wants to buy it, actually," Dale said, "and the offer came in from that investor's lawyer under their company. It's not uncommon for buyers to use their businesses as a shield when purchasing properties, or whatever else. It adds to their portfolio, and also gives them a bit of protection. They can write it all off as a loss for their business should the need arise."

"Like a shell company?"

Dale shrugged. "You could consider it that, yeah."

Huh.

"And this company—"

"Has quite a portfolio of businesses spread across the state, and elsewhere," he said.

Well, then …

Haven *had* said she wanted good news, and this certainly fit the bill. She did another quick scan of the contents inside the folder, taking her time to look over each paper, and memorize the details.

Part of her thought, *do you really want to do this?*

Do you really want to get rid of this place?

A louder part screamed, *one step closer to getting out of this city.*

Wasn't that what she wanted the most?

"Okay," Haven said, pushing the folder aside, and giving Dale her full attention once more. "Where do I sign, and how do we get the ball rolling on taking this offer?"

The man laughed. "I will call the buyer's contact as soon as I leave here to let him know everything looks good, and you're a go on taking the offer."

She clapped her hands together. The relief was a sweet sensation clawing through her bloodstream. "Okay, good."

"But you should be warned ... the lawyer who made the offer was clear on the buyer's wishes, and it could take a bit of time to get through all of that."

Ah, shit.

Haven gave the man a look. "And what exactly does that mean, now?"

"The buyer is pretty particular and picky about the businesses they purchase, I guess. They have to make sure everything is on the up and up. They don't want to buy a place only to find out it's two steps away from being condemned. Never mind, building code violations and health code issues—that all spells fines and problems."

Haven *tried* not to be offended. She really, *really* did. It was fucking hard. "Safe Haven is up to date, follows all the codes, and there isn't even a goddamn *shingle* loose."

Dale put his hands up in mock surrender. Okay, so maybe she could have curbed her attitude a *little* for that one. But probably not—this place had been her father's baby, and now it was hers, too. There was no way in hell that Haven *wouldn't* get offended at someone suggesting the place was a fucking dive.

Unreal.

"It's pretty standard for all of this stuff to be checked out during a sale," the realtor said. "I promise it's not personal."

Haven sighed, and rested her chin on her palm as she stared at the shiny bottles gleaming under the lights of the built-in bar.

"I take it that you didn't have to worry about those things when you bought the place?"

"I bought it from my father—we had inspectors, but all the reports went straight to the bank, and we already knew the place needed some work. I agreed to have it all done before re-opening, and I did."

Dale made an understandng noise in the back of his throat. "Well, it'll be a little bit more extensive this time around. You usually *could* just make a call, and shell out the money to have inspectors come in to check out the place, but the buyer requested *their* chosen inspectors do so. Which is where the time thing comes in ... depending on how long they want to fuck around with getting all of that done, we could be looking at a couple of months."

Jesus.

But the offer ...

The money ...

It was too good to ignore. She could easily take one of the other two offers, but she kept going back to that extra money, and the idea of how helpful and useful it could be for her mother in the end. Being the smart,

53

reasonable woman she was, Haven couldn't turn it down even if it did mean she might be stuck in this goddamn city for another couple of months longer than she originally planned to.

Details, she supposed.

Those were all just details.

Haven could deal with it later.

"Accept the offer," Haven said, deciding on her choice but still not entirely *settled* with it. Funny how that worked. She bet this would be yet another decision of hers that would keep her up at night to overanalyze and consider. Like she didn't have enough shit already on her plate to do that, for fuck's sake. It seemed like she was making decisions that lingered with her in all the wrong ways a lot lately. "And let's get this thing started."

Dale gave her another wide smile as he slipped off the stool. "You got it, Haven. Congrats on this, huh?"

Yeah.

Congrats.

Why didn't it feel like something worth celebrating?

That was the better question.

• • •

Haven paid the cab, but even as she said goodbye to the man who had been regaling her with stories about his toddler-aged granddaughter, her attention was on something else. Or rather … *someone* else.

A man stood at the end of the walkway leading up to Haven's small Brooklyn home. She recognized him immediately even though she had only seen him in passing maybe once or twice. She'd had a single conversation with him on the side of a street not very long ago when he'd been tasked with diverting her attention so that she didn't run into Andino's mother coming out of his restaurant.

Pink, she thought the man's name was.

All she knew about him for sure was that he looked like a goddamn linebacker—which in itself was a bit intimidating—and that he worked for Andino. That was it.

It wasn't so much that Pink was standing on her walkway that bothered Haven as it was the *why*. Why the fuck was he here, and what did he want? Not to mention … *why* did he have a small bouquet of winter flowers in his hand? It all made Haven think Andino was somehow involved because how could he not be?

And she didn't like that at all.

It got her irritation spiking all over again.

Stepping out of the cab, Haven took a minute to fix her coat, and watch the black and yellow checkered car drive away. It was only once she couldn't see the cab anymore that she turned to greet the man standing on her walkway with the flowers.

"Pink, right?" Haven asked.

The man nodded. "That's me."

Haven eyed the flowers in his hand. "Let me guess—Andino sent you?"

"You would be right."

Great.

"Do you often run flowers to women all over the city for him?"

Ouch.

Even she could hear the heat in her tone. Haven had no reason to believe Andino was running around with multiple women. In fact, she believed that he wasn't simply because he told her that. Even so, she couldn't resist taking a cheap shot just because the opportunity presented itself.

Maybe she was a little petty.

Pink lifted a single brow, saying, "This is the first time I have ever delivered flowers for him, actually. He thought you might appreciate a familiar face rather than a random delivery man."

"Well, he thought wrong."

Not that she didn't *like* Pink. She didn't have a reason to dislike him, as far as that went. That was not where Haven's problems originated. Her issues all stemmed right back to Andino, and the fact the man seemed to be playing some kind of game with her. She was *not* up for that at all.

He wasn't giving her a choice, either.

"My apologies," Pink said quietly.

Haven let out a sigh, and crossed her arms as she came closer. "It's not your fault. I know you're just doing your job."

"I am. Would you like me to carry the flowers in, or ...?"

"I can handle it."

"Lady's choice."

Pink carefully handed the flowers over, and Haven didn't miss the small card sticking out from the top. This time, it *was* Andino's handwriting staring back at her. A simple, single sentence with his initials attached at the end.

I thought your other ones might be starting to wilt. —A.M.

"Thank you," Haven said.

Pink nodded. "Have a good day, Haven."

Probably not.

Not with these goddamn flowers staring back at her. Wasn't it bad enough that she still hadn't gotten rid of the ones on her table even though they were actually starting to wilt a bit? Wasn't it bad enough that the first note had now migrated from her kitchen table to the stand beside her bed?

And now she had more ... more to look at and ponder and *over-fucking-think* because Andino couldn't seem to let her go.

She didn't have time for the games this man wanted to play with her. She wasn't strong enough to fight back, and she didn't know where to start even if she actually *did* want to fight back. Although, she *didn't*.

Like he's giving you a choice, girl.

Her mind was extra punishing today.

Haven waited until Pink had slipped inside his car, and was driving down the road before she walked up to her house. She juggled her bag, and the flowers in order to be able to unlock the front door. Once she was safely inside her house—as empty as it fucking was—she felt a slight bit better.

No one to see her confusion.

No one to watch her cry.

Just her.

Alone.

What a place that was.

Haven glowered at the flowers and the note all the way to the kitchen. She set the bouquet on the island, and wished her gaze alone was enough to make the damn things disappear. She couldn't be so fucking lucky.

Before she could think too hard about it, Haven grabbed the flowers, and dumped them into the open garbage can next to the island. She *loved* flowers. All kinds of flowers, really. She didn't like them, however, when they felt like a bid to entice or tease her by a man that she wasn't even sure if she wanted to see his face ever again.

What a complex that was.

She loved him.

And she hated him.

With the flowers in the garbage, Haven tried to go about doing *anything* else. She made herself a coffee, and even pulled out a few items from the fridge to make something to eat. And still, her mind continued to travel back to the flowers in the trash can. She couldn't even stop herself from looking back that way, either.

Although ... mostly at the note.

So weak.

Before Haven could talk herself out of it, she snatched the note out from the top of the flowers, but left the rest right where they sat.

She'd keep the note.

Fuck his flowers, though.

SEVEN

"You learn how to be a diplomat over time," Dante said as he and Andino crossed the street. "Because this business doesn't give you a choice. You're not muscle—not the enforcers on the street who threaten and use their fists to get things done. You are the *boss*. And you must talk like one. You're expected to talk all the time to get what you want, and to make sure things get done properly. You learn how to do that over time."

Andino gave his uncle a nod, but he wasn't really sure what Dante wanted him to say. Well, he did know, actually. Dante wanted him to stay quiet, and *learn* something. He wasn't looking for an actual response.

"Are you ready?" Dante asked as they neared the entrance of a restaurant.

Andino shoved his hands into the pockets of his slacks. "As ready as I will ever be."

"Good. This is a long time coming. It's time to put an end to it. Remember that. It's every reason why we're here."

He gave his boss a look, but said nothing. Again, that wasn't what Dante wanted. He pulled open the door to the business, and let his uncle go in first. It took Andino's vision a moment to adjust to the change in light. The quiet restaurant was nothing to get excited about, but one couldn't scoff at it, either. There were no patrons enjoying breakfast at the place— apparently, it was one of those that didn't open until noon, anyway.

The men of the hour—Andino was sure *they* felt they were the men of the hour, anyway—waited at the table in the middle of the main floor. Both were standing, and chatting quietly with one another although they silenced the moment Dante and Andino came inside the place.

Kev and Darren Calabrese.

They weren't the only ones there, of course. Dante had several men posted outside, and one inside who had entered before them. *Muscle*, and nothing more. Or that's how his uncle put it. Someone to watch their backs because one couldn't trust the fucking Calabrese brothers with an inch when they were sure to take a mile when a man wasn't looking.

For the Calabrese side, it looked as though Kev and Darren had followed the same line of thought by only having a few of their men there to keep an eye on things. Enforcers that Andino recognized from their organization.

Neither Dante and Andino, nor the Calabrese brothers had invited anyone with any real *pull* to the meeting between their families—no one

57

who could speak up and use their voice to cause trouble. Just the bosses, their underbosses, and that was it.

Andino wished he could say that he was surprised the Calabrese finally agreed to a meeting and were entirely willing to allow Dante almost all the say in how the meeting went down, but he couldn't. Again, the Calabrese were fucking predictable. They'd been working for a long time—long before John killed their boss—to get something from the Marcello family be it power, or standing through their name.

It was who they were.

It was what they did.

Kev had taken over the Calabrese faction after his father was killed. It was almost amusing how the man was quick to slither into his father's seat like the man had never been sitting there to begin with. But what could one really expect with this bunch?

Closed mouths didn't get fed.

Wasted time was gone forever.

It wasn't as much the men that surprised Andino but the quiet woman sitting at the table next to where her brothers stood.

Siena.

It had been a long while since Andino had seen the woman. Ever since her brothers came to John's house that night, and demanded she be returned. Andino had to take Siena in a second time just to make sure he *was* seeing the same woman because ... here, like this ... she didn't seem like the same woman at all.

Downcast eyes.

Quiet.

Hunched shoulders.

Perfectly made up in her dress, hair, and makeup.

Oh, sure, the woman was beautiful. He was sure that was the very thing that his cousin had first noticed about Siena. But quiet, meek, and submissive? Andino didn't think those sorts of things would interest John at all.

Since he knew Siena *had* been quiet since that night she was returned to her family, he was starting to wonder if that wasn't by her choice.

Andino didn't get the chance to think on it for long. Dante moved forward, and Andino went with his uncle silently. Kev was the first one to stick his hand out to reach for Dante's, and shake. The boss always went first. Andino couldn't help but pass the two bosses a look when they shook hands—he couldn't hide the disgust that slammed through him at the simple action of two men shaking hands.

Why?

Simple.

Kev Calabrese was nowhere *near* the man Dante Marcello was, and he would never be. That was just fucking fact. There was no way a Calabrese man could have even a fraction of the honor in his pinky that a Marcello man radiated constantly. They were two entirely different breeds of men.

There was a long-standing, unspoken rule in Cosa Nostra that when two or more bosses were in the room, they became equals in a sense. That way, the rest of the men who were watching didn't feel like they had a reason to cause trouble.

The problem with that for Andino was the fact *no*, he didn't think a boss who was clearly above another and had been for years should lower his fucking standards for someone else. And he did not plan on being one of those bosses when his time did come.

"Andino," Kev greeted him, letting go of Dante's hand and looking like he might try to shake Andino's. "The underboss position suits you, old friend."

Friend.

Right.

Andino almost fucking scoffed.

He did manage to keep his hands firmly tucked inside his pockets which was enough of a hint for Kev to not try and shake his hand. Thankfully. Dante didn't miss Andino's sneaky move if the look his uncle passed him from the side was any indication, but he didn't say anything as the meeting was moving forward, and he had more important things to deal with at the moment.

Small blessings.

The last thing Andino wanted was to sit down and make nice with these fucking fools. Hate was a strong word to use—he tried not to unless it was absolutely needed, but damn him if it didn't fit for the Calabrese.

He *hated* them.

"Let's get this started, yes?" Kev asked, gesturing at the table and the waiting chairs. "The sooner we get this finished, the sooner we can get back to the things we all want to be doing."

"I agree," Dante murmured.

Andino allowed his uncle to choose a seat at the table first, and then Andino took the one next to his uncle. It was only once he had sat down that Siena finally lifted her head. He didn't miss the way her gaze drifted to him, but just as quickly, dropped to stare at her hands resting on the table.

"Let's get right to the point, shall we?" Dante asked, leaning back in his chair and folding his arms over his chest. "The violence needs to stop between our respective organizations before it goes too far, and we both lose more than we can afford to."

Kev arched a single brow as he stared hard at Dante. "A little late for that, isn't it, Marcello? Your nephew took our boss—our *father*. I like to think that he was someone we couldn't afford to lose, and yet, here we are."

Andino didn't miss the scowl that drifted over Siena's mouth, but just as quickly, she hid it by glancing away from the table altogether.

Yeah, Matteo Calabrese was really a *loss*.

Fucking fools.

"Did we not offer to make peace somehow after that event?" Dante asked. "Did I not apologize for the misstep?"

Darren's gaze blazed from where he sat next to his brother. "You call killing our father a *misstep*?"

Dante blarely glanced at the man. "Are you willing to act as though neither of you had any hand in attempting to manipulate John and his mental state into a worse place for your own gain, then? I mean, if you're going to play the saints, you should at least make sure you're *saintly*, Darren."

Silence covered the table, and the men stiffened a little more in their seats. They were now balancing on a very delicate line, Andino thought. One that could quickly turn from calm voices and a reasonable conversation to shouts and promises of more violence. Andino wouldn't mind that as much, but it was not what Dante had come here to do.

"It seems to me," Dante said quietly, "that we have both found ourselves in a ... difficult situation. One of us wants to be in the right while the other one simply wants all this to stop. It's not difficult for you to come over to the other side, Kev. As a man who has sat in my seat for far longer than you have been sitting in yours, take my advice when I tell you the thing you want to do is the *right* thing in stopping all of this by whatever means you can. Is going up against a family like the Marcellos really how you want to mark your tenure as the boss of your family?"

Kev blinked, and opened his mouth to speak.

Dante was quick to interject before he could with, "Is a war where we tear your organization apart, even if you do land a few shots on us, how you want to be remembered when I make sure your family buries you?"

Yes, talking.

Bosses had to *talk*.

But it was all in using the right words.

Kev's jaw tightened as he stared at Dante for a good minute without saying anything. Siena stayed mostly unmoving at the end of the table while Darren, on the other hand, kept throwing glances at his brother like he was waiting for the man to stare back at him. Kev never once looked away from Dante.

"Well?" Dante asked.

"What is peace worth to you?" Kev's question came quietly, and seemingly innocent. Andino knew it was anything but those things. "Your wife's life, Dante? Your *daughter's*? How about your brothers', or their families' lives? What is it worth?"

Dante had a weakness.

Only one.

Them.

The Marcellos.

"It is worth the time and effort it took me to come here today to have this meeting with you," Dante replied calmly, "instead of blowing you to fucking bits when you walked out of your brownstone this morning, Kev. Shall we continue with a path that will end this feud between our families, or not?"

Finally, Kev looked away from Dante to glance at Darren. The two brothers shared a quiet look before Kev nodded, and went back to the conversation as though he hadn't even left it to begin with.

"We have *two* issues to handle on our side of things, actually," Kev said.

Dante waved a single hand. "By all means, tell me. I apparently have all the time in the world to listen."

If Kev heard Dante's low-grade insult, he didn't behave like it.

"It is more than just our father that we have to deal with in some way," Kev said, tipping his head to the left as if to direct attention to the quiet woman sitting there. "You see, we also have a woman who has been *badly* stained by the actions of a man in your family. She will never be seen as proper or respectable for a wife now—not after everything. What are we supposed to do with that?"

Andino scowled. "Let her have free will to do what she wants?"

That seemed obvious.

And *normal.*

Dante lifted a hand as if to silence Andino for a moment. "I can see where you might consider that to be a problem, but not how it becomes *my* problem, Kev."

"I think," Kev drawled slowly and with a cold smile, "that I could fix *two* of my issues by simply making peace with you, actually."

"How?"

"Isn't it obvious?" the man across the table asked.

"It is," Dante returned, "but I don't play word games, and if you're willing to do what I think you want to do, then you can be man enough to *say it*, so that the woman you're ready to trade can hear you say it, too. If you're going to be that man, then be that man, Kev."

Andino glanced at his uncle at the same time Siena's head snapped up, and her eyes widened. Her mouth opened to speak, but Kev was quick to talk first.

"A marriage," the man said, pointing a thick finger at Andino, and then down the table at his sister. "Between Andino, and Siena. It will make peace, and also, save my sister's reputation. I think it's a good d—"

"Absolutely *not!*"

The words all but exploded out of Siena's mouth. That shocked expression she had worn just a few moments before was gone now, and in its place rested rage and disbelief. She stood fast from her seat, making the chair topple over backward behind her. All eyes at the table were now on her, but she wasn't looking anywhere except at Kev.

"You won't have a choice," Kev murmured.

Siena didn't even *think* before she picked up the glass up full of water on the table, and whipped it at her brother. It crashed over the side of Kev's face, but to the man's benefit, he didn't even flinch.

"I will kill myself before I *ever* marry him, or any other man you put me in front of, Kev," Siena hissed. "Mark my words, I *will.*"

Kev's jaw tightened, but he stayed quiet. Lifting a hand, he gestured with a finger at his sister. One of his men who had been quietly sitting at another table stood fast, and crossed the floor. He took Siena by the arm, and was quick to remove her from the restaurant. Or at least, out of the main room. She didn't even try to fight, or protest with her voice.

Andino's attention went back to the table because his uncle was speaking, but not because he actually wanted to talk anymore.

"How do you feel about that, Andino?" Dante asked.

"Not Siena," he returned. "It cannot be her."

Not for himself.

Or even for *her.*

But for John.

Andino would *never* do that to John even if the last thing he intended to do was marry someone just because the fucking Calabrese wanted him to.

Dante nodded once, and looked back at Kev. "Who else is there?"

It took Kev a second to control the emotions flitting over his face, but somehow, he managed. "I have other sisters—two are too young. One is not. They are not ..."

Dante chuckled lowly. "You mean, Matteo's bastard girls."

Kev sighed, and nodded once. "Ginevra, specifically."

"Ginevra Calabrese," Dante said, his gaze turning on Andino again. "She's young, mind you ... but for the most part, appropriate. It would serve you well."

Well ... that was debatable.

Andino didn't see where he had much of a choice at the moment, and while an arranged marriage would put a bit of a kink in the rest of his plans … it was simply something he would need to deal with.

"I'll do that one," he agreed.

Dante went back to Kev. "There you go. Well?"

"The violence will stop," Kev said.

Andino's uncle was quick to stand from the table then. "I am glad to hear it. We will be in contact to set dates, and … get the details worked out for the marriage. Have a good day, Kev. You made the right choice today."

Dante turned to leave, and Andino didn't waste time getting up to follow. Outside the restaurant, a black car pulled up, and Dante slipped inside the back but not before giving Andino a look and parting words.

"We'll tell the rest of the family tonight. *You* also made the right choice."

Had he?

It didn't feel like it.

Andino nodded, and his uncle closed the door. The black town car for Andino was quick to pull up then, too, but he hesitated in getting inside only because Siena came out of the restaurant like a bat out of hell. There was no man following behind her, but a car was waiting across the road with the back door open—likely for her. Apparently, she hadn't entirely left the business earlier.

He had to figure out a way out of this.

Why not start with *her*?

After all, Siena had things she wanted, too.

"Siena," Andino called.

The woman stopped on the sidewalk, and gave him a look that burned.

He smiled, and winked. "You should take up a new hobby—yoga, even. Get yourself out of the house. You never know who you might find away from your brothers."

Her brow furrowed, and she said nothing as she kept staring at him. Andino only nodded, and then got into the back of the car.

There, he'd planted a seed.

She just had to let it grow.

• • •

"Well, how did it go?"

The first question came from Lucian damn near the second Andino and Dante arrived at the mansion, and entered the dining room. Food was already spread out on the table, and everyone was waiting. His father, and mother. Aunts, and grandparents.

They had all been waiting, it seemed. They hadn't even started to eat despite the fact it was well after the time their normal supper would happen.

"It went well," Dante replied.

Lucian passed a look down the table at Andino's father. "How well?"

"Yeah, what's happening from here on out?" Gio added.

Dante said nothing as he took his seat between his wife, and greeted her with a kiss to the top of her red-head. His aunt, Catrina, simply smiled over at Dante, but kept quiet. It was only once Dante was settled into a chair, and Andino into his own as well that the conversation started again.

"We've come to an agreement," Dante said. "Something that works for both of our families, and will end the violence in the city. No more fighting, everyone gets what they want. I would consider that a win, wouldn't you?"

"Yes, but *how* did that come about, son?" Antony asked from the head of the table.

Dante looked at his father, and shrugged. "A marriage."

Antony's old face didn't even crack with a single emotion to give away how he felt about that particular news. "Between who, exactly?"

Despite the fact his grandfather asked the question like he didn't already know the answer—there was really only *one* person in their family who was currently single and able to enter into an arranged marriage—all eyes at the table drifted to Andino.

He stayed quiet.

"Andino and a Calabrese daughter," Dante said.

"Which daughter?" Lucian asked calmly.

Despite his tone, Andino didn't miss the sharp edge to his uncle's tone. Always looking out for his son, even when John didn't know it. There was no way in hell Lucian would be okay with Andino marrying Siena … not after everything.

"Ginevra, wasn't it?" Dante asked Andino.

Andino nodded. "It was."

"Isn't that …" At the other end of the table, his grandmother, Cecelia, frowned as she looked at her own husband. "Antony, isn't that the mistress's oldest girl? Matteo's mistress?"

Antony cleared his throat, and nodded once. "As far as I know, yes."

Before anyone else could say something, Dante was quick to hold up a hand. It didn't matter that he was in another man's house or that their family often let everyone have a voice when it came to things like this. When he decided to speak, everyone else was quick to be quiet, and listen.

Boss's right.

"It's been done, and decided," Dante said. "This was the best course of action. Andino had his choice, before someone asks, and he agreed. It is *done*."

"So, they got what they wanted, then," Lucian murmured.

"I beg your pardon?"

"The Calabrese. The *snakes*." Lucian shook his head, and smiled bitterly. "They got what they wanted brother—they got *in*."

"It's a marriage, not a business agreement, Lucian."

Lucian nodded. "Right now. What comes later?"

That was a damn good question.

"Andi."

The soft murmur of his father's voice beside him took Andino's attention away from the men glaring at each other across the table. No one noticed Gio talking, it seemed.

"Yeah, Dad?"

Gio frowned, but his face returned to a passive state when he asked, "Is this what you want?"

"It's what has to be done."

"That's not what I asked."

"I have to protect our family."

And himself.

He had to protect himself, too.

• • •

The voices of Andino's family filtered out from behind him even as he left the mansion's dining room. They'd been debating and going over the Calabrese deal for longer than he figured was necessary.

It was done.

It would happen.

Or so they think.

Andino had his own plans to work on. He didn't think anyone even noticed him leaving the dining room, which was just fine with him. He had other things to deal with at the moment, and he no longer wanted to sit around and discuss the fucking Calabrese, or his newly arranged marriage to Ginevra.

Who he didn't even know.

It wasn't long before Andino stepped outside the mansion onto the large marble steps. He glanced up at the inky sky, and ignored the cold biting at his skin beneath the silk dress shirt he wore. He hadn't even bothered to throw on his coat.

He wouldn't need it.

"Pink!"

Like the good enforcer he was, Pink materialized out of practically thin air. Despite his size, the enforcer was good at blending in and keeping out of sight unless he needed to be seen. He followed Andino around—or whoever he was directed to watch by Andino—daily, and he rarely even saw the man.

A lit cigarette dangled from the man's mouth as he asked, "What can I do for you, boss?"

Andino eyed the cigarette. "Didn't Antony make rules about you all smoking on the property?"

Pink shrugged. "It's been a long day."

Wasn't that the fucking truth?

Andino let the cigarette thing go.

For now.

"Where's Snaps?"

"Sleeping in the back of the Lexus," the enforcer replied. "I turned it on."

"Good, good."

Pink took one last drag from his smoke, and then stubbed it against the heel of his boot. Wordlessly, he dropped the butt into his pocket. "So, what's up?"

"I need you to do something for me. I don't want word going beyond you and me about it. Like usual, you report back to *only* me about what's happening, and what I want to know. Got it?"

"Sure. What do you need me to do?"

It was time to put Andino's plans in motion. Or rather, some of them. Sometimes, shit just worked out for him. His father liked to say he was a lucky fuck like that, but Andino didn't know if that was actually the case or not.

Either way, it was time to get started.

"I need you to follow Siena Calabrese for me. Report back on where she goes on a daily basis, who she talks to, and what she's doing." Andino shoved his hands in his pockets in an effort to keep out the cold. His fingertips had already turned numb. Maybe he should have grabbed his coat. "I will be specifically interested in knowing if she starts to do anything different—say, joins a gym ... or something."

Yes, or something.

That worked.

Pink's brow furrowed, and he glanced away. "You want me to watch Siena Calabrese."

"That's what I said."

"Not your wife-to-be?"

Andino kept his face passive, and unreadable. "No, only Siena."

"All right."

Pink still sounded confused, but like the good made man he was, the enforcer didn't ask questions. He knew better than to demand details when Andino gave him a job. He was simply to do it, do it well, and nothing more.

"Start tomorrow," Andino said.

Pink nodded. "You got it. Reports daily?"

"Until I say otherwise, yes."

With that conversation done, and his plans moving forward, Andino was satisfied. He dismissed Pink before heading back inside the mansion. By the time he slipped back into the dining room where his family was *still* debating the Calabrese and the deal like it mattered, no one seemed to notice he had even left.

Or so he thought.

"Where did you go?" his father asked next to him.

Why was Gio so fucking observant?

"Stepped out for a breather," Andino said.

It wasn't a complete lie.

His father didn't question it or push, but then again, the conversation at the table took a lot of their attention, anyway.

"This is just another way for them to get *inside* our family in some way," Lucian said.

At the head of the table, Dante gave his brother a pensive look. "It's a woman, Lucian. We're not inviting the men to dinner, or doing business with them."

"*Yet*, Dante. We're not doing that yet."

"He has a point," Antony murmured from the other end of the table. "There is a reason why I kept our family so guarded and closed off from the Calabrese faction. They have always—*always*—wanted a piece of our business. They have never once stopped trying to get into our ranks in someway. I don't like that … essentially … you've given them an opening."

Dante opened his mouth to say something, but Antony was quick to raise his hand. It never failed to amuse Andino how even at his grandfather's age, and the fact he had stepped down from being the boss *decades* ago, when Antony spoke, he still headed the room. People gave him the chance to speak, and allowed him to take the floor without issue.

"I know *you* don't see it as an opening, son," Antony said, his gravelly voice dipping in tone. "But you don't have to see it as one. *They do*. And that emboldens them, and gives them the permission they think they need to … well, behave like the snakes we all know them to be."

"What is more important?" Dante was quick to ask. "Keeping the Calabrese far away from the Marcellos, or continuing to maintain peace in this city between all of the organizations? Go on and tell me. I'll wait. We have time."

Antony sighed.

Lucian scowled.

Dante only nodded. "Exactly. I am not giving them an opening. I am offering to make peace with them in this way. I know that it *seems* like an opening to them, but that doesn't mean it actually is. Nothing will change."

"Except Andino will marry one of them," his mother spoke up.

That wasn't like Kim.

She didn't even *try* to hide the contempt in her voice.

Dante passed Kim a look. "And your son agreed this was the best course of action. It also helps his standing considering he *does* need a wife when he finally takes my seat as the boss."

Kim looked to Andino. He saw her silent question even though she didn't voice it out loud.

"I have to protect the family," Andino told her. "I'll always protect my family, Ma."

It was *how* he chose to protect them that might differ from his uncle's plans. It simply wasn't time for Andino to explain that little detail, though.

They had other problems.

EIGHT

Haven sat on the park bench, and slapped the card she held against the palm of her hand. She didn't need to read the words on the card again to know what it said. As it was, she had probably read it one too many times already.

March 10th, noon. Be at the place where I first found you. —A.M.

She didn't need clarification about where *that* was. And as much as she wanted to rip that note off her front door when she first found it, Haven hadn't been able to do that, either. She took the note as a fucking sign, maybe. This was her last chance to say goodbye, and make it count. To really get Andino to *understand* whatever game he was trying to play with her was over now.

Maybe.

Nothing was ever that simple, though.

She heard footsteps approaching on the trail, but didn't need to look up to know it was him. She had always been able to feel his eyes on her long before he ever spoke to her. Despite everything, that was one thing that hadn't changed. Even if she wished it would.

"Right on time," Haven said, glancing up from her hands in her lap.

Snaps stood close to Andino's side with a stick in his mouth the size of a human arm. His dark eyes stared at Haven, waiting for her to greet him. She couldn't help but put her hand out to the dog who then dropped his stick, and came forward all at once to get his love from her.

Short, yet soft, fur met Haven's fingertips as she took her time greeting the pup. Snaps sat like the good boy he was, and accepted her silent hello with a wiggling tail against the cold ground.

Andino, on the other hand, had yet to say a word. Not that Haven was very surprised about that. She focused on Snaps for the moment. It was easier. The dog was far less complicated than the man he was always walking beside.

Or, that's what she found.

Finally, Andino spoke. And even then, Haven chose to keep her attention on Snaps. "I wasn't even sure if you were going to come today."

"I shouldn't have," she replied.

Andino made a noise in the back of his throat. "That's fair. But here you are, so that's what matters, isn't it?"

Was that what he thought?

Haven had news for him.

"You seem to be under some kind of impression that just because you make a demand, Andino, I must always follow it," Haven said, glancing up at him. Unsurprisingly, he was staring right at her, entirely unashamed. In some cases, that made it easier for her to see what he was truly feeling when he made such a great effort to hide it, but not today. Now, he was a blank slate, and she hated that more than anything else. "I'm my own person, Andino, and I have my own life. I came today because I wanted to, and nothing more."

Andino cocked his head to the side a bit, and his brow dipped. "Why did you *want* to come, then?"

"Maybe to tell you enough is enough. Or to ask my own questions. There's a lot of reasons, Andino. And I doubt that even one of those reasons will match up to yours."

He gave her one of his crooked smiles. A look she thought could do wonders for a woman's body without meaning to at all. She was no fucking exception to that rule, even if it did make her weak to admit it.

She *could* hide it, though.

Therein lied the difference.

"But you didn't have to come today to say anything to me or ask me a question if that's what you needed or wanted to do," he countered. "You have my phone number—though you barely use it anymore—and you know I'll answer for you. If all you wanted to do was get something off your chest, and make sure to stay the hell away from me, you easily could have made a phone call. You didn't need to come all the way out here in the cold to meet me on jogging trails, Haven."

Did he want a pat on the back for figuring that out?

A congrats of some sort?

She was all out.

"You're right," she murmured, "I didn't."

"Then, again, why did you come?"

"Because I wanted to look at you." Haven stood up from the bench, and Snaps was quick to get up on all fours, and move next to Andino again. She stared right at Andino, and refused to drop his gaze even when his face barely cracked with an expression or emotion. "Because I wanted to see your face when I asked you why you keep doing this to me. *Why?*"

Andino blinked. "What do I do to you, Haven?"

How could he not know? How did he act so blind?

She let out a bitter laugh, and waved a hand between them. "*This.* This right here, Andino! I thought I made it clear more than once that this was done—we're *finished*. And yet, you keep inserting yourself into my life time and time again. Flowers on my doorstep, and notes on my door when I get home."

Andino's gaze drifted over her face in that slow way of his that made her feel like he was taking all of her in, and appreciating her at the same time. It served no purpose, really, other than to heat up her body and make her *insane*.

"Yet, you don't actually tell me to stop doing those things," he murmured.

Haven stiffened. "I have—"

"You have not. Like this, you rant and rave. But I think that's more for yourself, than it is for me. It makes you feel better and not so fucking confused about why you smile every time you do find flowers, or a note. But you don't call—you don't send the flowers *back*."

Haven gave him a look she hoped burned. "I shouldn't have to do those things. My feelings should be clear."

"They're not. They're far from clear."

"A lot like yours, then, I guess."

Andino nodded, and glanced down the trail. "Walk with us?"

Haven thought to refuse, but two things stopped her from doing exactly that. One, the way Snaps was looking at her in his expectant, happy way. And two, the way she felt inside. Exactly as Andino had said. He was good for that ... calling her out when she didn't want to face something.

Despite wanting to be done ... they weren't.

They were so far from fucking done.

"Walk with us?" he asked again.

Haven sighed. "*Fine*."

• • •

"Your house hasn't sold yet?"

Andino's quiet question drew Haven's attention away from Snaps who had found a spot along the side of the trail to dig. "How did you know—"

"My man mentioned seeing the sign."

Oh.

"No, it hasn't sold yet," she replied. "The club is in the process of a sale, though."

Andino raised a brow high. "The club, too?"

"I can't run it from Florida, can I?" Haven shrugged. "At least, not hands-on like I would if I was here. That's a problem for me, so I would rather just liquidate what I can, and use that money to help my mother pay for her cancer treatments and whatever other bills might come up. They don't have a very big safety net."

Andino cleared his throat. "I'm sorry. I didn't realize she was sick again."

No, she supposed he wouldn't. She hadn't told him.

71

"I didn't know either," she admitted. "They hid it from me when I went to visit, and … well, I think they didn't want me to worry or uproot my life to go and help her. Not that it mattered in the end."

"Because that was the first thing you chose to do," Andino said.

"Yep."

How could she not?

"Besides," Haven added in a sigh as she looked back at him, "it's not like I have very much in New York to keep me here. Nothing is tying me down. Maybe a fresh start is exactly what I need."

His green eyes blazed, but he said nothing other than, "What about your friend? Valeria, and her child?"

"Gone."

Andino blinked. "I'm sorry?"

"Val is gone—took off one night. She didn't say goodbye, and didn't leave me a note to explain where she went, or why. She warned me once that she might do exactly that if she felt she had to. She wasn't *legal*, if you get my drift. It was still a surprise, and it hurt, but she did warn me. I have to give her that."

The two continued walking on the trail side by side in silence. He was so close to her that she could feel the heat radiating from his body. And still, he didn't try once to reach out and touch her or do anything more than just *walk* with her.

Haven appreciated that.

She also wanted everything else, too.

Fuck.

Why was she such a mess?

Why did this man make her this way?

"If the club sells, will you go even if the house hasn't sold?" he asked quietly.

Haven nodded. "I will. The house can stay on the market for months, for all I give a damn. I won't really be losing out when the mortgage is already paid, you know? It's just a waiting game to sell a starter home in the current market."

"I'm surprised the club hasn't sold already. Businesses like that—proven ones—tend to fly off the market."

"That's what my realtor said, too."

"And yet, yours is still there."

Haven scowled. "I have a buyer. He—or she, who fucking knows since their lawyer is doing everything for them—is just dragging their ass through the process. But the offer was far better than the other two I was given, so it would have been stupid to refuse."

Andino said nothing.

Haven was fine with that.

She went to take another step on the trail, but Andino was quick to stop her. It was only his hand snaking tight around her wrist and then tugging hard to spin her around that shocked Haven the most. She hadn't been expecting him to do that when throughout their walk, he'd not once tried to touch her.

His kiss, however, didn't surprise her at all.

That was *most* familiar.

He pulled her into his arms, fisted the loose strands of her hair, and closed the distance between them with a burning, searing kiss. His lips were haunting to her, she thought. Each graze, and stroke they made over hers. Soft, at first, and oh, so slow. And then faster, but harder, too. His tongue struck out to lap against the seam of her lips, testing the waters before she parted her mouth and let him inside.

That was all he needed, really.

What could have been an innocent kiss burned far hotter when he had an all access pass to love her mouth exactly how he wanted to.

The way she loved his kiss the most.

Deep, and aching, and *true*.

The taste of him on her tongue.

Salt, and man, and musk.

Those fingers of his tightened in her hair, and kept her close. Like this, though, there was very little chance she was going to push him away. This was predictable between them. Haven was not very good at refusing him—or herself—when they were this close, and he was kissing her.

It was the last thing she wanted to do.

That kiss of his slowed until he pulled away altogether. Still, even as she spoke, they were close enough for their lips to touch. His nose grazed hers, and their foreheads pressed together.

"I will be going soon," she whispered. "When the club sells, and the ink dries. I have to go, Andino. I need you to let me do that, okay?"

There.

She said it.

Haven couldn't be clearer.

Andino nodded. "*Then*, you will go."

"And you'll let me go."

It was more than letting her leave.

More than knowing she would be gone.

It would be the end.

Of them.

An official end of whatever they were, and whatever they might have been. There would be no coming back from that because once she was gone, Haven wouldn't be turning around.

Ever.

"I will let you go," he murmured.

She still wasn't sure she believed him. Or maybe that was just her heart wishing for things that could never be. Not now, anyway.

• • •

"You didn't have to walk me to the house, but thank you," Haven said over her shoulder.

Andino stayed at the bottom of the steps leading up to Haven's house. Snaps had fallen asleep in the back of the car, and barely even moved when Andino got out to walk Haven to the door.

"Didn't I?" he asked. "Who else is making sure you get home safely?"

She had the door unlocked, and the knob turning under her hand. She should have left his words alone, and just went inside the fucking house like a *smart* woman. She shouldn't have turned around to look at him—for just one more peek—because then she wouldn't have seen the darkness clouding his features. As if the jealousy coloring his tone wasn't enough … no, she had to see that, too.

Goddammit.

Weak.

She was so weak.

Haven was a lot of things, but stupid wasn't one of them. Yet, when it came to this man, that's exactly what she turned into. A stupid woman with little morals, and no real control over herself, or her wants. He took all of that away, and more.

"No one is walking me home," she whispered, "or anything else for that matter."

"But someone will eventually," he countered, "and that someone won't be me. That's what kills me."

Fuck him.

Fuck him for doing that to her.

For saying that.

Fuck her, too, for being this weak.

Without thought, she spun away from the door, and moved down the steps. Andino didn't move until she was right in front of him, and leaning in close. Only then did he reach out to grab her, but she was already making her next choice.

The next fucking mistake.

It could only be a mistake, after all.

With the way they were going?

How they would end?

Of course, it was a mistake.

In one second, she was kissing Andino on the bottom of her steps. And in the next breath, the two of them were inside the house, and one of them had slammed the door. It was hard to think when his lips were on hers. It was impossible to make good choices when his hands were snaking under her clothes, and those rough palms of his were touching her in all the right places.

One hand tugging at her jeans harshly. The other, palming her breast after pushing her lace bra away. It was his fingertips tweaking her hardened nipple into a firm peak that made her pull away from their kiss just long enough to gasp.

He didn't seem to mind.

His mouth went to her neck instead.

"*Fuck*," he breathed against her skin. "Can't fucking get enough of you."

His hand had gotten her pants undone, although how, she wasn't fucking sure. All she knew was that his hand was in her pants, and stroking her overtop her lace panties in the best way. He knew how to work her body with the least amount of goddamn effort to get her crazy, and ready to beg. She never understood how he did that.

"Wet already, Haven." His tongue struck out against the hollow of her throat as his fingers slipped under the gusset of her panties. "You want my fingers, baby? My fingers, and my mouth, and then my cock? How do you want me?"

Wasn't it obvious?

"Oh, my God," she whined. "*All of it.*"

Was a flat surface close?

Fucking anywhere?

Andino's hand ripped away from her body at the same time his mouth did. Haven didn't get the chance to voice her disapproval over his loss because in the next breath, she was in his arms. He moved through her house like he'd done it a million times before. He climbed the stairs with fast steps all the while kissing her when she threaded her fingers through his hair, and pulled him in for another.

She wanted more of him.

More of his taste.

And then his kiss was gone, too.

Haven felt the way her body dropped through the air when he let her go. A brief moment in time when she felt suspended before her back hit the bed. Andino didn't even give her time to realize what had happened entirely before he was on her. Those hands of his tugging and grabbing and *pulling*. Dragging her to the very edge of the bed before yanking her pants down fast and hard enough to make her muscles ache.

He didn't need to spread her wide. Not when she did it for him.

She pulled her shirt up over her head, and discarded it somewhere behind her. She had to take her eyes off him for a single second to do it, which was a fucking shame. She didn't want to miss the sight of him looking like he did right then.

All wild, green eyes trained on her. *Coming for her.* A muscled, firm body leaning over hers as he loosened his tie, tugged his shirt open, and she got a good eyeful of his chest and the path of lickable abs leading down to the hard-cut V of his groin. He discarded that shirt and tie on the bed, and popped open his pants with a flick of his hand against the button.

And even if just the *look* of him wasn't enough for her … it was how he looked at her. How he took her in with a slow gaze, and the grace of a predator. Like he'd found exactly what was his, and he was coming to get it whether she was ready for him to or not.

He was perfect.

And fucking terrible.

Everything she wanted.

And nothing she could have.

Loving this man had the worst kind of consequences for her. It was unforgiving, and careless. Entirely too reckless, and bad for her health and heart.

There was no escaping it.

She knew it.

Andino let out another one of those hard groans of his that could make her wet from the sound alone when he peeled her panties down her legs. She was *soaked*—he didn't need to confirm it for her to feel her arousal dampening her thighs.

Leaning between her spread open thighs, he was quite a sight. His broad shoulders filled the space, and his gaze was trained on her pussy. His tongue peeked out to swipe over his bottom lip, and that only served to make Haven *shiver.*

"Let me hear *all of it*," he murmured. "I want it all. It's *mine.*"

Like this, it was.

She could give him that much.

The second his mouth connected with her pussy, Haven's body reacted on its own. Her back arched hard off the bed, and her hands flew out to find anything for stability. That just happened to be his shoulders.

Not that he seemed to care.

Andino was too busy eating her pussy like it was the last meal he was ever going to have to notice how hard her fingernails dragged across his skin. Every strike of his tongue against her clit accompanied one of those husky, approving groans of his.

Nothing made Haven hotter than that.

Just by his noise, she knew he loved the taste of her cunt on his mouth. It was only made better by his hands pressing hard against her thighs to open her up more, and the way he buried his face even firmer between her thighs.

He went back and forth between working her clit, to tunneling that tongue of his inside her slit. Licking and lapping up every bit of her juices, and keeping her thighs open for him all the while. Even when her gasps turned into high cries, he didn't let up.

He only drifted away from her pussy just long enough to say, "Fucking shake for me, Haven. *Scream for me.*"

Those delicious sparks were back to light up her skin when his mouth was on her cunt again. They made her hot, and took away her breath. It didn't matter how much air she tried to suck into her lungs, it wasn't enough.

Every inhale burned.

Every exhale ached.

Heat shot through her body like a raging inferno.

She came so hard. Shouting his name just like he wanted, and entirely spun. Unable to catch her breath, and with her thoughts a jumbled mess.

Haven barely even registered being flipped over, and it was only when Andino's substantial weight pressed into her from behind that her vision started to clear.

"Deep breath," she heard him say. "And trust me."

She did.

It was all she could manage to do.

Silk wrapped around her throat in two tight loops. Haven didn't even have to ask what it was—his *tie*. A twist of his hand at the back of her neck, and the tie tightened more. Not to a painful point, but enough that her breaths were measured, and her body felt like hot lava.

"There's my good girl," he murmured along the back of her neck. "You look good like this, Haven. Ass high for me, thighs wet with your cum, and bound up in my tie. *Fuck*, too good, really. Do you want my cock now?"

Even her words had to be measured.

She chose the right *one*.

"Please," she breathed.

"And you'll lick me clean just the way I like when I'm done, won't you?"

"*Yes.*"

Hell, she would beg to do it.

If that's what he wanted.

There was nothing quite like the taste of her on his dick after he'd been fucking her.

"That's what I want to hear," Andino said.

It only took one flex of his hips, and a hard tug of her body into his, and he buried his cock into her aching pussy. Slick enough to take him, Haven relished in the way her body was stretched open for every inch of his cock, and the way he held her tight to his cock once he was balls-deep. That first thrust was accompanied by his palm slapping her ass.

With the next thrust, another slap.

And then another.

"Jesus Christ," Haven whined.

She thought her voice was too high—too lost.

And yet, she didn't care at all.

Not when he was fucking her like he was.

Deep, hard thrusts that shook her bed, and had her body aching for more. The tie around her throat kept her hyperaware of every single move he made. From the movement of his hips driving into her from behind, to the way his cock glided along her G-spot with every thrust. It only added to the bite of pain from his hand cracking against her ass with every other thrust, and she was so hot that it almost felt unbearable.

Except it wasn't.

It wasn't even close to enough.

Her cries became a catacomb of noise to her own ears—sounds that melded and mixed with the slap of skin on skin, and his rough words in her ear.

Who else is going to fuck you like this?

Who else owns you like this, Haven?

Who owns your body?

"You," she choked out through the second orgasm that ravaged her senses. "*You do.*"

That was the terrible part of all this.

She was never going to escape him.

Not entirely.

NINE

Andino moved quietly around the bedroom as he picked up his discarded clothes from the night before, and shrugged them on. Snaps waited patiently by the bedroom door, never moving unless Andino called him in. He'd went out and brought Snaps in once he figured Haven was going to let him stay the night.

The dog *never* got to sleep in Andino's bed. It was a rule he'd made when the pup was little, and once peed in the sheets because he was too scared to jump down.

Not when they were here, though.

At Haven's, Snaps got to sleep wherever the fuck he wanted. And the dog made sure to get right up on the bed, and put his big ass body between Andino and Haven for the *entire night*. It would be cute ... if it wasn't a cockblock.

He should have gotten up earlier, and headed out of Haven's place if only so that he could make a trip home to get something decent to wear. A dress shirt that wasn't as wrinkled, or just an entirely new suit.

Who the fuck was going to notice?

He *should* put in the effort for today; it was a big day. God knew Dante would expect him to seem like he knew it was important, and to behave like it. The least he could do was act like he gave a damn about it all, but even that was asking for a little too much from Andino.

Besides, while he was still there with Haven, even if she was still sleeping and entirely unaware that he was about to slip out of her house, he was *there*. With her, and no one else. He didn't even want to think about what was coming once he left her house.

One thing at a time.

Andino sat on the edge of the bed, and kept watch on Haven over his shoulder as he toed on his loafers. With her back turned to him, all he could see was the blonde strands of her hair fanned out along the expanse of the pillow and the shape of her curves tucked under a white sheet. It took every ounce of his willpower not to wake her up ... even just to say goodbye.

His reasons for leaving her asleep were entirely selfish—he might as well just admit that right now. If he woke her up, and she asked why he was leaving so early, then Andino was going to have to lie. He surely couldn't tell her the fucking truth without Haven throwing something at his head.

Not that he wouldn't deserve exactly that.

He would.

Andino knew he was hurting this woman. Probably more than she could take even if she did put on one hell of a brave face for him. He didn't want to keep hurting her, so instead, he was stuck in this cat and mouse chase with Haven until his plans finally came together ... and he was able to get what he wanted.

Her.

That was Andino's only end-goal right now.

Just Haven.

She still wouldn't understand why he had to do what he had to do today. It would still hurt her. He opted for the coward's way out instead.

Standing from the bed, Andino shrugged on his suit jacket, and made quick work of buttoning it up the front. At least then, no one would notice the vest and tie underneath were the same navy blue silk from the day before, and his slightly wrinkled shirt would also be hidden. He considered that a win.

Andino's feet seemed to turn into cement when he rounded the bed to Haven's side. Despite not wanting to wake her up, he also didn't want to fucking leave. All that served to do was make him feel heavier than ever.

He didn't miss the items on her nightstand beside the bed. Every single note he'd left her in a little pile—it was really his only way of safely getting a message to her, but also, he thought it felt more personal. At least, for him.

He wrote to *no one.*

He wrote to her, though.

She kept those notes like she kept the flowers on her table. Even if the flowers were wilting something terrible now. It would be easy—he figured—for her to throw the flowers away since they were dying anyway, but she didn't.

She kept them.

It kind of felt like them, in a way.

He was sure this woman—this amazing, beautiful woman with her brilliant, bright soul—thought this thing between them was also dying. But fuck her if she wasn't going to try to hold onto them for as long as she possibly could.

Andino didn't blame her.

Bending down, he grazed his fingertips along her bare shoulder before pressing a quick, light kiss to her forehead. Haven didn't move, and her eyelids didn't even flicker. He almost wished she would get up, but this was better.

Before Andino could convince himself to stay one more second longer, he gave Haven one last look and then slipped out of her bedroom. Snaps followed behind—it was only the click of his nails against the hardwood floor that could be heard. Andino's steps were quiet and quick as he headed through the house.

As he passed by the kitchen, he stopped and glanced in. The flowers looked lonely as fuck sitting by themselves on the table. Really, other than a few boxes that had been taped up, the table and flowers were the only thing in the kitchen besides a few dishes that rested on a cloth on the counter.

He hadn't mentioned it the night before, but her place was terribly empty. All the art and photographs that had lined the walls and given the place a *lived-in* kind of feel were gone. Nearly all of her furniture had been moved out at one point or another.

It just didn't feel like Haven's place.

Andino supposed … he was partly to blame for that.

He stepped into the kitchen before he could think better of it. Grabbing the notepad and pen on the island, he scribbled down one more note for Haven to wake up to. He should leave her with something even if it might piss her off more.

A risk he was willing to take.

Ripping the note off the pad, and he set the yellow piece of paper under the wilting flowers. Another one for her to add to her collection.

I had to go, sorry.

And then, just beneath that, he'd written, *We're real, Haven. —A.M.*

Andino didn't miss the goddamn time staring back at him from the clock on the wall. Hell, he could feel the watch on his wrist ticking down to let him know he was already running late, and by the time he got into the city, he might make it to breakfast by the skin of his fucking teeth.

Jesus.

He gave one last look around Haven's place, and then slipped out of the kitchen, and the house altogether. Snaps darted ahead, and waited for Andino to open the passenger door of the car before he jumped in.

Andino checked his watch, not that he needed to.

He really was late.

Fuck.

He wished he cared.

• • •

"Where were *you?*" Dante asked harshly.

Andino didn't even look up from the phone in his hand. Instead, he opted to answer his lawyer back before his uncle.

We could close anytime, the lawyer had messaged while Andino drove across the city.

No, that wasn't going to work for him.

Continue to take your time, Andino texted back.

"Are you even listening to me?"

Trying *really fucking hard* not to roll his eyes, Andino shoved the phone into his pocket, and gave Dante the attention his uncle seemed to want. Standing outside of a restaurant, this wasn't exactly the best place for the two of them to get into one of their rows together ... but hell, if that's what his boss wanted.

"No, I had something else to handle," Andino said.

Dante scowled as he glanced down at Snaps. "Where were you? And also, he can't come in. I don't care what Lucian says when he's here, but not today."

Jesus Christ.

"Pink is coming to get him. Don't mind my dog. He's always taken care of."

Spoiled, really.

Not that it mattered.

Dante let out a noise, and passed Andino a look. "Do you think I am that stupid? That's twice you didn't answer my question. *Where were you?* You're almost late this morning."

Andino tugged on the sleeves of his suit jacket, and shrugged. "Woke up late."

Lies.

Dante didn't look willing to argue, and Andino wasn't about to go and offer his uncle the truth. So, unless the two of them wanted to stand there for any longer and discuss things that weren't actually going to get discussed in any great detail, this seemed like a giant waste of Andino's time.

And he hated wasting time.

Gesturing at the waiting restaurant, Andino asked, "Are we ready?"

Dante gave him another one of *those* looks. "Act appropriately today. The way I know your mother and father taught you to behave, Andino. This is important not just for you, but for her. Make her comfortable."

That time, Andino did roll his eyes. He didn't even try to hide it, and he didn't give a single fuck what it made him look like.

"Do I seem like the kind of man who wants to make his future wife uncomfortable?"

Because *yeah* ... that's what he was there to do. Have breakfast and meet his wife-to-be for the first time.

Should be fun.

"I don't know what kind of man you are sometimes, Andino," his uncle murmured as he moved past him when Andino opened the front door.

Yeah, him either.

Funny how that worked.

"You know, your mother might have enjoyed being here this morning," Dante said as a hostess directed them through the business. "You could have invited her along."

Why?

So, then his mother could meet and try to like a woman that Andino had zero intention of actually being with, never mind making a life with?

That seemed ... wrong.

"Just me today," he said. "Had I been able to have this breakfast go *my* way, you wouldn't even be here."

Dante scowled again. "You're in a mood, I see."

He always was, lately.

"Dante, Andino. We thought you weren't coming."

All it took was the sound of Kev Calabrese's voice drifting across the quiet restaurant for Dante to finally take his attention away from Andino. He was both grateful, and extremely fucking annoyed because of it, too.

Christ.

He hated the Calabrese brothers.

Kev and Darren stood on either side of a young woman who looked no older than twenty-one, or so. Hell, maybe she was younger than that.

Too young for me, Andino thought.

Nobody would care about that, though.

Kev was saying something else, but Andino tuned the man out. He didn't give a shit what Kev had to say, or how the asshole wanted this whole breakfast to go down between them. He was more interested in the quiet woman with her gaze turned down toward the floor, and her shaking hands clasped tightly together at her middle.

Oh, they'd dressed her up, sure.

An appropriate purple number that showed off her curves, and womanly appeal. Her long, dark hair had been let down in soft waves, and someone had taken time to do her makeup with care to make her look natural and fresh. He could see that she'd taken her hair color and the shape of her mouth from her dead father, but the rest? He suspected that came from her mother.

Whoever and wherever that woman was.

Ginevra Calabrese was a beautiful young woman. There was no doubt about that. Right then, though? She was also *terrified*. Andino could see it.

"Do you prefer Ginevra, or Ginny?" Andino asked.

He was quite aware that he spoke to her before he'd been allowed to—that her brothers hadn't even introduced her to him, and that was out of line. Andino didn't give a shit. All he saw was a scared young woman who didn't want to be there, but was quiet and doing what she was told *because* she had been told to do it.

That bothered him.

83

All eyes turned on him, including his uncle.

"Well?" he asked quietly.

Ginevra looked up, and her brown eyes landed on him. "Either is fine."

"But which do you prefer?" he asked.

"Ginny."

Andino smiled. "Okay."

Ginevra glanced down at her hands—her shaking had stopped, at least. "I'm very happy to meet you, Andino."

No, she wasn't.

Scared out of her wits, likely.

Not *happy*.

"I'm sure," he murmured. "Let's eat."

And maybe in that time, he could figure out a way to also get this poor girl out of the hell she had found herself caught up in. There was no doubt in his mind that should something happen with this arrangement, Ginevra would be moved to another man to satisfy her brothers' needs, or whatever the case may be.

A shame, really.

Fuck him for having a heart.

God seemed to like having a good laugh at his expense lately. Why not add one more laugh to the bunch?

• • •

Andino was not missing the way his mother kept passing looks at his father like she expected Giovanni to do or say something to his son. That was the thing about Kim—she wasn't very good at being subtle.

This whole silent attempt at conversation by his mother had been going on ever since he walked into their house an hour ago for supper. And he still hadn't even had supper.

Andino was over it.

"What?" he finally asked.

His mother glanced at him, but quickly went back to cutting the fresh bread on the island. "Nothing, Andi."

Gio chuckled under his breath, but kept quiet.

"Right," Andino said. "So, we're going to pretend like you haven't been shooting Dad looks all night or something?"

Kim sighed, and smiled a little. "I was just thinking … well, it's been a few days, hasn't it?"

"A few days for what?"

"Since your breakfast."

Oh, that.

Fuck.

He blamed his mother's curiosity about the whole Ginevra and marriage thing on the fact she really wished Andino would hurry up, and settle down in life. Then, she could have a half of a dozen grandbabies to spoil.

He didn't want to break his mother's heart, but there was no way on God's green earth that would be happening with the Calabrese daughter. It wasn't that there was anything necessarily wrong with Ginevra except for the fact she wasn't *Haven*.

And that was a whole host of problems for him.

"How did it go?" Kim asked.

She tried to sound flippant, but her tone came off entirely too sly for that nonsense. Andino gave his father a look—a silent plea to *help him*—but Giovanni acted like he hadn't even seen a damn thing.

Nothing new there.

Gio was far more likely to indulge Kim, anyway. Not to mention, Andino was sure his father was also curious about how all that had went a few days ago, and what would be happening now.

"It went fine," Andino settled on saying.

"*Just* fine?"

"Ma."

Kim shrugged one shoulder, and leaned against the island as she stared at him. "Don't blame me for wanting to know about her, or how you feel. I worry, Andino. It wasn't like this happened over time. It was quick."

To say the least.

"I feel fine," he lied. "And the breakfast went well."

Gio made a noise under his breath. "Even with the Calabrese there?"

Andino didn't even try to hide the scowl that slipped over his mouth at that question. "Well, they made things interesting."

Yes, that was a good way to put it.

Why the fuck not?

"And you like her, then?" his mother asked.

Oh, great. We're back to that again.

"Ginevra is ... pleasant," Andino replied.

He knew that was the wrong choice of words the moment they slipped past his lips, but there was nothing he could do now. They were out there, and his mother heard them. Which meant she also heard the fact he didn't actually compliment his wife-to-be, or offer anything that might show he held some kind of affection.

Kim was not going to miss that.

At all.

"I see," his mother murmured.

Gio sighed heavily and said, "It'll take time, I think, to get past the ... uncomfortable part of this whole arrangement."

"You mean the fact she's been told to marry me, and doesn't want to?"

Kim frowned.

Gio, on the other hand, nodded. "Yes, that."

"She does seem like ..."

"What?" his mother asked.

"Nice, Ma. She seems nice."

Which wasn't a lie.

Ginevra had been sweet, and entirely pleasant during their breakfast. She hadn't talked out of turn even once, and she was nothing less than respectful to him. Andino assumed—and probably rightfully so—that it was more because of her brothers than because she actually cared to be nice, but that was another issue for a different day.

He had to handle shit one thing at a time.

The ringing of a phone in another room sent Andino's father off the stool at the island. He was gone from the kitchen without a look back, leaving Andino alone with his far too curious mother, and all her questions.

God, he loved his ma.

He *did*.

Andino also didn't want to hurt her by refusing to answer her questions, or even telling her the sad truth. It seemed like his mother wasn't really going to give him a choice, though.

"Well," Kim said, "then what *can* you tell me about her, Andi? You wouldn't even let me go to meet her, and who knows when I will? Give me something to go on here. I want to ... like her."

Of course, she did.

Because Kim was *wonderful*.

Andino scrubbed a hand down his jaw, and used the moment he had to decide what he needed to do. He decided to give his mother what she wanted, but not about *who* she thought he was describing.

"She's independent in the ways she can be," Andino said, smiling. "And strong, I think, all things considered."

Kim's familiar gaze lit up. "Oh?"

"I appreciate that in a woman. One that can probably give my shit back to me as much as I throw it at her."

"She will certainly have to be able to handle you."

"I think she can," he returned. "She's smart, and quick. Capable of handling her own business, it seems. And she's beautiful. In the obvious ways, but in her own unique way, too."

"Hmm."

A small hint of a smile played at the edges of his mother's mouth. She had no idea that the woman he just described was one he had been in love with for months—one he fell in love with simply because she was who she was—and yet, couldn't have.

Kim didn't know Andino meant Haven. He wished he could tell her the truth.

"Snaps loves her," Andino added quieter.

His mother's gaze jumped up to meet his. "Snaps was there?"

"Outside."

Kim nodded. "That's a start, Andino. I know that this wasn't what you wanted … you had different plans for your life, but this could be good, too."

Oh, he doubted that.

Andino only smiled.

Thankfully, the beep of his phone allowed him to take his attention away from his mother without seeming rude. Or like he was *trying* to find a way out of the conversation. He turned his back on Kim, and checked the message. He hoped it was Haven, but like the stubborn woman she was … well, she hadn't once called or messaged him since he left her house a few mornings ago.

No surprise there.

Andino was giving her time.

Instead of Haven, it was a text from Pink. The enforcer keeping an eye on Siena Calabrese, and reporting back when something interesting came up. Andino was still trying to figure out what to do with that woman, after all, and how to get her *safely* back to his cousin.

Where she deserved to be.

Siena took up yoga—same time every week on Wednesdays and Fridays.

Andino looked over Pink's message again, and nodded to himself. Good, the girl did know how to listen, and follow directions.

That spelled good things for her.

Instead of replying to Pink, Andino sent off a message to John's father instead. A simple, *I think I might go visit John.*

Lucian would know what it meant.

• • •

"Yoga seemed like a good fit for you," Andino said as the woman of the hour stepped out of the changing rooms with her gaze turned to the floor. It was the sound of his voice that finally made Siena Calabrese take note of her surroundings, and who was near. Her eyes widened when they landed on him leaning against the wall. He gave her a quick smile, and when she glanced down the corridor with visible fear, he said, "Your enforcer is still outside like the dumb fuck he is."

Siena relaxed a bit, but not much. It had been a good while since Andino had seen this woman, and the last time ... well, it was when her fucking brothers dragged her away from John's house that awful night.

She looked better.

And yet, she still looked sad.

Not surprising.

Andino was hoping he could make things better for this woman, and maybe ... she could help him out, too. A tit for tat, kind of thing, if everything went well.

"Your yoga class starts in what, ten minutes?" he asked.

"About that, yeah."

"How long is it?"

"Hour and a half, sometimes a little less."

"Does the enforcer come in to watch, or check on you?"

Siena shook her head. "He hasn't so far."

"Good." Andino pushed away from the wall, and gave her a second look. "Do you want to change back into your other clothes, or are you good with the yoga pants and tank top?"

She only blinked. "What?"

"We've got places to go, and people to see. Do you want to change, or are you good?"

That fear in her eyes was back in a blink.

"I shouldn't leave," Siena whispered.

Andino arched a brow. "Not even to see John?"

That had her perking back up again.

He smiled.

"See, I thought if I could get you away from your brothers for more than five minutes at a time, we might be able to work on this whole mess we're in now," Andino explained. "Yoga seemed like a good fit for you, all things considered. You listened, and so here we are. It's a risk—you going with me, I mean—but is it one you're willing to take?"

Siena's hands tightened into fists at her side. "For John, yes."

Of course.

Love was crazy like that.

Or so Andino was learning.

"I have to be careful," Siena was quick to say.

Andino gave her a look. "Do you think I'm stupid?"

"No, but—"

"Good, then let's go."

Siena didn't move. "My brothers aren't stupid either, Andino. And they're not playing games anymore. Do you know they killed Ginevra's mother when she tried to step in and help her daughter when it came to the marriage to you?"

Andino stiffened.

Siena barked out a laugh. "I guess you didn't know that, huh?"

"No, but that explains a lot," he replied.

"Like what?"

"Why she seemed so scared when she had to meet me."

Siena glanced away from him. "She—and her sisters—are good girls. They've never really been involved in the mafia like the rest of us. My point is ... well, you get the point, don't you?"

"You have to be careful," he said. "Yeah, I get it."

"Good." Siena frowned, and that sadness came back into her eyes even as she tried to hide it by looking away. "They're never going to let me be with him now. Not after everything ... and now, with our families working together. Well, what's the point, Andino?"

He made a noncommittal noise. "The point, is that you never give up. Not until someone puts you in the ground, and at least then, you know the rest was worth it because you did all you could. Don't you remember what I told you that night when your brothers showed up and took you away?"

Siena nodded. "Yeah."

"What was it?"

"This isn't forever."

Damn right.

"Keep that in mind." Andino waved a hand at the exit door down the corridor that led outside the building instead of to the yoga class. "Care to surprise John with me? I think he could use a smile. If so, let's go. We're running out of daylight."

Siena didn't need to be told again.

TEN

How was it even *May*?

Haven blinked at the calendar on her phone for a third time even though the date still hadn't changed. It seemed like the entire month of April passed her by without any sort of warning, and here she was, in a whole new month.

"So, yes, another inspection," the realtor said.

She finally looked away from her phone at that to give the man her attention. It was him mentioning the date that had put her in this goddamn daze in the first place. She simply meant to check her phone to see how long it had been since she started this process for the buyer who offered her well above the asking price for the club, and instead, got lost in wondering how an entire month passed her by.

"*Another* one?"

"The buyer assures this will be the last one. You should get a call sometime this week to set up an appoint—"

Haven made a frustrated noise, and tossed her phone to the bar. "Yes, an appointment that will take *weeks* to actually show up, and get done. It'll be into June before that actually happens. You said I would have this place sold by now."

The realtor shrugged, and his face remained passive. "You very well might have sold it by now, but you chose what I would call an investor instead of a passionate buyer. They do their homework, and they don't mind dragging out the process. We can still go back to the original offers—one was willing to wait, if you changed your mind."

The thought was appealing. Maybe a bit too much, really. Haven was absolutely willing to take the cut in money if it meant she could get out of New York quicker, and down to Florida where her mother was still sick, and in need of help. At the same time, the idea made her feel selfish as hell.

Her mother *was* still sick. Her parents still needed help. Financial help, even if they weren't openly telling her that. Shit, Haven had seen all the medical bills from the first round of cancer years ago, and how it crushed her parents under its substantial weight.

They couldn't afford for her to take the drop in price.

"What would you like me to do?" the man asked.

Haven didn't answer him right away, instead taking a moment to glance away, so he couldn't see her face while she gathered her thoughts. She took in the empty club's floor, and all the tables and chairs that were waiting to be filled for the night. She had another two hours before the club would open, but she thought coming in early might help to take her mind off things if she stayed busy.

A fleeting hope, apparently.

Her mind was still as chaotic and confused as it ever was, now. That seemed to be her one constant. The thing she couldn't escape from no matter how hard she tried.

She had to keep busy—or try, even if it was a failed effort—because if she didn't, then she focused on all the things that *weren't* happening in her life. Like Andino, and his missing presence over the last month.

He didn't call, but he did send a text once in a while. He never showed up at her club, or house.

He had sent her one vase of flowers on her birthday with another one of his notes attached in the middle of April, but other than that … radio silence. She was being smart, and taking that for what it was.

This thing between them was dying.

Or … it was already dead.

Haven wasn't really sure which one applied, but nonetheless, it was happening. His distance, even if he occasionally did reach out, made her think that perhaps he knew the truth, too. Especially if she wasn't engaging him.

Not that she didn't *want* to.

Christ.

Haven wanted Andino more than anything, but she also didn't want to be hurt over and over again. Too much had happened between them for her to just … forget it all. Whether or not he understood that was a whole other matter.

"Well?" the realtor asked again. "What would you like me to do?"

It almost amused Haven how all she needed to do was get Andino on the brain, and suddenly, nothing else mattered. Work and life flew away because he took up all the space in her mind and heart, and left no room for anything else.

Why did it have to be like this?

"*Try*," Haven said pointedly as she turned her gaze back on the man sitting at her bar, "to get the buyer to speed things along. I don't want to go back to another offer if I don't have to. So yeah, try to get him—or her—to speed things up."

"I can try, but the buyer's lawyer is a goddamn pit bull. He's stuck in what he wants, and he doesn't budge very much."

Yes, so she was learning.

Haven was starting to get curious about the mysterious investor behind the company name on the paperwork sitting on the bar. She hadn't thought to look in to it before—there really wasn't a need. A part of her wondered what she might find if she did. Was this their normal standard when it came to buying a business? Fuck someone around until they were at their wits end?

Another day.

Now was not the time.

"Just try," Haven said. "As the saying goes, closed mouths don't get fed."

The realtor pushed off the stool with a nod. "I will try."

That was the best she could ask for.

As the realtor made his way out of the club, Haven seriously considered cracking open one of her top-shelf whiskeys just to take a couple of shots to ease her edginess. It wasn't like she needed to be in a mood once her workers started filtering in for their shift.

It was only the ringing of Haven's phone that stopped her from moving behind the bar. She picked up the phone from where she'd tossed it away earlier, and didn't bother to check the caller ID before answering.

"Haven here."

"Hey, sweetheart."

Haven wished she could say that at the sound of her father's voice, all of her stress fled as fast as it had come. She couldn't, though. Now, every single time her father called, she found herself on edge thinking that something might have happened to her mom.

It was constant.

It *sucked.*

"Hey, Dad," Haven said, keeping her tone cheerful.

Or as much as she could manage.

"How's Mom?"

"Good," Neil said. "She had a good day. The treatment wasn't easy today, but she didn't get as sick afterward. And she wanted ice cream."

Haven smiled.

That was good.

Usually, chemo left her mother unwilling to eat entirely. Sometimes, for days after. Sure, the doctors had her on meds that should increase her appetite, but Haven thought it was also a mental thing. No one could have much of a desire to shove food into their mouths when they knew the only thing that was going to happen soon after was the food coming back out … and not very pleasantly.

"That's great," Haven said. "Is she around? Let me talk to her."

"She's sleeping right now," her father said.

Damn.

"Well, don't wake her up. Let her rest."

God knew her mother needed it.

"How's things that way?" Neil asked. "The club doing well?"

"Of course. The realtor was just here. We were going over—"

Her father made a harsh sound on the other end of the line. *Fuck.* Haven shouldn't even have brought the realtor up, really. She knew better.

"I wish you wouldn't sell the club," her father said quietly. "You worked *so hard* to save that place after everything, and you shouldn't just give it up. You know your mother and I will be fine—we want you to live your life, Haven. This is *your* life."

"And you're a part of that," Haven returned easily. This was the same conversation they had been having for months. Nothing about it had changed. Her parents wanted one thing, but she knew that she had to do another. It was as simple as that. "You and Mom are a big part of my life, and every reason why I took over this club to begin with. And now, things have changed again. I should be where I can be most useful to you and her, but I don't think that's here, Dad."

"You should be *happy*."

Haven blinked.

She didn't know how to tell her father the truth but … she hadn't been happy for a long time. Sure, her mother's cancer coming back hadn't helped with that, but it was mostly everything else going on in her personal life that kept her down.

Her father didn't need to know that.

"Mae doesn't want you to sell the club, and uproot your entire life just because she's sick, Haven," Neil said, refusing to let this go. "She also wants you to keep living your life. It is not your job to take care of us—we can do that. We have been doing it just fine ever since we left New York."

But wasn't that exactly her job?

"Could we talk about this another day?" Haven asked.

When her father wouldn't let something go, then deflecting onto something else was Haven's next best defense. She was sure her father knew that she was doing exactly that, but he wasn't likely to call her out on it.

"For the record," her father said, "my opinion on this isn't going to change just because it's a *new day*, sweetheart. Neither will your mother's opinion. It's more stressful on Mae to think that you're giving up things you love for no other reason than you think she's dying. Do you understand that?"

Haven hesitated.

She hadn't, actually.

That one was new.

"I don't think Mom's dying …"

"You don't sound very convinced," Neil replied.

Yeah, shit.

"I just want to help," Haven settled on saying. "That's all, Dad. I need to help."

"You can help by living and being happy. That's what we want the most, sweetheart."

If only it could be that simple.

Haven knew it wouldn't be.

• • •

"Take five," Jackson said as he slid behind the bar.

Haven gave the man a side-eye that could rival the Devil's. "Does it really look like I have time to take a five-minute break?"

Jackson was quick to take the mixing shaker out of Haven's hands, and his posture said that she was not fucking getting it back anytime soon. Goddamn him.

"We also need to keep people coming into the club, Haven," Jackson said. "And you've snapped at the last three patrons who came up to order drinks."

Had she?

Jesus.

Usually, she didn't mind busy nights. They were the best kind to work, frankly. Tonight, however, seemed to be the night when literally *everything* was willing to test Haven's very kind patience. She blamed it on the visit with the realtor earlier, and then the call from her father. After all of that, she really wasn't in the mood to put on a happy face, and serve already drunk people more liquor.

The littlest things put her in a bad mood lately.

"Take five," Jackson repeated firmly.

No room for argument.

Haven nodded, defeated. She was quick to slip around the bar, and head across the club's floor. She barely passed the girls working their pole a look, and she didn't even bother to stop and say hi to a familiar face she recognized sitting at one of the far tables.

Before long, she was closing the door of her office, and dragging in a deep breath. Putting her back to the wall, she counted back from ten, and willed her nerves to relax. It should help. It always did before.

It didn't this time.

Haven pushed away from the door, and dropped into the chair behind the desk. Maybe what she really needed more than anything was a fucking vacation. Time away from just *being*.

That sounded heavenly.

And it tasted like guilt.

Fuck her life.

The first thing Haven thought to do was bitch about her life. To open her mouth, and let all the stress come out of it in a vomit of words that would leave her with less things on her mind. It was something she found helped.

Usually, she would do it with Valeria.

Except … Haven glanced up to find the office empty. Like her home, and her heart. She was never more aware of Val's missing presence in her life than she was lately. The more shit that piled onto Haven's shoulders, the worse she missed her friend.

Where was she?

Was she okay?

What about Maria?

Those thoughts were a constant plague on Haven's mind now. It was just one more thing to add to the hell that had become her life. She didn't have answers, and no way to get them, either. It was quite a fucking place to be, really.

Haven wasn't sure how long she stayed in her office, but it was definitely longer than the five-minute break Jackson had told her to take. She wasn't any less stressed, but she was slightly more relaxed. More willing to put on that happy face for her customers, anyway.

That was something.

Jackson popped his head in the office doorway after knocking *once*. But hell, at least he fucking knocked. That was more than he used to do.

"Yes?" Haven asked, rubbing her fingertips into her temples.

"The patron for the private room is here."

Haven's brow furrowed. "All right."

In the entire club, there was just *one* private room. Haven didn't like the sleazy appeal of private rooms where the girls could take customers and do whatever the hell a man was willing to pay for. That wasn't what she wanted Safe Haven to be known for beyond the walls of this place. She also didn't like the idea that a patron might take advantage of a girl behind closed doors when no one was there to help the woman.

It all left a bad taste in Haven's mouth.

So, she culled any chance of that by simply not allowing for private sessions between a dancer and a patron.

They did, however, have a private room that was used for things like parties and whatever else. Security was *always* present, as was at least one member of management. They didn't use the private room very often, and when they did, Jackson was the manager who handled all the details and making sure things were on the up and up.

Haven rarely touched it at all.

Jackson didn't move from the doorway. "It was booked last week, remember?"

"Not particularly."

That shouldn't be a surprise, though. A lot of things were slipping in Haven's life lately. It only served to leave her feeling like a giant fucking failure, but maybe she would get used to feeling like this after a while.

Who knew?

"The patron who booked the room asked specifically for a meeting with *you*, not a dance or anything," Jackson said.

Haven's gaze narrowed. "What?"

The man shrugged.

Something felt off for her.

Maybe she didn't remember Jackson telling her about the private booking because he actually hadn't told her at all. That seemed more likely considering she *never* did a private dance. And all meetings she had were held in her office, or at the bar before the club even opened for the night.

"What's going on?" Haven demanded.

Jackson cleared his throat, and glanced away. "Listen, he was very persuasive when he called in, and I didn't think you would mind me saying yes."

"*He?*"

"Your friend—Marcello."

"*Andino?*"

Jackson nodded. "That's the one, yeah."

Holy mother of fucking *Christ*.

Haven had the distinct feeling Jackson had only been trying to help. Most likely her, but also Andino in a way. The man had no idea about the shit that had happened between her and Andino. All he could know was that Andino didn't come around the club as much as he used to, but even that could be explained away with simple excuses.

She tried not to get mad at Jackson.

Tried being the keyword there.

"He's in the private room, then?" Haven asked, her tone rough.

"Yeah. Sorry, did I fuck up?"

Haven stood from the desk. "More him than you … but don't do it again."

"Noted."

• • •

"Is this supposed to be a joke?"

Andino met Haven's gaze from across the private room where he was currently sitting on one of several red velvet couches. He gave the server handing over what looked to be a glass of whiskey a quick smile.

"Thank you," he told the server.

"Anything else?" Kandi asked with one of her signature smiles that tended to have all the men tipping her generously. "Just ask."

Kandi really was a sweet girl. Her name was far more than appropriate. Usually, Haven appreciated the fact that the girl made the patrons comfortable, and happy. She did not, however, like the way Kandi was currently smiling at Andino.

"No, that'll be quite enough, thanks, Kandi," Haven said.

A little too sharply, maybe, if the way the young woman looked over her shoulder at her boss was any indication. Haven wished she had taken a second to cool the raging jealousy flooding her body at nothing more than the sight of a woman—who was *just* doing her job—paying Andino a bit of attention.

How could a woman not pay him attention?

He looked like sin had come into her club, and sat down on a velvet couch wearing an Armani suit, shiny leather loafers, a Rolex on his wrist, and a smile that screamed sex. The man didn't even have to try. He filled out his tailored suit in the best way, and he fucking knew it, too.

That was *before* Haven moved onto his good looks, and charming nature.

She shouldn't *be* jealous. There was no fucking need for any of that nonsense. They weren't even really a thing anymore. Sure, she might not be seeing someone else, but that didn't mean he wasn't out fucking God knew who.

Jesus.

Was he doing that?

"Sorry," Kandi said as she passed Haven by. "I'll leave you two alone, boss."

Haven glanced up at the ceiling, and prepped to give the girl an apology. She didn't get the chance—Kandi was gone from the private room before Haven could even open her mouth again.

Great.

"That was awkward," Andino murmured.

Haven's gaze flew back to the man of the hour, and her anger was back in a blink. "That was nothing. Why are you here?"

"Really, *nothing?*"

She wished the lump in her throat wasn't so goddamn thick. "You didn't answer my question."

"I think we should talk about how pissed off you just were because I smiled at a woman, and she smiled back at me. That seems far more interesting."

"I would rather not."

"Pride's a bitch, huh? I know all about that."

Haven clenched her jaw. "Could you *not* right now?"

"Who else will call your shit out when I don't?"

Good point.

That didn't mean he had to make it, though.

Haven went back to her first question instead. "What are you doing here? And did you really think booking the private room behind my back to get a few minutes with me was a good idea?"

Andino didn't blink at the face of her anger. "I don't expect you to understand, Haven, but I am trying to be discreet in the way I do things lately. A hazard of my current position. I wanted—and needed—a few minutes with you, so this seemed like the best way. I don't have to stay."

God.

She hated how the first thing she wanted to do was simply say *don't go, stay.* That she so badly wanted to ask why he wasn't calling her nearly as much, or know what was happening in his life that was keeping him away from her.

Because even if a part of her did want him to just leave her the hell alone, another part of her wanted nothing more than to have him keep being ... this man that was in front of her.

The man that didn't stop. Didn't take no for an answer. The man that showed up in her life, and inserted his presence there like that's exactly where he was always meant to be whether she fucking liked it or not. This man—this infuriating, confusing, and strange man—who could put her on edge, take her to the top of the world, or crush her entire heart all in the same breath.

Andino had no idea the things he was capable of where Haven was concerned. He didn't know—couldn't possibly understand—the power he had over her. He didn't have a single fucking clue how much she *loved him.*

God, she loved him.

And she hated him, too.

"I came to give you something," he said, standing from the couch. For the first time, she noticed the folder that had been resting on his thigh when he flashed it with a wave of his hand. "And then be on my way."

Haven swallowed the words in an attempt to keep them in, but the bastards still managed to slip out anyway. "Whatever that is—is it the only reason you came?"

"Of course not," Andino murmured, coming closer. "I miss you. I always miss you, baby."

She blinked.

Fuck my whole life.

Once he was close enough to hold the folder out to her, he did just that. Haven took it, but she didn't look inside right away. Instead, she looked at him.

"The place still hasn't sold, huh?" he asked. "Strange—this club should have flew off the market."

"The buyer is a prick."

Andino smirked. "I see."

"What's this?"

She waved the folder.

Andino shrugged one broad shoulder. "You mentioned your friend … Valeria … and I figured it must have been weighing on you that she up and went without a word. You're that type of person, aren't you? You give entirely too much of a shit about everybody else, and not nearly enough about yourself."

He knew her too well.

"You looked into Valeria?"

"As much as I could," he replied. "This might help to get you started if you want to look elsewhere, or try to find her. I didn't want to give this to you."

Haven's gaze narrowed, but Andino was quick to shake his head.

"Not for the reasons you probably think," he was fast to add, "but because there are things that came up about Valeria Gomez that quickly turned dangerous, and murky. And if you go looking in those places … not even I could keep you safe, I don't think."

She stiffened, and looked down at the folder in her shaking hand. "Oh."

"But here it is," Andino said, "whether I want you to look or not isn't my choice. I didn't even have any business looking into her history to begin with but the idea that something was bothering you killed me. So, I made a few calls, and pulled what I could. That's what I came here for—I hope it helps."

Haven blinked, unsure of what to say.

Andino didn't really give her the time to figure it out before he moved to pass by her, but not before he stopped, and gave her a soft kiss on her temple. That gentle press of his lips was enough to send a blaze lighting up over her skin. He really hadn't come to upset her life again, or to get in the way. He hadn't shown up to cause problems, or drag her to bed for yet another round.

He came because he cared.

He *still* cared.

And that just fucked her up more than ever.

"Could I replace your flowers again?" he asked, his lips still grazing her skin.

She wanted to ask if he would bring them himself this time, but she held back. He'd been the one who said he was trying to be discreet, after all.

She was sure there were things happening that she wasn't privy to, and maybe that was for the best.

Right now, Haven had a lot of things to figure out.

"You should," she said quietly, "the others are wilting."

Andino nodded. "Will do. And, if you want to chat about what you find in that folder … you know where to find me."

"Thank you."

He kissed her temple once more, and brushed his knuckles against her cheekbone before he left the private room altogether. Haven felt like her feet had suddenly turned into cement right there on the spot.

It took entirely too long for her to break from the daze and open the folder. Maybe she should have waited until she was back home again.

She couldn't.

She had to know what Valeria had never told her.

The second she opened the folder, she wished she would have waited until she was home alone so that she could absorb the information staring back at her on just the first page. It looked to be a newspaper clipping of some sort. She scanned the words, and the ones that seemed important jumped out at her.

Gomez Cartel.

Fifteen-year-old Valeria Lòpez marries the oldest son of Martín Gomez in a ceremony at Saint Basile Chapel only two weeks after her father's arrest for embezzlement.

Blackmail. Bribery.

Haven kept reading, and the information only became worse with each page. Who knew Mexico was so goddamn corrupt?

• • •

"I'm surprised it took you this long. Or rather, that it took you a whole week to decide to come and talk to me about the folder."

Haven sighed, and continued staring at the green shrubbery someone had placed in a terracotta potter beside Andino's front door. It was easier to stare at the small plant than at the man who managed to tell her that statement, and yet, still not sound smug about the fact that he said it without a hint of surprise.

Like he just *knew.*

She was going to come back here again.

"I had a busy week," Haven said. "Took a two-day trip to Florida to visit my mom, and work … well, work is work."

"How is your mom?"

Haven frowned, and finally glanced at Andino. There was genuine concern written on his expression, and not a hint of the arrogant man she expected to find when she knocked on his door earlier. She didn't quite know what to make of that. God knew it was far easier to deal with Andino—at times—when he was laying all of his cards out on the table rather than keeping them close to his chest.

She didn't know how to deal with him like this at all.

"Still sick," she said.

Andino nodded. "I'm sorry."

Haven shrugged. "It just upset her to see me there, anyway. She thought I was coming to stay right then, and hadn't told her. They would rather I keep living my life, and help from afar. They don't want me to uproot everything."

"And you just want to help."

"Yeah, well …"

That was the best thing she could think to say, as lame as it was. The visit to see her mom *had* helped a bit. Despite the chemo treatments being far more aggressive this time around, her mother was doing wonderfully. That counted for something.

Andino stepped back a bit from the doorway, and widened the door. "Do you want to come in?"

Haven clutched the folder in her hands a little tighter as she stared at the dark hallway behind Andino. The sight was as familiar as it was uncomfortable. His entire life was hidden in his home. Haven had learned that over time. She also learned that he guarded his private life more carefully than most.

Yet, he had no issue with inviting her in, and letting her make herself at home. She craved the comfort of this place—filled with furniture, things, and *life*—as much as she did Andino, in a way. Compared to her own house currently, it was far warmer.

Even if the man in front of her was the source of heartache for her.

"I don't know if I should," Haven said.

Andino chuckled, and gave her a look from the side. "It's just a house, *donna*. One you've been inside time and time again. Stop looking at it as though it might come alive and bite you."

Funny.

That's exactly how it felt.

"Don't be patronizing," Haven said, moving past Andino in the doorway to enter the house. "It's not a good look on you."

"First of all," he said behind her as he slammed the door close, "any look on me is fucking great. And secondly, I wasn't being patronizing. I was being *funny*. If you're looking for the right word to describe that, it's *wonderful*."

Haven shot him a condescending smile over her shoulder. "Is that what your mother tells you? You did say you were spoiled being an only child and all."

Andino's mouth curved at the edges with one of those sexy smirks of his before he tossed his head back, and laughed hard. There was something beautiful about this man when he let loose, and separated from the hard shell that he seemed to always keep front and center.

It was distracting and disconcerting to Haven. Just the sight of him laughing was enough to make her breaths quicken, and her heart ache. How different things could have been between them if only shit had worked out.

She needed to get away from those thoughts, and fast. That was not why she had come here, and she wasn't about to indulge that nonsense.

"Let's sit in the living room," Andino said, seemingly noticing Haven's change in mood. "I was doing some paperwork."

As she headed that way, she asked, "Don't you have an office for that?"

"I thought a change in scenery might be nice." Andino was close enough behind her that Haven could *feel* the heat of his body. And yet, he didn't reach out to touch her or anything of the sort. She wasn't sure which pissed her off more—that she *wanted* him to do exactly that, or that he didn't do it at all. She really was a sad state of a mess. "And also because my cousin mentioned he'd missed the last few episodes of his favorite show, and wanted me to fill him in."

"John, you mean?"

That was the only cousin Andino ever really talked about.

"John," he agreed as he dropped down on the couch. Haven stayed standing even when Andino glanced up, and quirked a brow. "Do you just want to stand, or ...?"

"I don't plan on staying."

"Shame."

The word came out of his mouth like a soft murmur. Whispering to her in all the wrong *and far too right* ways.

Haven knew it then ... she was going to be fucked—probably in more ways than one—before this night was over.

ELEVEN

Andino wasn't sure what Haven reminded him more of in those moments as she stood just a couple of feet away from where he sat on the couch. Like maybe a skittish deer that was ready to bolt away from the thing that terrified her … or a woman ready to jump his bones.

It was amusing … and sad, too.

"Sit," he said again. "You have questions, right?"

"Maybe," she countered, "but how many of them do you plan on answering?"

Andino smiled.

Smart woman.

"As many as I know the answers to, Haven. I promise." She still hesitated to move, and kept an even tighter grip on that file. Guessing by the way the spine of the folder had been cracked again and again, Andino figured she had looked through the contents more than a few times. And because she was a smart woman, he knew she would have done her own research, too. Or, as much as she could by way of an internet search, probably. "I'm not going to bite you—you *can sit*, baby."

Haven gave him a slightly bitter smile. "Not unless I *ask*, right?"

Well …

"You said it, not me."

The slight shake of her head was all he got in response before Haven moved to sit on the couch beside him. She still kept an inch or two of space between them even as she opened the folder on her lap, and stared down at the contents. Andino leaned forward, and rested his clasped hands over his knees.

"There's rumors that her father was arrested because he wouldn't allow the cartel to *buy* his loyalty. I don't understand."

"He's … or was, because he's dead—"

"Like her mom, too," Haven said softly.

Andino nodded. "Her mom was killed in what *looked* to be a car accident less than thirty days before she married the son. Her sister was killed after she took off, it seems."

"I noticed that. And her dad was killed within a month after being married."

"Being a politician in Mexico is a dangerous endeavor but especially when there's major cartels who control *everything*. And I mean everything, Haven. That's how cartels work. They integrate into every aspect of their country or territory that they can to control their business, and the business

103

of those around them. Police. Government. The coffee shop down the street."

"So, they wanted to control her father, and he wouldn't take their ... bribes?"

Andino made a noise under his breath. "I don't think bribe would be the right word when it comes to cartels. More like ... look at her mom who was killed and then shortly after, she married. Coercion and violence. *Threats*. That's how they work."

He could see that statement clearly made Haven uncomfortable, but she simply stared down at the file again and kept talking.

"Do you think she married the son of the cartel leader to help her father?"

"I would almost *count* on it, yeah."

Haven flinched. "She was only fifteen, though."

"I'm not sure if that matters to the man she married."

"Obviously," Haven whispered. "She had Maria when she was seventeen—she took off when she was pregnant. She told me that much."

"I think the only way for Valeria to stay safe is to keep moving," Andino said. "That's just based on what I know about this particular cartel, and people who escape from them. They can't stay in one place for very long."

"She'd been with me for a while, though."

"Maybe that's why she left, then."

Andino didn't know if that was the case, however. He didn't like the alternative to that option, though, considering that meant the cartel caught up with Valeria and forced her back to Mexico, and her husband.

A man who Andino suspected *wasn't* a good man.

Why would a woman—a *pregnant* woman—run from him otherwise?

Nonetheless, Andino wasn't done looking for Valeria Gomez yet. He simply had to be careful given the things he knew about her now. It could be dangerous for him—and her—if the cartel found someone who was actively searching for the wife of the man currently running the operation.

Given the way Haven looked right then next to him, sad and so unsure, he figured it was worth the damn risk, anyway.

"What else are you wondering?" he asked.

Haven shrugged one shoulder. "That was it, really. About Val, anyway."

"What, you just wanted—"

"Confirmation of my suspicions, I guess. Yeah."

Andino leaned back on the couch. "I see."

"What did you get this information for—to leverage it against me?"

Wow.

That was a whole one-eighty there.

Andino respected Haven for having the guts to ask him, though. And considering everything that had happened between the two of them, he understood why she asked, too. Still, she was so far from the truth, it wasn't even funny.

He stood from the couch, and readjusted the rolled up sleeves of his dress shirt. "I did it because I knew it was bothering you, and maybe I could help. That's all. Do you want to stay for dinner, or do you have somewhere to be?"

Haven blinked up at him. "I shouldn't stay, Andino."

Yeah, he figured she would say that. He also didn't plan on taking no for an answer.

"Why the hell not?"

She let out a laugh. "Because it always ends the same way."

Andino arched a brow. "I don't follow."

"We *fuck*, Andino. We fuck, and then I leave. We fuck, and it means nothing. We fuck—that's what we do."

Perhaps so, but she never said no.

Hell, *she* initiated.

"I don't see the problem."

Haven gave him another one of those smiles. "Of course, you don't."

• • •

Haven wasn't wrong.

It took very little time, the two of them simply working in the kitchen to make dinner, some flour tossed around, and then they found themselves trying to clean up in the bathroom, but ended up *like this*.

Andino backed against the cold tile of the bathroom wall, and Haven on her knees. She was quite a fucking sight down below him with his cock between her lips as she swallowed him right down to the base. There was something about her lipstick stains around his cock that made his fucking balls tight, and his spine hot.

Something about her mussed makeup, and his hands fisted in her hair. Something about the way she hummed around his shaft like the taste of his precum on her tongue was candy she couldn't get enough of. Something about the way this woman knew how to use her lips and teeth to tease the *life* out of him until he was ready to blow his load, and watch her swallow every damn drop he gave her.

She was good for that.

Loved it, really.

"Fuck, *yeah*," Andino grunted, his hips flexing forward in reaction to the way Haven let her teeth graze along his shaft. "Suck that dick, baby. Show me how much you love it, Haven."

She did. In the way her eyes darkened as she watched him from her knees, and how her lips curved into an attempt of a grin.

Little tease.

She was killing him like this.

All it took was Andino's hands tightening in Haven's hair for her to loosen her lips around his dick. She knew what that meant, and followed along *beautifully*. Like this, he could fuck her mouth as fast, deep, or hard as he wanted. He could feel the way her tongue flattened against the base of his shaft, and her muscles relaxed in her throat.

Every jerk of his cock sent him closer to the edge.

Almost ... almost ...

"Jesus Christ," he breathed when that edge finally came. It was swift, and unforgiving. An orgasm strong enough to make his fucking knees weaken from the intensity. Somehow, he managed to keep his eyes on Haven although he hadn't been able to give her a warning. Not that she needed one. The woman swallowed every drop, and then licked his dick clean with one of her sly smiles. "Holy *fuck*."

She was still on her knees. Still naked but for the panties and bra he hadn't quite managed to rip off of her before she got down to suck his dick. Still red-lipped from having her mouth fucked, and still dotted with the flour he'd all but thrown at her when she left a floury handprint right on his cheek. Still a mess.

Still so beautiful.

"Still mine," he murmured.

Haven's eyes flashed with something unknown, but she said nothing. Andino didn't really need her to. He was quick to pull her up from the floor.

Andino had Haven backed against the wall in the next breath, and his mouth descended on hers as his hand slipped under the waistband of her panties. She was so wet and fucking warm under his fingertips.

Slippery, needy flesh.

Fuck.

The sounds she made when his fingers stuffed inside her tight cunt, and his mouth latched onto that spot on her neck that she loved so much was *raw*. She always made the best sounds.

All it took was the feeling of her wet pussy clenching around his fingers, and his name in her mouth, and his semi-hard cock was at full attention once more. He needed all her sounds like he needed the air in his lungs.

And then the begging started.

"*Please.* Oh, my God, just fuck me, please."

When she sounded like that—breathless and high off him—then he lost all control. His desire to make her wait left just like that.

Haven laughed in that spun way of hers when Andino yanked her away from the wall, bent her over the sink, and ripped her panties down her thighs.

"*Open up and show me what's mine.*"

His dark demand was punctuated by his hand slapping against her inner thighs. She was quick to open for him—lost in a long sigh as he fitted himself between her thighs from behind, and thrust in.

One flex, that's all it took.

He was home again.

He found heaven again.

Her name was Haven.

How was he supposed to just ... let this go?

• • •

"Do you talk at all?" Andino asked.

Ginevra Calabrese glanced up from the unappealing salad that had been placed in front of her by a server at the restaurant. Not one of Andino's restaurants—the place belonged to Kev. Had it been his, that shit she was supposed to eat wouldn't be on the menu. At least, not as a single item. Who the fuck wanted to eat rabbit food with no real substance to help it go down?

"I do," Ginevra said softly, frowning. "I'm sorry."

Andino cocked his head to the side, surprised at her response. "Why?"

The young woman didn't seem to know how to respond, or rather ... what she was supposed to say to begin with. Andino, on the other hand, didn't know how he was supposed to deal with a woman like this at all.

Not that he wanted to.

"Why, what?" she asked.

"Why are you apologizing to me?"

Ginevra used the fork to drag through the salad. "For not being ... whatever you would like, I guess. That's what I was told to be today— whatever you would like. And with everyone else, that usually means staying quiet and out of sight, if possible. I can't exactly *be* out of your sight when I have to sit right in front of you at the table, so being quiet seemed like the way to go. Sorry if that's not what you want."

Andino's anger flared as his gaze drifted from Ginevra to the men sitting a few tables away. He asked for this dinner simply because he wanted her to be comfortable with him even if the last thing he intended to do was marry the woman because he needed for her to trust him. It was her brothers, however, that demanded they be there to supervise. Thankfully, he managed to get them to do that from afar.

He truly hated those pieces of shit.

Really.

"I neither want, nor need, for you to be a piece of art beside me. Pretty, but inanimate," he explained, shrugging when she glanced up at him. "If that's what they expect, then that's another story. When they are around, you can behave however they deem appropriate as to not cause yourself trouble. With me, you can be whatever you feel like in the moment."

"Right now," she told him, "I would prefer to be anywhere else."

Andino smirked. "I do appreciate a woman who isn't a liar, but for the sake of appearances, let's at least play nice."

"I don't want to marry you, Andino. I don't want to be *here*, and I certainly don't want to pretend to give a damn about anything you want to talk about right now. So, if it's okay with you, I would much prefer to sit here and occasionally nod when you talk so that you might think I give a shit. But really, we'll both know I don't."

Well, then.

Damn.

Good on her for being honest. Andino appreciated that, and honestly, that was the kind of fire he wanted to see from a woman like Ginevra in the position that she was. It spoke to good things for her.

"Oh, good. Then, we're on the same page."

Confusion flickered across Ginevra's face, but she opted to stay quiet. That was, frankly, the better choice for her. Andino chose not to point that out right now. It wouldn't help his case, or his plans at the end of the day.

"Did they choose the salad for you, too?" Andino asked. "Because I wouldn't willingly eat that without some kind of steak to weigh it down."

The hint of a smile graced Ginevra's lips.

Battle almost won, he thought.

"They did—heaven forbid you thought I ate too much."

Andino made a noise in the back of his throat. "I prefer women who enjoy themselves, actually. Not that it'll matter *what* I prefer from you. Some other man, perhaps, but not me. You would do well to remember that."

She glanced up at him again.

Andino simply smiled back.

He just needed this woman to trust him. The rest would come easily after that.

• • •

"How was your dinner with the girl?"

Andino glanced up from the work on his desk to find his father leaning in the doorway of the office. Just beyond where Giovanni stood, the hustle and bustle of the restaurant continued on. Gio waited with a measured expression for his son's reply.

"Bearable," Andino chose to say.

Gio's mouth quirked higher at the edge as he said, "That's not the answer I want to hear when you're talking about your wife-to-be."

"Seems like a fine enough answer for me."

"And why is that?"

Andino pushed away the work on his desk to give his father the attention Giovanni was so clearly looking for. Obviously, or his father wouldn't be here at all. Andino was not the only one with business all over the city, and his father's days were often busier than even his own. If Gio made a point to make time to come here and see Andino today, he did that with a purpose.

Clearly, information this time around.

Maybe for his mother, who knew?

"What do you want to know, Dad?" Andino asked. "If we talked, or if she's happy? If she's willing to meet Ma—frankly, she'll do whatever she's told because she's terrified of what might happen if she doesn't. What is it you want?"

Giovanni blinked. "Is she?"

"What?"

"Scared of you."

Andino scowled. "It's not *me*—it's them."

His father nodded once. "Her brothers, then."

"Calling them that in reference to their relationship with Ginevra seems like a stretch considering all she is to them is a pawn, Dad. She is something for them to use to get where they want to go, and very little else. They don't actually give a shit about her. I could be the worst kind of trash, and they wouldn't give a single fuck about it. Okay?"

Gio didn't bat an eye at Andino's statement. It was almost like that was exactly what his father expected to hear, and so, it didn't really come as a surprise.

Nothing in this life was a surprise, now.

"And none of that seems like a problem to you," Giovanni noted.

Jesus Christ.

"Don't mistake my apathy for a lack of empathy," he countered. "But I also know what's expected of me, and what I have to do."

Or make it look like I am doing.

That, too.

"For now, that's what matters," Andino added.

Gio tipped his chin up a bit. "*For now.*"

Ah, fuck.

"Is that because your attention is still elsewhere, and you still haven't committed yourself to the things Dante has asked of you, or no?"

Andino's jaw clenched. "Don't play word games. I hate that."

"Haven Murphy. You're still seeing her, I hear. And I only heard it because the enforcer you have trailing you at the moment thought to mention it to me the last time we spoke. You're still playing with *that* fire—as much as two days ago, even. She spent the night at your place. How's that for a word game?"

Fuck his whole entire life.

Pink was still busy elsewhere—the enforcer had to keep an eye on Siena from afar like Andino told him to do. Which meant Andino needed to have a new enforcer watch his back on a daily basis. One he didn't particularly like, and who didn't understand the meaning of being loyal to the person who was paying him. Instead, he was loyal to the family.

That was a problem for Andino.

He needed a lot of things from people—most importantly, he *demanded* their loyalty. That, and for them to be discreet about his business. Private, or otherwise.

Even if it was his father.

"Thank you for letting me know that," Andino said darkly.

Gio frowned. "What does that mean?"

"It means I have a problem that needs to be disposed."

"You're going to kill the enforcer because he spoke to me?"

"Don't be offended. It's not about you."

Gio chuckled. "No, it's about you, I suppose. You're going to make an interesting boss, son. I can already tell."

"That is the plan, apparently."

"Are you going to tell me what in the hell you're doing with Haven? And *Ginevra*? This deal—your uncle? What is going on, Andino? At least give me the respect of telling me what kind of shit I might step into before I put my whole foot in the pile. Allow me to ... well, be on your side, son. Please."

Andino had planned to do this alone—whatever he needed to do, that was, to get what he fucking wanted. He didn't need help. He just needed the means and the time to get shit done.

Still, as he stared at his father, he had to wonder ...

Was that the right choice?

"I want her," Andino said.

Gio dragged in a deep breath, and took a moment before he spoke again. "Haven."

"Yes."

"All right."

"All right?"

Gio smirked. "If you're going to pick a hill to die on—why not that one? Yeah, why not that fucking hill, Andino."

Hey, at least it was a beautiful hill.

TWELVE

Haven was entirely distracted by the report from yet another inspection of the club sitting in front of her. The hustle and bustle of a small Brooklyn café was practically nonexistent. Nothing more than a hum in the back of her mind.

"Are you looking at it?" Dale asked.

"Finally," Haven said. "Yes."

She'd printed off the report Dale faxed over from the investor's inspector just before leaving the club after a weekly meeting with the employees. He had offered to come over and go through the report with Haven, but her empty stomach wasn't having it.

Now, with a coffee and bagel in front of her, she felt a little more human and up to looking through the report.

The *final* report—or it was supposed to be. This was the last inspection that the investor wanted before the deal on the club could go through.

This was what she had been waiting for.

"So, what exactly am I looking at, then?" Haven said.

The official documents seemed like a lot of nonsense and legalese. Nothing that she cared to wade through to find the keywords she needed to say everything was good to go. That's what Dale was working for, anyway. He wanted his commission. He could earn it, too.

"*Basically*," Dale said, "the inspector gave the green light on everything. The investor is good to go whenever he is ready to sign the check, so to speak."

Haven blinked.

Yeah, that's what she wanted to hear. And yet, it was still a little surreal when the words finally reached her ears. All this time, and just like that, the wait was over. She didn't really know what to do about it, or how to feel.

"Oh," Haven said.

The realtor chuckled on the other end of the line. "You don't sound happy."

Haven rubbed at her forehead, and shook her head even knowing that the man couldn't see it over the phone. "No, I am. It's just … been a while since we started this process, I guess. Maybe I expected them to drag it on for another few months."

"Well, the check isn't signed yet."

She heard the joke in the man's tone, but she didn't find it very funny, all things considered. Nonetheless, she let it slide.

"How long is it going to take to get the paperwork drawn up, signed, and finalized?" Haven asked.

"At most, a week or two. Probably closer to two."

Two weeks.

That was all.

"I can do two more weeks," Haven said.

Her house still hadn't sold yet—a couple of low offers that made her roll her eyes before, sure. She was starting to think that maybe she should take a lower offer just to get the house off her hands, too.

That would make things simpler …

"Okay, well, I will get on the phone with the—"

"Haven?"

Dale's voice cut off entirely in Haven's ear even though she knew he was still speaking because she suddenly found herself staring up at someone she didn't expect to see. Well, at least not in some random tiny Brooklyn café.

Andino's father.

Again.

What kind of shitty luck did she have to keep randomly running into this man? At least with Andino, she was the one who went to him. With his father, it seemed like the world was just having a good fucking laugh at her expense.

"Giovanni, hi," Haven said.

The man smiled warmly.

On the phone, Dale's voice filtered back through Haven's shock. "Are you still there?"

Shit.

She gave Giovanni an apologetic shrug of her shoulder, and pointed at the phone before mouthing, *just give me a second.* "Yeah, Dale, I'm still here. I have to go—something came up." Or *someone*, rather. "Give me a call when you need my signature."

"Will do, Haven. Have a great day."

"You, too."

Haven shut the phone off, and tucked it into her purse at her side. By the time she gave her attention to Andino's father again, the man was staring at the paperwork from the inspector and the investor with a dip in his brow, and a curious smile.

Haven cleared her throat, and Gio glanced at her. "Do you come here often?"

"A couple of times a week. They have my wife's favorite Danishes."

"Ah. I just needed something to eat fast, and this was the closest place."

"It's a good choice," Gio replied, still smiling kindly. "They have great food."

"Good to know." Haven closed the folder, which again drew in Gio's gaze, and then proceeded to pack the stuff into her oversized purse. "Also, for future reference, because it seems like we keep running into each other … but you don't have to say hello to me just to be polite. I know you probably wish you didn't have to see me at all, so—"

"Oh, you couldn't be more wrong about that," Gio interrupted her with a soft laugh, "but I suppose, all things considered, you can't be expected to know anything different. Right?"

Haven blinked, and looked up at the man. "I beg your pardon?"

Giovanni shrugged his shoulders beneath the well-tailored black blazer he wore. Just like his son, the man was broad-shouldered, tall, and classically handsome. He also gave off an air that screamed bad news, old money, and a lifetime worth of secrets he probably wasn't willing to share.

It was almost funny how alike he and his son were in those ways.

"I mean," Giovanni said, sliding into the chair across the table from Haven without even being invited, "that I think it's a shame we haven't really been able to have an actual conversation. Knowing *some* of the things I do about you, that seems like it's my loss."

His loss.

His loss to not *speak* to her.

"Uh," Haven said, still unsure.

Giovanni flashed her a wide smile. "I always thought … well, knowing my son and how he is, the woman who eventually came into his life and took it over would have to be something amazing. Mind you, all the men in our family have managed to find a wife that fits him just the way she needs to. They're all amazing in their own ways. But my son? He went out and found someone I never expected, but I still can't find it in myself to be surprised."

"Why?"

She didn't want to ask the question, really, but it still managed to slip out. Damn her curiosity straight to hell and back. It only served to get her hurt.

"Because Andino is not average, and he does not come from average men," Gio said like it was the most obvious thing in the world. "He is not the *exception*; he is exceptional. You see, I always thought my son was more like his uncle—the one you met at the club with me, Dante. A stickler for the rules; always toeing the line; never questioning his place or the demands put on him. Certainly nothing like *me*."

Gio laughed in that way again—dark, and deep. "Not like me, Haven, who broke every rule I could, and caused the *most* trouble for my family. Not like me who went after a woman I was not allowed to have, and nearly got myself and her killed for it in the process. No, he wasn't like me at all. He was smarter than me, and better than me. It was for the best, anyway. Someone decided when he was just sixteen that he was going to be a king-in-waiting, but they didn't want to tell him, then. He didn't need to know then. Either way, he was going to do great things while I had only done the bare minimum. He was destined to be someone I could never be. I only managed to keep myself alive. *That* was a feat in itself, believe me."

Haven didn't know what to say.

Gio wasn't looking for a reply, apparently.

He shrugged, and reached for the menu that had been placed on the table. Looking it over, he said, "It turns out, my son is a hell of a lot more like me than I thought. I'm not sure whether to be surprised, or terrified for what might happen because of it, but here we are."

"You do know that I don't understand a lot of what you're telling me, right?"

The man grinned slyly. "In time, you will. I expect so, anyway."

Haven frowned. "I think you're confused about some things, then."

"How so?"

Giovanni met her gaze, and despite the warning she found there, she didn't look away.

"Andino and I ..." Haven struggled to come up with the right thing to say that wasn't too personal. "We're not together. That was a choice he made, and one I'm trying to deal with now even if he does confuse the hell out of me constantly. That's not important, though. We're not a thing, and we're not going to be. Ever."

"Not together?"

"No."

"You two seem to end up in the same spaces for people who are ... not together."

Haven let out a bitter laugh.

What else could she do?

"How do you even know that?" Haven asked.

Giovanni kept an innocent expression as he replied, "Because I look out for my son even when he thinks I am prying and spying. He deserves—and *needs*—only the absolute best people surrounding him. Those who will give him absolute loyalty and nothing less in this life. Even when it's someone like his father looking for information. Anyway," he said with a wave of his hand, "when I was dealing with something else for him, I learned you were still around. I guess we just haven't run into one another again since the last time I found you coming out of his house, huh? But we both know you've been back there."

Haven's cheeks pinked. "*Yeah.* Let's not and say we did."

115

"Mmm." The man only smiled in that sneaky way of his. "You don't even know why you keep going back to him, do you?"

"Not the slightest clue."

Giovanni nodded. "I didn't think so."

"He keeps drawing me back, I guess."

"I bet." Gio stood from the table, then, and fixed his jacket. "By the way, how is your mom?"

Haven glanced down at the folder in front of her. "Still sick."

"I'm sorry. I'll pray for her—I don't think God cares much to hear from me anymore, but who the hell knows?"

Haven smiled a little. "Thanks."

"Is that why Andino is buying your club? You didn't get a better offer, and he was willing?"

Her head snapped up and her gaze narrowed. "I'm sorry?"

Gio's expression blanked as his gaze drifted from the folder sticking out of her bag to Haven's confused face. "The inspection report in that folder—I saw the company name. Your club is still for sale, isn't it? That's what I assumed it was for."

"Not *that*. The other thing—the Andino thing. What did you mean by him buying my club?"

"The company on the inspection report."

"*What about it?*"

Gio's brow lifted. "That's the shell company my son uses to invest in different businesses. His lawyers handle the buying, selling, and other paperwork. He just deals in the cash."

Haven blinked.

What. The. *Fuck.*

"Andino's company," Haven murmured.

"That's what I said."

Yes, it was.

Jesus fucking Christ.

How could he?

How *dare* Andino?

• • •

Where are you right now?

The text seemed innocent on the surface. Nothing to suggest Haven was raging mad, and out for blood. She had carefully measured each word she sent to Andino so that he didn't think something was up. She didn't *want* him to know something was up yet.

His response had been almost automatic with, *At my restaurant in Manhattan. Busy today. Want me to call you later?*

Haven hadn't even bothered to reply back to that question. No, she didn't want him to call her back. After today, she didn't ever want to see his fucking face again.

She had figured out long ago that Andino could be a little manipulative when he wanted to be. That if a situation called for it, and he knew it would work out to his favor, he had no issues with playing *very* dirty to get what he wanted.

Haven never thought he would try that shit with her. Well, not to this goddamn extreme. Not to the point where even *knowing* her mother was sick, and that she greatly wanted to get out of New York for her mom, and to put distance between him and her ... he still stepped in her way behind the scenes to make sure she wasn't going anywhere.

She never thought he would do this to her.

How was that *love*?

Maybe an unhealthy love. An obsessive, crazy, and nonsensical love. One meant to covet, hurt, and destroy. One that Haven didn't want at all.

She didn't want love if it meant *that*.

Usually, Haven would take a cab when she was traveling through the city. That, or the subway. It was faster, and easier. The thing was—she hadn't even cared to wait long enough for the cab to get to her place after her meeting with Giovanni sent her flying home in a rage. She'd grabbed her keys, and took her car out of the garage for the first time in months.

Worst purchase of her life, really.

She never even needed a car in the city.

Today, though, the car was coming in handy for once. Except she was forced to sit in gridlocked upper Manhattan traffic while the warm May sun beat down on her windshield. The second she got a chance to pull off the road—she was only a couple of blocks away from Andino's restaurant now—she did just that. Even knowing she was likely going to have her car towed, she parked it right where she stopped.

Fuck it.

They could keep the goddamn car.

Haven didn't *care*.

She stepped onto the sidewalk, and blended into the crowd of people going in all different directions. She barely even saw their faces. It was all a blur as each one of her steps took her that much closer to a man she wanted to hurt like he had hurt her.

Time and time again.

He just hurt her.

The two blocks it took Haven to get to Andino's business passed before she even fully realized it had happened. She was lost to her own anger and thoughts. She couldn't even think about anything else.

Haven never once considered that this might be a bad idea. She didn't even bother to consider that she should at least offer Andino the decency and respect of confronting him somewhere less public, and unattached to his name.

She didn't think about any of that.

Why should she?

He'd never once thought about her. Not her heart, or that the things he did might hurt her more than he could ever truly understand. He never cared about those things—*apparently*—so why should she give a fuck about him now?

She didn't.

Not at all.

Haven climbed the steps of the familiar restaurant, and flung the front door open. She didn't bother to spare a glance at the changes since the last time she had been there, if there even was any to mention. The girl at podium smiled brightly—she was a new face, clearly, as she didn't recognize Haven at all—but Haven walked right past her without as much as a hello.

"Excuse me, Miss! If you have a reserva—"

Haven flipped a hand over her shoulder in reply, but said nothing otherwise. She wasn't here to eat, and she didn't give a shit about reservations. She didn't even care about asking where Andino was, for that matter.

She'd figure it out on her own.

Besides, he could only be in one of two places. As he usually was whenever he was in the restaurant. Either in his office, or the private dining section. She didn't think the man had ever even done a job in the restaurant that was a part of *owning* the fucking place. Certainly not cooking, or serving a table. Maybe some paperwork, and coming out to shake a hand or two.

That was it.

Haven figured—only because Andino said he was busy—that he was probably in his office. That's where she headed first, but she had to pass the private dining section of the restaurant in order to slip through the kitchen to get to the back office.

She almost stumbled in her steps when she caught sight of Andino in the private section. Apparently, dining with two other men dressed in dark suits. One she recognized as Andino's uncle, Lucian. The other man, she didn't know at all. All she could see of Andino was the expanse of his broad shoulders, and the back of his head.

That wasn't what made her stop.

Or stumble.

No, it was the fact that his arm was so carelessly tossed around the back of a chair where a woman sat next to his side. *Close* to his side, actually. Very fucking close.

She couldn't see much of the woman given her back was turned to the doorway. Just the woman's long, wavy dark hair, and the low cut back of the dress she wore. The delicate line of her shoulders, and then her profile when she turned to smile at something Andino said.

A *soft* smile.

It could mean anything. It could mean nothing.

And yet, Haven didn't think that was the case at all. Maybe it was the way Andino smiled, and nodded back to the woman. Like he was comfortable sitting there like that, and didn't mind having the woman so close to him. Or it could have been the way he fixed a stray strand of her hair with a chuckle, and then the woman dropped her gaze with a pink tint coloring her cheeks.

Too close.

Too fucking personal.

Too much for her.

Haven *blinked*.

That rage she had been feeling ever since she left the café blinked out for a fast moment. What was left in its wake was a sharp, stinging pain that sliced through her body with devastating intent.

A pain like no other.

God.

She thought he had broke her heart before, but that was not the case. This was far worse. So much worse, really.

It was like she forgot how to breathe all of the sudden. The floor tilted under her, and the room became entirely too hot. Nothing felt right, and everything was horribly wrong. It was an awful way to feel.

She hated him for making her feel like this.

Haven wasn't sure what gained the attention of the people inside the private section. It could have been the noise that escaped her suddenly raw throat. A mixture of pain, and disbelief at the sight in front of her. Or it might have been one of the two men sitting on the opposite side of the table with full view of the doorway, and her standing directly inside of it.

Either way, they noticed her.

Andino turned to glance at her first, then the woman.

Haven was too busy looking at *him* to give a single fuck about her. She should tell the woman good luck—warn her that she was going to need all the luck she could get where Andino was concerned. The man didn't give a shit about anyone but himself.

That much was clear.

She didn't bother.

Useless, wasted words.

What was the point?

"Haven?" Andino said, confusion thickening his tone. He was quick to stand from his seat, and move toward her in the doorway. "What are you—"

He was too close.

Already.

Even being ten feet away with another second or two before he could reach her, she felt like he was too goddamn close to her. She didn't even want to be close enough to share his air, or see his face.

None of it.

Look at what he'd done to her.

Look at what he *did*.

"Don't," Haven snapped out in a rasp, holding one hand up to stop him from coming any closer. "I don't want you near me, Andino."

The hard set of his jaw flexed, and something flashed in his eyes. Confusion and pain, she thought, but it was hard to tell. He was good liar—said so himself. Nothing he did or said could be trusted. Not anymore. Haven learned that lesson and learned it *well*. Even if it was the last thing she wanted to know.

Andino's gaze darkened, and he took one more step closer to her. "Why are you—"

Haven glanced at the woman, and then back to him. If his shifting feet were any indication, Andino didn't miss the way her stare moved. Uncomfortable was not a good look on this man, but fuck him, because he deserved it.

And that woman?

Fuck her, too.

Except, she wasn't even the reason why Haven was there. She was just a second realization—a byproduct of Haven coming here, and nothing more. She was the confirmation that Haven needed to know this was the end.

"My club—Sandstone Investments. Ring any bells?"

Andino stiffened, and his face blanked. "Haven, I—"

"Oh, don't try for an excuse. Don't *lie*. You stepped in with the offer under the guise of your company in order to *keep* me in New York, and with you. That's what you did. I don't need you to fucking lie about it, Andino. I have had enough of your lies to last me an eternity. Thanks."

"Would you give me a minute, *please*?"

"No, I'm good," Haven replied. "We're done. You and me, it's over. Don't ever come near me again, Andino. Leave me the fuck alone."

She had so much more she wanted to say. There was a hell of a lot more she could have said. She could have made a far bigger scene, and let all that anger and pain out in words that would cut him to the ground.

This felt better.

This felt final.

Haven let it be done, and before Andino could respond, she had already turned her back to him and walked away.

It has to be done.

THIRTEEN

We're done.

Leave me the fuck alone.

Andino was more than aware that he couldn't afford to be lost in his thoughts in that moment, and yet, the only thing he could manage to do was stare blankly at the doorway Haven had just vacated.

He'd fucked up.

Oh, damn.

He'd fucked up *badly*.

The pain that had saturated Haven's words when she spoke was still echoing in his mind. Even as the chairs scraped behind him, and bodies shifted to stand, he was still lost in the sound of Haven's words banging around in his head.

Like knives and hammers.

Cutting and demolishing.

He hadn't meant to do this, and certainly not to her. That had never been his intention, not to hurt her, or bring her into this mess. He wanted her, but he didn't want to break her in the process. And yet, he thought that might be exactly what he had done.

"*Nipote*," Lucian murmured from somewhere behind him. "Do you need a minute to—"

"What was *that*?"

Kev Calabrese's voice grated on Andino's nerves like nothing else. It made his back and shoulders stiffen with the rage that swelled hot and heavy in his gut. More than anything, he wanted to turn around and tell Kev to go fuck himself. That the deal was off—not that he ever intended to follow it through in the first goddamn place.

Yet, he was still stuck.

Still *quiet*.

"Andino," Lucian said again.

Andino simply held up a hand for them to see over his shoulder. A silent way of asking for them to be quiet, and give him a second. Who knew what he fucking looked like right then? He didn't want to turn around and give anyone—but especially Kev—any more ammo to use against him than what Haven had just handed over.

Fuck.

She didn't realize what she just did.

He couldn't even blame her.

"Andino, I don't have time for this *shit*," Kev snapped.

Fuck him.

Andino turned around with a sardonic smile plastered on his face. A *forced* smile, really. The most he could offer right then. "What's the problem, Kev?"

The Calabrese man's gaze narrowed in on Andino like he had found the target he was about to shoot at. Andino might actually welcome the fucking bullets with the way he was feeling. Right then, though, he needed to get a handle on this situation in whatever way he could.

Kev gestured at the doorway. "*What is the problem?*"

"That's what I asked."

Andino was acutely aware of the way his uncle had reverted into something akin to a statue. Lucian was blank all over—no expression, and nothing to give away. He most certainly knew who Haven was, and what her showing up there meant. And yet, his uncle stayed unreadable as to let Andino handle the situation however he wanted to.

He was grateful.

One less issue for now, anyway. No doubt, he was going to have to deal with his own family for this at a later date. That was always going to happen—it would have been unavoidable in the end. Andino simply didn't know if he was ready for it *now*.

Too late to be considering that, he supposed.

"The problem—" Kev cut off with a disgusted noise. He pointed at the doorway yet again. "Who was that woman?"

This was what Andino had wanted to avoid the very most. He didn't want Haven on the Calabrese radar for any fucking reason. They were snakes—they couldn't be trusted with a single inch. If they thought they could use her to get to Andino, or the rest of the Marcellos, there was no doubt in his mind that they wouldn't even think twice about doing exactly that.

These fuckers were predictable.

He'd worked so hard to keep Haven away from these people. Sure, in a way, it ended up keeping her away from his people, too. It probably made her think she was his secret—how many goddamn times had she said that exact thing to him?

She didn't know, though.

He couldn't explain.

This was why he needed her to stay away. This was why he kept her separate, and made sure that no one ever touched her simply because she was attached to him and his name.

Not until he could *protect her.*

Fuck.

"Who is she?" Kev asked again. "Because I am going to assume—and probably rightfully so—that she is someone you're involved with considering the things she said. Tell me I'm wrong, Andino. I dare you."

"Oh, her?" Andino shrugged. "She's no one."

All lies.

Lies, lies, and more lies.

A sneer worked its way over Kev's mouth. "No one. *Really?*"

"That's what I said."

And that was all he was going to fucking offer, too. Wasn't it bad enough that Andino had said Haven's name out loud, and all Kev would need to do was a little bit of fucking digging to find out exactly who she was?

Because he thought it was.

Andino glanced at Ginevra who was quiet, and had turned her gaze down on her hands. She'd been uncomfortable for the majority of the dinner. He assumed something happened before she and her brother showed up because she came in looking like a damn ghost, and as silent as one, too.

He'd been *trying* to make her feel a bit better just before Haven walked in—he still needed this woman to at least trust him so that when the right time came, he could use her to help himself, and her, too.

Fuck my whole life.

"Andino," Lucian said quietly, "are you sure you don't need a minute?"

He heard his uncle's unspoken question.

Do you want to end this?

"I'm good," Andino lied. "We were getting dessert, weren't we?"

He sat back down at the table beside Ginevra. Kev, on the other hand, looked ready to blow his fucking top. Well, that seemed like a Kev problem and not an Andino problem at the moment.

He had other things to deal with.

"Are you going to sit?" Andino asked Kev.

Kev glared. "Are we going to have a problem, Andino?"

"I don't know—are we?"

The man didn't respond.

Andino figured … that was self-explanatory.

He glanced over at Ginevra. "Cheesecake, then?"

The young woman stared at him for a while, saying nothing. He could see the questions in her eyes. He wondered if she knew just by looking at him that he was in pain, and that the love of his life had just walked away from him.

Maybe forever.

Who knew?

Ginevra swallowed hard, and then nodded subtly. "Cheesecake sounds great."

Smart woman.

Andino might be able to still help her yet. But how in the hell was he going to help himself? And *Haven*?

That was the better question.

● ● ●

"Damage control," Dante said, shooting Andino a look that burned.

Andino didn't need that fucking look from his uncle. He'd been hearing Dante rage at him all week about Haven showing up at the restaurant. The first thing Kev had done was call Dante and ask about the blonde, tattooed *whore*—Kev's words, and ones he would probably die for—that Andino was involved with.

Dante had made his feelings more than clear to Andino. He was disappointing his uncle at every turn. Big fucking deal.

"Damage control is what we need to focus on right now," Dante continued.

"How do you suggest we do that?" Lucian asked, dropping into the chair beside Andino's father. "Give them something else they want, brother?"

Dante didn't miss Lucian's cutting tone if the way his gaze sliced to his brother was any indication. The older men stared at one another for a long time without saying anything. That whole *cut the tension with a knife* came to mind.

So was their life lately.

The Calabrese were good for that—fucking shit up. The Marcellos weren't immune to that nonsense, either. For as strong as their family unit could be on a good day, it only took one single issue that could bring up a differing of opinions on all sides to make them put a bit of distance between each other.

"I do not have the patience for this tonight, son," Antony said, pushing out of the chair behind the large oak desk. "This is for you and your brothers—" Andino's grandfather stopped talking as he shot him a look. "And Andino, I suppose, to figure out now. You don't need me here to do it, and I don't care to listen to you all bicker back and forth for hours on end."

"We're not—"

Antony held up a hand to quiet Dante. "I don't care."

Apparently, they were back to using Antony and Cecelia's mansion as a meeting hub. Really, it was supposed to be their usual Sunday family dinner. No business on Sundays was the rule, but exceptions could always be made. Andino was a reason for *a lot* of exceptions lately.

Or that's what Dante had pointed out time and time again this week. Andino was starting to become numb to this shit.

Once Antony was gone from the office, Dante turned his attention on Giovanni instead of Lucian. "And what about you?"

Gio quirked an eyebrow high. "What about me?"

"Do you have anything you want to say about all of this?"

"Why should I say something when you've been shouting at my son enough for all of us lately, Dante?"

Dante stiffened, and straightened on the spot. "Excuse me?"

"You heard what I said."

Gio held his ground, and Andino was surprised. It wasn't often that his father and the boss went head to head on something. Gio was happy in his place as Dante's consigliere, and the two rarely argued.

That was changing, it seemed.

Andino didn't need to wonder why, either. His father's position was always clear where he was concerned: what Andino wanted, Gio also wanted. His loyalty to the family was never in question, but he, like Andino, knew that the family wasn't just the wants of one man, but all the men. It couldn't be just about Dante when there were other people in the equation, too.

"Do you expect me to be *pleased* with the fact Andino is still running around with that woman even after this agreement was made—"

"I think you can't expect my son to be like you," Gio returned, stopping his brother from saying anything more. "And you're still expecting exactly that in a lot of ways. You expect him to be fine and faithful to a woman he didn't choose and doesn't love. You expect him to do what you were willing to do for Catrina—except he isn't you, and I won't be someone else who puts those expectations on him."

"So, you're fine with him having—"

Enough of this.

Andino could and would fight his own battles, but he really just wanted to move the hell on at the moment. "It's over."

Dante turned on him again, quiet for a passing second before he asked, "What is over?"

"Haven and I."

Andino didn't offer more because frankly, he didn't think he needed to. What more needed to be said other than that? Oh, he sure as fuck didn't actually *mean* it. He wasn't anywhere near done with Haven. He loved her to the ends of the earth and back, even if that meant killing himself to finally have her.

But for now?

Well … for now, he needed to keep her as safe as he could. He needed to keep attention away from her.

That meant he needed to stay away.

Dante folded his arms over his chest, and replied, "I think you can understand my disbelief when you say that, Andi."

"Sure, but the fact remains the same."

"I don't think it's *his* choice when he says it's over," Lucian murmured from his seat. "The young woman made it quite clear where she stood."

Dante glanced over his shoulder briefly at that statement, but quickly gave his attention to Andino once more. "Would you give me your word on that, then?"

"Is that what you need?"

"Andino, I refuse to clean up another mess for you if your only intention is to go ahead and make another one when my back is turned. You think I haven't noticed that seems to be a common thing for you? Funny—we always said you were nothing like your father, but it seems we all had that backwards, didn't we?"

Or maybe he just finally found something—*someone*—that he was willing to break all the rules for. Haven was worth that. She was worth everything.

Dante would understand, but not now. He would understand why Andino lied, and then lied again when it was all said and done because he too had a wife he loved. And sure, while his wife was considered appropriate for their life, that didn't mean Dante wouldn't have fought tooth and nail to have her if someone told him that he *couldn't* have her.

That was the thing …

That was why his father had his back—Gio was being his *dad*, and not a made fucking man. It was why Lucian was quick to side with Andino when needed, too; he'd married an outsider himself. That was why his uncle would understand that when push came to shove, Andino was going to get what he wanted one way or the other; Dante loved his own wife enough to do anything for her, too.

Andino loved Haven.

Nothing else mattered.

"You have my word," Andino lied. "No more problems."

Dante nodded once, murmuring, "I'm starting to think I should be more concerned about the problems you might cause once you finally are the boss rather than the problems you're causing now, all things considered."

Andino shrugged. "Well, by that time, it won't be any of your business, will it?"

That was sort of the point.

Dante said nothing.

• • •

"You good?"

Andino nodded over the glass of whiskey he'd been nursing for a half an hour. "Fine, Dad."

Gio frowned. "Then, why don't you look like it?"

"Shitty week?"

A chuckle answered him back.

Andino sighed. "It's fine, really."

"It isn't."

No, it wasn't. But that didn't mean he wanted his father to get stuck in his head about it, either.

"Don't step in between Dante and me, all right?" Andino asked. "Just … let me handle him on this."

Gio tipped his head back, and folded his arms over his chest. Behind his father, the voices of their family filtered into the living room area from the dining room. Dinner was still in full swing, but Andino just wasn't in the mood.

He had shit to consider.

Things to work through.

"You lied to him earlier," Gio said quietly.

Andino shrugged one shoulder. "I'm telling him what he wants to hear. That's the only way to get this shit done and over with. What do you want me to do?"

"I want you to *not* make this family into something it isn't, Andi. Don't turn the Marcellos into something they have never been. Don't cause enough of a fracture between us all in your effort to be happy that we can't come back together again in the end. Do you understand what I'm saying?"

He did.

"I'll try," he offered.

"There you two are."

At the soft voice of his mother, Andino relaxed a bit. He took another sip of his whiskey as Kim came in through the doorway. She gave the two of them a look that said she knew their secrets. She probably did, knowing his father.

"Rough night?" she asked.

Andino laughed. "Rough life, Ma."

Kim grinned, but it quickly faded. "You've been busy this week."

"Work."

He said that even knowing that it was far more likely his mother knew the truth. That no, he hadn't been busy with work at all, but more his uncle, and dealing with the mess that had come after the Haven debacle. There

128

was no way in hell that Gio kept that information from Kim. And even if his father hadn't told her, news traveled fast in their close family circles.

She had to know.

So, she had to also know he was lying.

Gio shot him a look.

Andino didn't return it.

"You know," his mother drawled, "I genuinely thought you might like that woman—the Calabrese woman, I mean. Ginevra. You spoke kindly about her. Men who run around with someone else don't tend to ... well, do that. Or is that the kind of man you are, Andi?"

Ouch.

He chuckled dryly, and set his now-empty glass aside. "Ma—"

"He was talking about Haven Murphy that day," his father said. "In the kitchen at our home. You told me about it after, Kim. He was talking about her even if it seemed like it was about Ginevra."

Andino shook his head, and scrubbed a hand down his face. Yeah, fuck his whole life. Because this was a mess he was never going to get out of. Or so it seemed lately.

Kim's brow rose higher. "Haven."

"Yeah, *Tesoro.*"

"Oh."

That gentle, soft-spoken word felt laced with a heavy sadness that Andino didn't want to hear at all. This was why he hadn't wanted to bring his parents into this mess at all.

Yes, they were Marcellos. They were loyal to the family and the name. They knew this life.

But they were also his parents—they loved him so much. Far more than anyone else in his life ... except for maybe Haven. All that meant was that the pain he felt or the struggle he dealt with would be *amplified* for them as they had to watch, and were unable to do anything.

They'd allowed him to live exactly the way he wanted to for so long. To grow, and be whoever the fuck he needed to be. They never stopped him from doing anything, and they never stepped in to change his direction.

Why would this be any different?

"What are you going to do, then?" his mother asked, her soft gaze turning on him. "What can we do?"

He wished he knew.

This was something he was going to have to do alone.

They wouldn't understand.

• • •

There was no missing the smug smiles that Kev and Darren Calabrese wore as Dante and Andino met the two men at the bar. He couldn't wait to wipe those fucking smirks from their faces, but now was not the time.

No, now was the time to *play nice*.

God knew how long that would last.

"June twenty-fifth," Kev said.

Dante quirked a brow as he and Andino came to a stop in front of the two men. "For what, Kev?"

"The wedding. A month from today. We decided on the date, and thought you would appreciate knowing. Maybe have a drink with us to celebrate. Invitations were printed this morning by that place your wife suggested, Dante. Thank her for us. And some were already hand delivered. We will, of course, make sure your family has invitations for your side of things."

What?

Did he just walk into the Twilight Zone?

Andino could feel his uncle's gaze shift to him, but he didn't respond in any way. They'd called them in for a *drink*? And to give a wedding date? What kind of fucking garbage was that? Andino wished he could be surprised, but he really wasn't. This would be just like the Calabrese to make a show out of something like this.

They'd been in a fit for a good week or more about the Haven issue. Kev had gone as far as threatening to end the deal between their families. And even earlier, when he'd called to ask for this meeting, Andino was right there listening in when Kev told Dante he wanted to discuss the issues at hand, for Christ's sake.

Lucian had been right.

When it came to the Calabrese, they were all about their own standing and appearance. They thought they had gotten something from the Marcellos—some kind of upper hand with this marriage arrangement—and they were going to use it to the very maximum that they could.

Jesus.

"I thought this meeting was for something different," Dante said. "That was the impression you gave when you called and asked for it, Kev. Are you usually this unstable? I'd like a fair warning next time."

Kev's jaw ticked, but he was quick to hide it with another one of those smiles. "There's nothing to handle, Dante. We made a deal—the marriage between Andino and Ginevra. It will go forward. We've decided that."

"You were quite adamant about the *issue*—"

The issue being Haven, Dante meant.

Kev waved a hand to stop Dante from saying anything more. "Oh, that? We've handled that, I assure you. And besides, we are aware that what a man might do in his private life is his business as long as it's … kept quiet."

The man looked to Andino, asking, "Isn't that right, Andi?"

"Andino," he corrected Kev. "For you, it is always Andino."

Andino could tell that this was not what Dante had expected to happen for this meeting. He'd forewarned Andino to stand at his side, and keep fucking quiet as much as possible. They were still working towards peace with the Calabrese, after all. That was supposed to be the most important goal.

Kev got in his feelings about Haven's little show at the restaurant for a while, but now it seemed like he was over it. Andino knew it couldn't be that simple. Nothing with these snakes was that simple or easy.

And Kev had said …

"What does that mean?" Andino asked the man.

Darren smirked. "Oh, us handling the issue?"

Andino hadn't asked the youngest of the two asshole brothers, but he also didn't give a shit who answered his question as long as somebody did.

He didn't like what it implied.

His rage was rising again.

"It means we handled it," Darren said slowly as though he were talking to a small child and not a man who could easily beat his skull into the bar behind him. "And we have no doubt that the problem will correct itself now."

"Interesting woman you chose to be fucking, though," Kev added. "Former stripper. Current business owner. Pretty thing—if it weren't for all the tattoos. A bit much, really. I can see why your family wouldn't want you running around with that all over town, even if she is quite nice to look at."

Dante tensed beside his nephew. "That's out of line, Kev."

He didn't need his uncle stepping in for him.

At all.

Andino's jaw ticked when he said, "First, if you insult Haven again, it will be the last thing you do. She has nothing to do with this, or us. Second, if you *think* to touch her in some way, I will make it my first and last mission every day to make sure anyone with your name is in a grave."

"Andino," Dante warned.

He never took his gaze off the Calabrese men.

"It's not a promise," Andino said, "it's a fucking guarantee. Test me."

Kev only smiled in that fucking way of his again. "Oh, I don't think we need to worry about that now, Andino. As Darren said, we believe the issue will correct itself from here on out. We handled that."

Yes, but what did that mean?

Andino didn't think he would like it, but he was going to have to find out.

Not right now, though.

Kev gestured at the bar. "A drink?"

Andino wanted to say no.

Dante answered for him, instead. "Sure, a drink sounds fine."

They were still playing nice, it seemed. Andino was really getting sick and tired of this bullshit. His time for playing nice was just about over.

FOURTEEN

"Haven, let me in. Come on, baby, *please.*"

The banging on the door continued. Even as she ignored Andino's pleas. Even as his fist came down harder on the wood. Even as he begged for her to talk to him for even a *minute.* No, she ignored him.

Well, she tried.

It was fucking hard.

She pressed her back harder against the door, and stared up at the ceiling. She tried to daze out from his voice so that her heart didn't have to hear him speaking. So it would stop beating so fucking fast and *wish, wish, wishing* she would answer him back.

It was so goddamn traitorous.

This heart of hers hurt.

She squeezed her eyes shut, and thought about plugging her ears. Then, this stupid soul of hers that wanted this man so badly would stop twisting and burning and trying to tear its way out of her fucking body just to get to him.

Why?

That's what she kept asking herself: why.

Why, after all he had done to her, did she still love him? Why couldn't she just walk away from the door, and turn off all the lights? Why couldn't she even *pretend* like she didn't give a shit about him?

The paper cardstock with its fancy script, and a woman's name under Andino's announcing their *marriage* should have been enough. That should have been her hard fucking limit. Her *no more, we're so fucking done.*

They should be done.

She had every reason to be done!

And yet, it was him and his voice in her head. It was her, and her stupid heart and her weak soul *breaking.*

Fractured, and ruined, and entirely *gone.*

Gone, now, because she'd given it to him. Oh, sure, she'd tried to take it back. But fuck all of him because he still had it. She didn't even own herself anymore. Surely not her *love.* That was all his, and look at what he'd done with it.

Look at how he lied. How he hurt. *Look at what he did to her.*

"Go away, Andino," Haven mumbled against the palms of her hands.

She hated that she cried. Hated that her face was streaked with hot tears, and her palms tasted like salt under her lips. She hated that somehow, she had allowed a man to have this kind of control over her.

This was not her.

This was some awful, horrible version of her.

This was his version of her.

She hated it.

His banging continued.

So did his voice.

"Just go away!"

"Please, Haven … *please*. Let me in; let me talk—*something*."

Go, she wanted to scream. Go, go, just fucking *go*. That awful, horrible part of her screamed, *stay, please, stay.*

"Haven, just open the fucking door!"

"Go away."

"Open the door!"

"*Go.*"

"You think I won't break this fucking thing down, baby? You think I won't move heaven and hell for you? You think you know what I did? You don't know anything—you can't because I couldn't let you. Let me explain, please."

Maybe it was his whole *you don't know anything* that pushed her over the edge. Maybe that was what made her so fucking angry that her vision blackened, and her breaths stopped altogether.

She didn't *know*?

She was living it.

"Haven, just—"

She pushed away from the door fast, and spun around to throw it open. Andino's hand was already raised to knock again when the door flew wide. He looked *wild*. Probably a hell of a lot like she looked in those moments.

Messy, and crazed.

Pissed.

"*I don't know?*" she all but screamed at him. "I fucking know!"

Haven threw the invitation at him. It bounced off his still-as-stone chest, and fell to the threshold of the doorway keeping the only distance between them.

She'd been holding the invitation ever since a man knocked on her door, and handed it over with a sadistic smile after he introduced himself as Darren Calabrese. The last name rung a bad bell for Haven, but the first name … she didn't know it at all.

It didn't matter.

The invitation had been enough.

On the ground, the invitation stayed where it had fallen, untouched and unwanted. By her, anyway. It being there—and too close—was enough to taunt her.

Andino still hadn't said anything. He didn't move, or even glance away from her. Certainly not to look down at the invitation on the ground. That was enough to tell her he didn't actually have to look at it.

He knew exactly what was on it. He knew the words she had read again and again while *willing* them to disappear, or be some kind of cruel joke. He didn't have to pick up the invitation to know anything about it at all.

Haven didn't give a single shit how she looked standing there in nothing but an over-sized T-shirt, and very little else. She hadn't been expecting *anyone* to show up, but least of all this man. He always was a little too goddamn cocky for his own good.

Finally, he spoke.

A second too late, and dollar short.

"It's not what you think."

Haven barked out a bitter laugh, and wiped the stray tears from her cheeks. "It's *exactly* what I think it is, Andino. You're getting *married*."

"It appears like—"

"*Married!*"

Andino glanced away, and shook his head. "You've got to let me talk for five seconds. Just let me talk, Haven."

No. She really didn't want to hear anything he had to say at all.

"Was it all this time? Was this happening since the beginning?"

Her voice came out raspy and aching. That happened when you cried this hard; when you hurt *this much*.

Andino's jaw ticked. "You know better than that."

"Fuck *you*," Haven spat. "I don't know anything about you at all. You've shown me that time and time again. *When someone shows you who they are, believe them*. Right? That's how the saying goes. My fucking mistake, Andino. It won't happen again."

Taking a wide step back, she grabbed the edge of the door and prepared to slam it closed. He could stay right where he was for all she gave a damn. Far away from her, and on the outside of her life. Forever.

"Go away, and stay gone," she told him.

She swung the door to close it, but no fucking surprise, Andino was there to stop it. His hand crashed into the door, and pushed it open hard. The force was enough to make Haven stumble in an effort to move away fast enough so that it didn't hit her.

The fucking *asshole*.

"Get out!" she screamed.

If he heard her—and there was no way he didn't—Andino acted like she didn't say a thing. He slammed that door behind him, and swung around on her. Haven was already reacting; her emotions hit their limit.

She *broke*.

Her palm connected with his face with a slap that echoed and sent his head snapping to the side. The red imprint of her hand left behind said he had to *feel* it, and all Haven felt was the greatest sense of satisfaction at that fact.

Good.

He should feel it.

Like she did.

Andino sucked air in through his teeth that sounded like a hiss before his hands were on her. One grabbing firmly to her waist, and the other curving around her neck. She couldn't even protest before his lips crashed against his.

She didn't want to respond. She wanted to push him away, and hit him again. Yet, her anger was only stroked tenderly from a small flame into a raging inferno with his kiss. The rage wrapped tightly around the lust and love she always felt for this man whenever he was near.

His kiss was not like it used to be, though. It was something wilder—something more desperate. Hard enough to hurt, and crazy enough to take her breath away. His fingers dug into the back of her neck like his hand on her waist, and he dragged her impossibly closer.

If he wasn't such a good liar, she might think he was trying to give her his soul with that kiss. Like he was offering it in bleeding, blackened hands for her to take.

Except he was who he was.

She believed *nothing*.

"I love you," he said hoarsely when he finally pulled away. "*I love you so fucking much, Haven.* I love you too much. I love you enough to destroy *everything*, but you don't know that at all because I haven't been able to tell you. I love you, woman. Let me explain—let me *show you*. Don't you get it? Just let me—"

Sure, and quiet, and strong, Haven whispered, "You don't love me at all. Love doesn't do these things to someone else. This isn't love."

"*Haven.*"

God, why did he have to sound like that?

Fuck him.

"What you've done to us is *not* love," she said, refusing to budge even an inch. She was not going to give him that, not for this. "You're not love."

"Haven, *listen to me.*"

"There's nothing to listen to because there's nothing to say."

"There is!"

Haven shook her head slowly. They were so close that she could see the darker flecks of green and gold in his eyes. God, she had loved those eyes of his once. Loved how they seemed to only see her even in a room

136

full of others. Deep, and expressive. Even when the rest of him was as cold as ice.

But right now?

She didn't love them at all.

A lot like him.

All she wanted to do in that moment was hurt him in the way he had hurt her. Make him feel the same kind of pain, or even a fraction of it so that maybe he could understand the hell he had created in her life. She was fine before him; she was going to be fine after this man, too.

Haven kissed him again. The same way he'd kissed her—like the world was gone, and she was handing her sound over with every stroke of their lips, and tangle of their tongues. She kissed him like nothing else mattered, and nothing ever would.

Because it would be the last time. That was her promise.

She was going to use him like he'd used her time and time again. She wasn't going to regret it for even a second—nothing after everything.

Haven reached for Andino's pants, and it was the only time he hesitated to answer her back. His wariness lasted as long as it took for her to get his pants undone, and slip her hands beneath the waistband. She found his cock hard, and heavy inside his briefs. Against her lips, he grunted out her name followed by a soft apology as she stroked him with a tight fist.

That apology only pissed her off more.

It was enough to make her want to hit him again, but she didn't even have time for that before Andino was lifting her against the wall. His mouth attacked the column of her neck—tasting and kissing all those spots he knew she loved—as she wrapped her legs around his waist.

The hard ridge of his erection pressed against the thin fabric of her panties. *Damp* panties. She was already wet, ready to take him, and willing to so they could finally be done with this dance that had been going on between them for far too long. Unashamed, she arched her body against his, and used the grinding of her hips to ease some of the ache between her thighs by rubbing against his dick.

Flames licked at her body with every touch of his mouth or hands against him. His palms slipped under that too-large T-shirt, and found her bare breasts. Haven tipped her head back, and let out a hard gasp when his thumbs and forefingers tweaked her hard nipples. His tongue lapped at the hollow of her throat, his hips flexed forward to grind his cock against her wet panties, and she was *flying*.

For a second, she did forget how much she hurt, and all the things this man had done to her. Even through her lustful haze, she could feel how frantic and desperate they were in their movements. Shaking hands, and hard breaths. Hard kisses, and stinging bites.

Haven all but blinked, and Andino was moving them again. His fingers dug into her ass as he moved into the kitchen. Her backside came to rest on the counter, and he spread her thighs wide. He only let her go long enough to peel those panties down her thighs. He wasted no time—there was no slowness in his actions. He loved to tease her, but not today.

His mouth was back on hers when he shoved his pants down. Then, his hands were on her thighs again to squeeze tight, and widen them until her muscles protested and her bones ached.

But fuck her, because she *loved* it.

"Just fuck me, and be done with it," she rasped.

Done with her.

With *them*.

Just done.

"Fuck," Andino snarled when his cock was right *there*. All it took was one hard flex of his hips, and he was buried deep in her slick cunt. Sensitive flesh became all that much more tender as he filled her full, pulled back out, and then slammed right back in again. Another brutal thrust came right after that one, and then again. Until he was just pounding into her with a tempo that drove her *insane*. "Look at me … *look at me*."

She didn't.

Couldn't.

Instead, she watched his cock slide through the wet lips of her pussy until his hand curved around her throat, and he forced her head back. Like this, she was forced to stare into those eyes again. She was forced to see things she didn't want to.

"Hate you," she breathed.

Andino's fingers tightened. *"Don't."*

"I hate you."

If anything, he just fucked her harder for that. Haven wished she could say that she didn't like it, but that would have been a lie. She loved it.

She raked lines over his back with her fingernails, and dug her heels into his back to force him closer. Even as she wanted him gone, she needed more of him, then, too.

She was such a fucking mess.

"Don't," he said again, shoving her head back against the cupboard. "Don't you *ever* lie to me."

Haven laughed breathlessly. "Like you do to me?"

She was so close to coming it was crazy. Almost at the edge, and ready to jump the hell off. Her nerves snapped with every meet of their hips. Trembling like a fucking leaf, and aching between her thighs.

His fingers dug in again, and he kissed her before biting down on her bottom lip. The shock of pain was enough to finally do it. It sent her tumbling over the cliff of bliss. The orgasm ravaged her senses, and made her numb to everything else.

She felt him grunt, and two hard thrusts later, empty himself deep inside her cunt, too.

Haven *breathed*.

She took a second, and just breathed.

Then, quietly, she said, "Now, please go."

The devil wasn't a man with red skin, hooves for feet, and horns on his head. No, the devil was the most handsome, charming man with hands that could make a woman sing, and lies on the tip of his tongue. The devil was a man who made her want to *die* for him, but all he did was fucking kill her instead. And he did it without a second thought, or regret. He did it unashamed of the heartache he caused.

He was sin, sure, but pain, too. He was not what the devil should be, but he was still his own kind of hell. He burned like it, too.

And right then, she was staring him straight in the face.

Andino, only a breath from her and trembling from head to toe, looked like agony materialized into a *being*. He looked like pain in the flesh, but she couldn't believe it. She couldn't believe anything from him anymore.

"I can't go until you let me explain," he finally said.

Haven shook her head. "That's the thing—I don't want you to anymore."

"That's not fair."

Life wasn't fair.

Nothing ever was.

"You're so good at this," she whispered.

Things that loved you shouldn't hurt you. Things you loved shouldn't hurt you. That wasn't how this was supposed to work. He needed to understand that.

"Haven, please—"

"You're so good at hurting me, Andino, but I don't want to be hurt anymore, okay? *I don't want to hurt.*"

"I'm sorry."

"No, you're not."

"*I am.*"

Haven shook her head, and more tears slipped from her eyes. The ache between her thighs, and his cock still hard and heavy there would have usually meant satisfaction and *love*. Right then, it only felt like shame and sadness.

"Just …" Haven dragged in a hard, ragged breath. "Just leave. Just go, please."

His hands on her thighs gripped tighter. Like he wasn't going to let her go for anything. His fingers were going to leave bruises, but she couldn't find it in herself to care about that. For now, she just needed to get this man away from her.

She'd wanted him close; now she needed him to go.

"You won't even let me explain," he uttered through a clenched jaw with his eyes blazing. "Let me fucking *explain*. This is not what you think it is, I swear it isn't."

"It's just another thing on an already huge pile, Andino. Please go."

"Baby—"

"The club is sold. The house is next to go. I'm leaving, and you're going to let me. You're going to stay far away from me in the meantime. You're going to do that, Andino, because I want you to. Do you understand?"

"*Haven.*"

Saturating his voice was pain. She was almost happy about that. She took a small sense of satisfaction in the fact that just *maybe* this man might understand all the hell he had put her through.

But who knew?

"Go," she said.

Barely above a whisper.

Barely there at all.

"Just go, Andino."

It took a second, and then two. It took another squeeze of his hands on her thighs, and his gaze nailing into hers—a silent plea. She answered none of it. She couldn't if she was going to somehow survive this crash and burn, and come out better for it.

Haven knew that much.

"You might not think so," he said quietly, "but we're *not* over, Haven. This can't be over. It was always real for me; it still is."

Finally, he moved away from her. Well, it was more like he tore himself away from her as though he had to force his body to move. All the while, even as he fixed himself and she remained half-naked on the cupboard with her thighs opened and leaking with the proof of their last mistake, he never once looked away from her.

That was fine.

She didn't look back. She didn't move, or breathe, or *think* until he was gone. She didn't cry, or beg, or break until he was already gone.

He couldn't see it, then. She wouldn't let him.

He didn't deserve even that.

• • •

Haven met the gaze of the man sitting across the table from her. It was almost amusing because he *looked* like the stereotypical private investigator. Right down to the rounded stomach, old leather jacket tossed over a cotton dress shirt with the top two buttons undone, and the aviator sunglasses that he'd pushed high on the top of his head. She'd never seen him actually have a camera in his hands, but if he did, he would fit the bill perfectly. She assumed he did have a camera, and whatever else he needed to do this job, but she never cared to ask.

She paid him money, and he gave her information. That was the deal, or it was supposed to be.

"Hot day, isn't it?" Wally asked, patting his sweaty forehead with a white napkin from the table. Haven was slightly happy that she had eaten before he arrived. That would probably make this whole meeting a little easier to handle. "June never gives me a break."

Haven smiled. "I like the heat, personally."

And she did.

She loved jogging on a hot day, and coming home to a cold shower. That was the best feeling in the world next to sex, she would swear on it. She wasn't about to tell this man that, though. They were sitting in this café for other reasons today.

"You called me saying you had something for me?" Haven asked.

Anticipation and anxiety curled thickly in her stomach like coils tangling around one another. The tighter they wove, the more she wanted to fidget or move. She'd felt like this from the moment she decided to hire a private investigator to find information on Valeria, or even where her friend was right now.

It'd never really left.

Wally cleared his throat, and nodded. His gaze darted around to take in the other patrons sitting at various tables, and fully lost in their food or discussions. Some had their faces shoved into tablets or phones. None of them were paying *any* attention to Haven and the private investigator.

Why was he so nervous?

Haven could have easily shrugged that off by saying it was just the man's ways. He probably preferred less public meeting spaces, or something like that. He didn't like doing business where anyone could overhear, or something.

Her gut said that wasn't it.

Maybe that should have been her first hint that this meeting was unlikely to go the way she had been hoping. Still, Haven refused to give up or give in to the anxiety that just wouldn't leave her alone.

This—trying to find something, or *anything*—on Valeria and Maria was one of the last things she needed to get done before she could get the hell out of this city. The club was sold, and she hadn't been back since the fucking ink dried. Her house had an offer put on it last week, and the paperwork was being started on all of that.

If all went well, she would be in Flordia with her mother and father by the end of June. She had a few minor things to tie up, but then she was gone.

Finally.

Haven was both sad and relieved about that fact. The heaviness that swelled in her broken heart every time she felt good about being able to put the distance between herself, and the man in this city that she knew she needed to leave behind was as confusing as it was infuriating.

It kept her up at night. And when she did sleep, she woke up with a tear-stained pillow more often than she cared to admit. Being alone was the most lonely place to be, Haven had come to learn.

This should be easy.

This was *right*.

Her heart didn't seem to care about any of that. All it cared about was the fact it had been broken again. Not that she hadn't expected to be hurt again, because she had. That didn't exactly help to make the hole in her chest any smaller, though.

"Are you listening, girly?"

Haven blinked at Wally's amused question. "Sorry?"

The private investigator waved the folder in his hand for Haven to see. He must have pulled it out of that black messenger bag he always carried around when she was lost in her thoughts. Silently, he set the folder on the table, and pushed it across to her.

"There you are," he said, "have a looksie, and tell me what you think about the things I found on your little friend."

Haven didn't see the point of this whole charade. He could easily tell her what was in the folder, but whatever. She flipped the folder open, and quickly scanned the contents on the first page. Her brow dipped as she read familiar words that she already knew about Val, and where she had come from, who she was married to, and more. Flipping to the next page, Haven found similar information that Andino had already provided to her about Valeria.

None of this was even *new*.

Peering at the man, Haven said, "I already know a lot of this stuff."

"Did you?"

"Yes."

"Then, I hope you understand why when I say I won't be taking on this job beyond what I have already done and provided to you, Miss Murphy."

Haven froze. "What?"

142

"You gave me a name, and some cursory information. You *mentioned* the cartel aspect, but I honestly thought that was simply another American who thinks every Mexican that comes across the border illegally must be involved with crime in some way. I did not expect to find that this woman is a runaway Cartel leader's *wife* who took his child."

A lump formed in Haven's throat—hard, and hot. No matter how many times she tried to swallow, it just wouldn't fucking loosen a bit.

"She didn't have the child when she left—she would have been pregnant," Haven forced herself to say.

"Fact remains, I am sure the man knew she was pregnant." Wally shrugged his beefy shoulders, and folded those thick arms over his chest. His perspiration on his forehead had picked up a bit. "You seem to be under some kind of impression that just because I am a private investigator, I will do *anything*. That is not the case. My safety is a priority, and these people," he said, reaching over to tap a finger against the paper, "are *not* the kind of people I care to find out I am looking into their business. I hope you understand."

Haven's jaw ached from how firmly she clenched it. "You're telling me that you won't look for her at all?"

"Listen, girly …" Wally leaned forward, and lowered his tone as his eyes scanned the patrons in the business again. "This is a stupid road you're trying to walk down, and I assure you that unless a private investigator has a whole army of guns behind him to take care of him, he is *not* going to take on this job. For reference, so you can save yourself the money and the hassle of trying to find someone else. It's a wasted effort on your part, Haven."

She didn't think so.

How could she think that?

"She's my friend," Haven murmured.

Wally coughed, and glanced away. "Yeah, well, your friend got mixed up in some pretty bad people. So, unless you care to get yourself mixed up with them, too, I suggest you scurry along and don't look back. That's my advice. Be smart, and *take it*. You don't have the kind of power or influence these people do. You are a regular woman in a very dangerous world. These people live a life that would give you nightmares. You don't have even a fraction of what you need to get you through their front door."

Well, *fuck*.

"Right now, you are not even on their radar," the man added quieter. "If you begin looking at them, you will become a blip. The second they know you are there is the very second you become their problem. And do you want to know how they deal with problems like you?"

"How?"

BETHANY-KRIS

"The easy way would be to kill you. The hard way would be to *keep* you. Now, you can keep that folder I gave you, but I suggest you burn it and pretend like you never saw it to begin with." Wally stood from the table, and gathered his things. Sliding his shades back down to cover his eyes, he turned to Haven once more with a simple, "Have a good day, Miss Murphy. Don't contact me again about this—I won't answer. In fact, I blocked your number after I called you this morning. I hope you understand."

That was that.

Haven was left sitting at the table alone, and staring blankly at the stupid information in front of her. She had wasted a lot of money for information Andino had given her simply because he wanted to, and she wasn't any better for it.

If anything, she was just *more* concerned than before.

She sat at that table for entirely too long before Haven decided enough was enough. She was quick to gather her things, and then leave the small eatery with the folder still tucked under her arm. Despite what Wally suggested, she had absolutely no fucking intention of burning the information.

She wasn't giving up on Val.

Not yet.

Since the eatery was only a few blocks away from Haven's house, and she hadn't been able to jog that morning, she had simply walked. She was halfway home before a prickling sensation covered the back of her neck. The kind of feeling that made all the fine hairs on her body stand up on end.

She peered over her shoulder, but nothing stood out. So, she kept walking. A few cars passed her by, but it was only when a familiar black sedan drove past her for the third time within two blocks that Haven finally noticed it.

The fourth time, the car drove slower.

She didn't recognize the shadow of the man sitting behind the wheel, but it left her with an uneasy and angry ball growing in her gut. Cars like those were all too common, she found, when it came to the mafia.

How many of the men who worked for Andino had she seen driving cars exactly like that one?

Jesus Christ.

She'd told him, hadn't she?

Wasn't she fucking clear enough?

Haven was a few steps from her house when the car drove by going at least twenty under the goddamn speed limit yet again. Done with that nonsense, she pulled her phone from the bag slung over her shoulder, and dialed a familiar number. Despite the fact she had actually deleted his

144

contact from her phone altogether, her stupid mind knew the number by heart.

Of course.

This was the one and only call she would make to him. And it was only to tell him to fuck *way* the hell off.

He'd done enough to her.

"Haven?"

Andino's voice filtered in her ear with a soothing, sexy quality. Fuck her body for feeling some kind of way about it, too. Haven pushed those thoughts aside as she turned to watch the black car coming her way.

"You're having me followed now?" Haven demanded. "Is that your next thing? Instead of you coming and going, you're sending someone else to do it for you, or ...? Because I don't appreciate it, and you can call them off at any fucking time."

"What?"

"Don't act like you don't know exactly what I am—"

"Haven," Andino murmured, "you made yourself perfectly clear, and even though you weren't willing to let me talk or explain some things ... I heard you. As best as I could. I swear to God, if someone is following you, it's not me."

Haven stiffened in place, and her gaze lifted to watch as the car came closer. "It's not you."

"No."

"Then, who the fuck is it?"

Andino cleared his throat. "It's probably the Calabrese just making sure things are as they want it to be."

"You mean ... we're not together."

"Exactly that. They know better than to hurt you, but I am sure they are just making themselves known. My advice would be this ... if they're watching you, Haven, then *watch back*. Make them know that you're aware they are there. Don't be afraid—don't let them think for a second that they're bothering you. Watch them as much as they watch you."

"Watch them."

That felt odd.

"As long as they're watching you, yeah," he said. "And Haven?"

"Yeah?"

"I'm still sorry. And I still love you."

Fuck him.

She didn't need to hear that.

He couldn't possibly mean it.

Haven hung up the call.

FIFTEEN

Three weeks to go.

The countdown was on.

A weight pressed down on Andino's shoulders as he stared at the place card that had been set in front of him alongside four different slices of cake. He was not a sweets person, really. He could do without cake, and sugar.

Not today, apparently.

Today, he had to cake test.

For his fucking wedding.

"The traditional flavors all have a nice twist, as you will all find once you begin the tasting. There's also our signature flavor," the baker said, leaning over the table to point at a chocolate cake that Andino was sure tasted exactly like it fucking looked. "This one here. Now, the final one ... The lemon cake has a zest—"

"Lemon is disgusting for a wedding cake," Siena said.

At the other end of the table, Kev made a noise under his throat, and tossed his oldest sister a glare. "You could at least let the woman finish speaking, Siena."

"I could, but nobody wants lemon flavor in their wedding cake, Kev."

"She has a point," Andino murmured, drawing the attention to himself. He would much rather pretend like he wasn't there at all, but here he fucking was. He might as well make the most of it. "But then again, no one thought to ask the only woman who should really get a say about it, yeah?"

All eyes turned on a quiet Ginevra sitting beside Andino. She, like him, had barely been paying attention throughout this whole charade as well. She didn't want to be there any more than he fucking did, clearly.

Not that he blamed her.

"I don't care," Ginevra said.

There she be.

Ginevra did well on her good days to pretend when it came to this marriage nonsense. She put on a smile, and acted like she gave a fuck. She didn't step out of line, or do something that might piss off her brothers' already thin patience. She was the respectful, dutiful wife-to-be, Andino supposed.

And then there were days like this.

Days when she didn't care to even try. She still managed to be somewhat kind to Andino and Siena, but he figured that was because they were the only ones who made an effort to look out for what she wanted or needed. Kev and Darren surely didn't give a single fuck about Ginevra, or what she was feeling.

They'd made that clear enough.

Kev passed Ginevra the same kind of look he had given to Siena just a couple of moments earlier. The man wasn't very good at verbal communication unless it was to tell one of his sisters or his brother an order that he wanted them to follow. Otherwise, he just glared and went on like a foolish prick.

Then again, that's exactly what Kev was.

A fucking *prick*.

Well, that was too bad for Kev because this wasn't about him. And even if the wedding would never happen—Andino was still working on that angle how he could—he didn't think this needed to be so goddamn traumatic for Ginevra, either.

Andino gestured at his fiancée—fuck, he hated even thinking that—and shrugged. "She doesn't care. Continue on, I guess."

"Yes, well, okay," the baker muttered.

Andino might have laughed at the woman's befuddlement on any other day, but really, he just found it fucking sad. Even she could tell that this whole tasting bit was pointless. She wasn't making a wedding cake for a couple that even *wanted* to get married, and it was palpable.

It made for an awkward tasting.

To say the least …

The baker waved her hands at the pieces of cake in front of everyone at the table. "Well, I will just leave you all to it. I don't think you need me here."

Or rather, they didn't want her there. It was probably obvious, like everything else, frankly.

Kev grunted, and heaved his heavy body out of the chair he had been sitting in. Passing the rest of them a look, he muttered, "I think we could all take a few minutes, actually. I'll be back—you two, fucking *mind*."

He said that with a beefy finger pointed at Ginevra, and then Siena. To Andino, however, the man only gave a nod. He fucking knew better than to open his mouth and spew some kind of shit to Andino. That wouldn't fly over well for any of them.

Had he mentioned that this tasting—like every other part of planning this goddamn sham of a wedding—had been awkward?

Because it *was*.

This was exactly why, even though his mother continued to ask time and time again to be allowed to help, Andino refused her. He knew Kim wanted to be involved in some way, even if she knew he wasn't happy with this whole thing simply because it was her son, and what they all believed to be his *only* marriage.

He would be married.

And *once*.

Not to Ginevra, though.

Nonetheless, his mother didn't need to be a part of this unholy mess. Kim was too good for that shit. He didn't want her to put effort into something that he only intended on ruining. He wasn't that horrible of a man to do that to his own mother.

"You up for a visit to see John soon?" Andino asked Siena the second he figured her brother was out of earshot.

It was only them, and Ginevra left in the tasting room.

"Next week?" Siena asked back.

Andino shrugged. "Maybe, or the one after. Depends on how much running I have to do for this fucking nonsense."

Siena gave him a look. "Be nice."

"Where was the lie, though?"

"Yeah, well ..." Siena glanced at her half-sister, and then back at him. "Just because it is doesn't mean you have to point it out. That seems cruel."

Andino dipped his head in Ginevra's direction. "She knows what this is, girl. God knows, she probably feels the same way. Right, Ginny?"

Ginevra glanced between Siena and Andino with a furrowed brow. Yeah, he bet that was some kind of crazy shit for her to now realize he communicated with Siena beyond this wedding nonsense. They were actually *friends*.

And allies.

Ginevra would learn that soon enough.

"It does seem pointless," Ginevra finally said, still looking entirely too confused. "They're going to pick whatever in the hell they want, anyway. What does it matter?"

Siena sighed. "Yeah, I know. Where's Snaps? Didn't you bring him?"

Andino made a face. "Outside with my man."

"Why?"

"For one, because they likely would have had a fit if I tried to bring him inside. And for another reason—"

"Because he doesn't like me," Ginevra muttered.

Andino made a noise under his breath. "Yeah, and that."

Siena's brow dipped. "Really? Snaps seems to like ... well, mostly everyone. Women more than men."

Wasn't that the fucking truth?

His dog was just in a mood lately. A lot like Andino, really. He knew exactly why that was, too. Snaps was quite aware that Haven was not around, and hadn't been for a while. About as long as the time his dog had been in this goddamn mood of his.

He was snappy—appropriate, for his name ... or fucking ironic—but especially toward Ginevra. Which was just strange considering she never tried to do anything but pet him.

"He's got some issues," Andino said as though he were talking about a child and not an animal. "I'm handling it."

"It's because I'm not her, isn't it?" Ginevra asked. "That ... Haven woman."

Silence drifted down the table with a heavy hand. Andino wished he could lie and say that wasn't it, but he was getting really tired of lying all the time. It was a lot of work, and Ginevra basically said it anyway.

What difference did it make if he confirmed it?

"Yeah," he murmured, "that's a lot of the problem."

She only nodded.

Ginevra was not stupid.

Quiet, yes.

Sly, sure.

Not stupid.

Andino planned on using that to his advantage. Glancing at Siena, he said, "We'll talk more on the John thing when I get something worked out."

"Sure," Siena replied.

"Should we try the cake?" Ginevra asked.

"Why bother?" Andino shrugged one shoulder, and stood from the table. "None of us are going to actually eat it."

Ginevra glanced up at him with a knot between her brows. "What does that mean?"

He simply gave her a smile. "You'll find out soon enough. Just keep doing what you're told, Ginny."

● ● ●

Five days to go.

Andino's life had been reduced to counting down the days to a wedding that shouldn't have been agreed to in the first place. He felt like a ticking time bomb that had almost reached its time to blow, but it wasn't coming fast enough.

He was ready to put an end to all of this.

For good.

But for now?

Andino held his arms out straight, and allowed the tailor to take yet another set of measurements. Not that the man needed it—Andino's size hadn't changed since his early twenties. Nonetheless, the man was particular, and demanded Andino be sized each and every time he came in to have a suit tailored.

But ... at least if he was here doing this, then he didn't need to be somewhere else handling the goddamn Calabrese brothers. That seemed like a fair trade to him. After all, he was going to have to deal with Kev and Darren more than he would ever want to soon enough.

"All right, Andino," his old, familiar tailor said. "I think I have everything. Dante, you're up next. And stop fucking scowling, Dante, you know I hate doing your measurements when you scowl."

"Maybe because you keep finding inches where there *are none*," Dante bitched under his breath as he pushed up from the couch.

The tailor still heard his uncle anyway. "That's what happens as we grow older. Things shift, and move. You still look fine enough for a man your age; as your wife hasn't left your difficult ass yet, we can all safely assume she feels the same way. Stop whining, and get up here."

Chuckles passed around the room between the Marcello men. For a second, Andino felt comforted by the familiarity of it all. Had this been any other day ... for *any other event* ... he might not have felt the nostalgia be chased away by the heaviness of his impending fucking doom.

Dramatic?

Maybe.

Still felt true, though.

Andino took a seat between his uncle, and his grandfather as Dante stepped up beside the tailor to be measured on the small platform. His boss eyed him from the position with a softer eye than usual.

Normally, Dante surveyed Andino like he was trying to get inside his head, or size him up for what might be coming next. It often made him feel like a bug under a damn microscope, but he was becoming numb to it. This was just Dante's way. Andino didn't have to like it.

"What?" he eventually asked.

Dante smiled. "Nothing, just thinking, *nipote*."

"Care to share with the rest of the class?"

Antony laughed beside him, and Lucian only smirked.

"You can talk if you can listen at the same time," the tailor warned Dante, "now widen those legs for me."

Dante widened his stance for the tailor, and shook his head at Andino. "I'm not sure if I want you to lose that attitude before you take over for me, or keep it and see where it takes you, Andi."

Andino rested his ankle over his knee, and leaned back on the couch. "I suppose it doesn't really matter once I'm the one calling the shots, does it?"

"No, I suppose not."

"That's the hardest part," his grandfather said beside him. "Watching the one who comes after you do all the things you wish they wouldn't. And making sure your voice doesn't even *attempt* to overtake theirs in the grander scheme. I suppose that's why bosses who have taken over after a death find themselves more comfortable than those who have the former boss constantly watching over their shoulder."

"I don't intend to watch over his—"

"You will and not even mean to," Antony interjected before Dante could say more. "I did the same thing for you—why would this be different? It's what you do or do not do, for that matter, which will make the difference in how the rest of them see Andino once he takes that position in front of them with you still remaining in the background."

Andino could feel his uncle watching him, but he kept staring at his grandfather. Antony made a good point, and he wondered if anyone else had thought to tell Dante what he had just been told. Andino didn't think so.

"Arms out," the tailor said with a tap of his tape to Dante's chest.

Dante did as he was told, but continued to stare at Andino even when he met his uncle's gaze, too. "I suppose none of that matters anyway, does it?"

"Why is that?" Andino asked back.

"Because I will be proud of you regardless of what you do as a boss," Dante said. "Because I am proud of the sacrifices you have made for this family, and how much you've stepped up to make sure everyone is protected the way they deserve to be. I will be proud of you for those things even when you do other things that I am sure I won't agree with, Andino. And I know you think I *don't* care or understand just how much you've sacrificed, but I do know, *nipote*. I wish things could have been different for you in that respect."

Andino stared unflinchingly back at his uncle. "You have no idea, *zio*."

Antony was next to get his measurements taken for any final touches on their suits that might need to be done before the wedding in a few days. Andino slipped out the shop when he had a chance, but mostly because his father kept texting his fucking phone nonstop.

Gio *should* have been there, but he hated going in for measurements more than even Dante did. It was almost amusing how even at his father's age, Giovanni still didn't give a single shit about what other people wanted.

"What, Dad?" Andino asked, putting the phone to his ear.

Gio chuckled. "You alone? Took you long enough."

"Trying to keep Dante amused. What do you need?"

"It's for you actually. An update."

"On ...?"

"Haven," his father murmured.

All it took was her name being said for Andino to flinch. It was like a sharp spike suddenly drove into his chest, and left a gaping, bleeding wound behind where his heart used to be. This was *so fucked up*.

Why was he so fucked up?

"Is now a good time?" Gio asked when Andino stayed quiet.

"Yeah, why not?"

Lies.

It was all lies.

Gio probably knew that, too, but like the good father he was … he listened to what his son said to do, and didn't press for more details. He'd been the one to offer to keep an eye on Haven from afar without following her to stepping in on her life. Andino's request. Mostly, he just wanted to make sure the Calabrese idiots left her the hell alone.

Nothing else.

Not yet, anyway.

"She's still being watched by them," Gio said, "and yes, it is definitely the Calabrese, like you thought. They're not approaching her at all, but they are watching her."

"That's a smart move on their part."

"Andino."

"Well," he uttered.

Gio sighed. "She flew down to Florida this past weekend to see her parents, but came back on Monday morning. Stopped into the club to say hello, I think, but she didn't stay. That's the first time she's been back there since it sold, according to the guy I talked to."

"Huh."

He bet that fucking sucked for her.

"The *For Sale* sign on the house has a sold marker," Gio added quieter. "I take it they haven't fully closed, though, as she's still there even though she's moving the rest of her things out slowly."

Jesus.

The air was gone from his lungs, and it was painful.

She was *this close* to leaving.

Too fucking close.

"All right, thanks," Andino said.

"I'm sorry. I know this isn't what you want."

"She's not gone yet. That's what matters. There's still time. I can still fix this once I finish with the rest. It doesn't matter. I'll fucking fly to Florida for all I give a damn. *I can fix it.*"

"I know you can, son," Gio murmured.

His father sounded like he believed him.

Andino wasn't even sure he believed himself.

Showtime.

Andino carefully balanced the large white box with the matching satin bow in his hands as he maneuvered through the halls of the church. He only set the box down long enough to greet his mother when she came out of her dressing room.

"Look at you," Kim said, smiling widely. She fixed his tie—though he knew it wasn't crooked because his father, uncles, and grandmother did the same goddamn thing earlier—and smoothed the lapels of his tux with the kind hands only a mother could have. Proud, he thought. She looked proud of him. "You're so handsome, my boy."

Andino smiled. "Thank you, Ma."

"Are you ready for today?"

"More than ready."

It wasn't a lie.

He was ready for today.

It was the beginning of the end, so to speak.

Kim's smile faltered for a brief second. "Really?"

Andino shrugged, and bent down to kiss his mother on her forehead. He stayed there for a few seconds, knowing this was what his mother deserved. She always wanted to make sure he was happy, and so he wanted to do the same with her.

"Really, Ma. Don't you worry about me today. All I want is for you to enjoy the show."

Kim raised a brow at that statement when she glanced up at her son, but Andino only winked. She patted his cheek, and said, "I better go find your father. You've got all of an hour before you need to be down at the altar. Got it?"

"No worries. I don't need a reminder."

Andino said goodbye to his mother. She went one way down the hallway, and he went the other. It took him another ten minutes before he was on the other side of the church where the bride-to-be and her family had been situated for the day.

He could hear the cheerful laughter of Kev and Darren Calabrese before he even opened the hallway door. That sound alone was enough to send Andino's rage spiking higher—he could not despise those two men more than he did—but he tampered the emotion down. He remained a blank slate as he pulled open the door to find the brothers sharing a drink in the hallway, and clinking beer bottles.

"Andino, what are you doing down this way?" Kev asked.

Entirely *too* happy.

Andino lifted the box in his hands. "I thought Ginevra might like a gift."

Darren cocked a brow. "Bad luck to see the bride—"

"I'm not superstitious, but thanks for your concern."

The younger of the two narrowed his gaze at Andino. "Well, I'm sure you'll have more than enough time to spend with Ginevra *after* the wedding, Andino."

"And right now when I give her this gift."

Darren didn't look like he was willing to back down. Neither was Andino, really. Darren was smart like that where Kev, on the other hand, was a fucking idiot. Maybe he felt something wasn't right—he would be correct—but it didn't matter.

Andino was going to do what he was going to do whether either of them liked it or not. He didn't need their fucking permission to give Ginevra her wedding gift.

Kev laughed, and slapped his brother on the back. "Relax, brother. This is a *good* day, huh? We've been waiting for this. Let him have a moment." Then, to Andino, Kev added, "We'll give you a few. Siena is helping Ginevra finish getting ready. We have to check on the other two girls, anyway."

Andino nodded. "I appreciate it."

Kev grinned in that way of his as he passed Andino by. This stupid fuck thought he was about to get everything he wanted. All the things his father had never been able to achieve as a Cosa Nostra boss was suddenly at the tips of Kev's fingers, and he was craving it something bad.

Andino had news for him … it was never going to happen.

It didn't matter.

Kev would learn soon enough.

Once the brothers were out of the hallway, Andino gave one last look over his shoulder before he headed for the bridal suite. Rapping on the door with two knuckles, he stepped back and waited for someone to open the door. No one did, but he did hear footsteps come closer to the door.

He knocked again.

"Jesus Christ, Kev," he heard Siena snap behind the doorway, "just give her a few minutes, okay?"

Andino raised a brow. "It's me, actually."

"Oh." Slowly, the door was opened. Siena popped her head through the crack, and gave Andino a look before her gaze dropped down at the box in his hands. She looked ready for the day all dressed up in her silk and chiffon pale blue gown that would match Ginevra's other two sisters' dresses as well. "What do you need?"

"A minute with Ginevra." Andino smiled. "And you."

Siena cleared her throat. "Now's not the best—"

"I really don't have time for this, Siena."

"Just ... give me a second, okay?"

Andino sighed. "Fine, but hurry. We're running out of daylight."

Not really, but he was running short on time.

Siena closed the door, and he waited. It was less than a few seconds before shouting started to filter out from behind the door. Yells, and crying.

Jesus Christ.

Andino shot a look down the hallway, and figured, he needed to get that noise under control before someone came looking to see what in the hell was going on. None of them needed that kind of problem.

Not if this was to happen the right way, anyhow.

Instead of waiting for Siena to come back to the door like she told him to, Andino opened it and slipped inside. He closed the door behind him quickly, and spun around to face whatever hell was happening inside the space.

Across the room, he found Siena *trying* to console a sobbing, messy Ginevra. Her makeup was ruined, and her white wedding gown had been thrown to the floor—entirely forgotten, it seemed. Or unwanted.

Yes, unwanted seemed like the better word.

"I can't, Siena," Ginevra rasped, trying to pull away from her half-sister. "I *can't.*"

"Come on," Siena urged. "Just breathe. It worked last time, remember? *Breathe.*"

Andino could have let Siena handle the situation, because by the looks and sounds of it, this wasn't the first time Ginevra had found herself in the midst of some kind of breakdown. The woman had been hiding it well, but today was the day, he supposed.

The end of the line.

There was no hiding it, now.

Andino crossed the room quickly, and kept a hold on the gift tucked under his arm at the same time. Siena caught sight of him coming their way, and her shoulders dropped before she took a wide step away from Ginevra. Andino didn't think about taking the place she had left.

Ginevra was in such a state that she didn't even realize Andino was in the room until it was too late. She laid eyes on him, let out a wail, and turned on her heel to dart for the bathroom just a few steps away. She was too late.

He had his arm wrapped around her waist before she could even try to run. She barely weighed a thing—maybe one-hundred-ten pounds soaking wet, he thought. Like this, she just seemed so fucking fragile, and not at all ready for the hell her brothers wanted to put her through.

He'd known that from the beginning, though.

"Stop," he ordered, dropped her onto a couch. "Don't you move."

Ginevra pushed up from the couch with her hands raised, and ready to slap him. "I don't want to marry you! *You can't make me!*"

Andino chuckled. "Good. As much as I like an angry woman, you're not the one for me, Ginny. Now shut the fuck up, and sit the hell down if you want to leave this church as a single woman."

Her eyes widened—still full of tears, and red-rimmed. "W-what?"

"*Sit.*"

She did.

Andino took the box out from under his arm, and set it on her lap. "A gift for you. Consider it your wedding gift, even if this wedding never happens. You're to use everything you find in it, and if you follow every direction inside to the letter … there is someone outside in a black Porsche. He's doing me a favor. You get in that car, use what I've given you in this box, and you stay gone until I say otherwise. Do you understand me?"

Ginevra's gaze drifted from the box in her lap, to Andino's face. "I don't … Why?"

"You're not the one for me," he murmured. "I'm sorry it went on this long. It shouldn't have happened to begin with."

She untied the bow, and opened the box. Andino didn't need to look down to know what she would find inside—paperwork and a fake identity to get her across the Canadian border. Money, and untraceable credit cards attached to said identity. New clothes, and even a sizeable church hat that would give her just enough of a different appearance to get her out of this place.

"His name is Corrado," Andino said. "And he was told to leave by twelve-thirty whether you were in his car, or not."

Ginevra looked up again. "Corrado?"

"Corrado Guzzi. He's a friend, and he owed me a favor. What time is it, Ginny?"

She didn't know.

Siena answered for her.

"Twelve-twenty."

"Ten minutes, then," Andino said. "You better hurry up, and make a choice."

"That's not enough time," Ginevra whispered. "Kev and Darren are—"

"Busy, at the moment. And I can keep them busy for a while longer."

"I'll help," Siena added. "I will, Ginny."

Ginevra was still staring at Andino, and the tears had started falling again. "Is he nice?"

Andino laughed. "Corrado?"

"Yeah."

"What does that matter? He's just going to help for a while."

156

"I just ... I don't know."

"Corrado is ... Corrado," Andino settled on saying. "And he's a hell of a lot better than what you're facing if you stay."

Ginevra nodded. "Okay."

"Good. Hurry up—time is running out."

Literally.

SIXTEEN

"What time does your flight leave?" her mother asked.

Haven slapped the ticket she'd printed off against her palm, and smiled even though her mother couldn't see it. "Supposed to be five, but you know how it goes …"

"Probably three delays, and before you know it, you'll be on the damn red-eye."

She laughed. "Yeah, exactly that."

Silence covered the phone for a moment. She knew that was just her mother overthinking again. She called them every single day. It didn't matter that she knew they were fine, she still had to *call*. Their conversations had been like this ever since Haven called to let them know the house had finally sold.

Then, this became real. This whole Haven moving to Florida thing. For a while, her parents believed she wouldn't. That she would do exactly what they wanted for her, and keep living her life because that's what they felt she deserved.

Well, it was happening.

Today was her last day in the house. Everything was gone now except her laptop, and a printer she was ditching as soon as she left. Her luggage was already outside in the trunk of the car. A car that would stay in the parking garage of the airport until a friend could drive it down to Florida next month.

It was all done.

Today was the day.

"How's Dad doing?" Haven asked.

"Outside mowing the grass."

"Bet his allergies are loving that."

Her mom made a quiet noise. "It's not so bad, actually. Allergy pills do wonders for him, I guess."

"Huh." Sighing, Haven stared out the bare kitchen window to the outside. It was a beautiful June day—bright, sunny, and hot. The kind of day she would love to get a run in before heading to the club for a night of work. That had been her life. Her entire life. And it was all about to change. "You have chemo tomorrow, right?"

Mae cleared her throat. "I do—noon, sharp."

"I'll be able to go with you, then."

"You don't have to do that, Haven."

"I know, but I want to, Ma."

Mae let out a heavy breath. "I wish you wouldn't put your whole life on pause for me, sweetheart. I'm *fine*."

Her mom kept saying that, but Haven didn't know if it was truth. That was part of the problem. Not that Mae understood, really. Haven had never properly explained it, she supposed. That wasn't her mom's fault.

Turning in the empty kitchen, Haven took another look around the space. The bare walls stared back, as did the freshly cleaned counters, and appliances. She'd opened the doors on the fridge and freezer to allow them to circulate air.

"I'm gonna miss this place," Haven said.

It was the first time she admitted that out loud to one of her parents.

Her mother made a sad noise. "I know, baby."

"But ... I have to get away from here. I can't be here anymore."

That silence was quick to saturate the line again. Haven wasn't sure how long it lasted before her mother broke it.

"Haven?"

"Yeah, Mom?"

"You're sad," Mae murmured. "Why are you sad, dolly?"

Haven smiled at the affectionate nickname her mother used to call her when she was just a girl. She'd been that peach and cream-skinned kid with big blue eyes, and pouty pink lips. Her blonde hair had fallen in ringlets down her back. Just like a pretty little China doll, she supposed.

Or that's what her mom always said.

Hence, *dolly*.

"I'm not sad," Haven was quick to lie. The last thing she needed to do was burden her mother with all the shit that had been happening in her life. She'd managed to keep Andino and that mess far away from their notice. She wanted to keep it that way, especially *now*. "I'm ... nostalgic. Yeah, that's the right word."

It worked, anyway.

Mae made a dismissive noise. "Do you know when you lie, you almost ask things as a question when you mean to state them?"

"I do not!"

"Okay," her mother drawled. "Haven, what's wrong?"

Her gaze caught the white cardstock sitting on the edge of the counter. It was crumpled now, and a little bit bent from being caught in her doorway a month ago when Andino showed up. She'd had no contact with him since then other than that one phone call she initiated. He listened, and stayed away. She was grateful.

Yet, that stupid invitation was still sitting there, and fucking *taunting* her. Nonstop. She couldn't seem to get rid of it. Even though it hadn't come from him, it was something. Just like all those other stupid notes of his were still stuffed in her journal—pressed safely between the pages where no one but her could read them.

"Haven?" her mom asked.

"I met someone," she whispered.

Mae sucked in a fast breath. "Did you? Who?"

"His name is Andino. It was supposed to be fun, you know? And then it turned into something else entirely. I love him, but he hurts me. I can't do that anymore. It doesn't matter. Point is, he wasn't who I thought he was, and … he was the worst mistake I ever made."

"Nothing is ever a mistake, Haven," her mom was quick to say. "*Love* is not ever a mistake."

Haven felt that familiar prickling behind her eyes. The telltale sign her tears were about to make another show of themselves, the fucking things. She hated crying. She was so sick and goddamn tired of crying.

Hadn't she done enough of that?

"Love can't be a mistake when it's one of the few things in life that can change us irrevocably in a second, Haven," her mother said. "Love is a lot of things, but a mistake is not one of them."

"Feels like it right now."

"Because you're hurting. That's not the same."

Haven let out a shaky breath of air. "He just comes from a different world than me, Mom. There's a wall there that I can't get over, and every time I tried, I ended up a little more broken when I fell. I'm tired of falling. I don't *fall*. I climb."

"Oh, Haven."

"What?"

She hated the pity in her mother's voice. The sadness there. This was exactly why she didn't want to bring Andino up to her parents. They loved her so much. And it didn't matter what she did, or what she chose for her life … they were going to say, *go on, girl, and live your best life. Be your best person. Be happy.*

Because they were wonderful.

She did not deserve them.

"How are you ever to learn if all you do is succeed?" Mae asked softly. "We learn best when we are challenged, and when everything seems the *most* impossible … when we are able to drag ourselves broken and bleeding out of despair, *that* is when we become the best version of who we are. You can only be a fraction of that person if the only thing you've ever done is succeed. Why would you think love was any different?"

"Love shouldn't hurt, Mom."

"Maybe not," her mother agreed. "But love is crazy, dolly. Love is unlike anything else, and it is worth a second chance. It is worth pain, and hurt, and everything else that comes along with it if you can still drag your broken and bleeding body out of the rubble it leaves behind. When the fire finally goes out, and all that's left is ash, what does the Phoenix do, Haven?"

"*Mom.*"

"What does it do?"

"It rises."

"It rises," her mom echoed. "And so does love, and so will you. If that's what you want."

Because it was her choice, she realized. Her choice to go back, and ask why. To finally give him that chance to explain. To decide to leave the rubble alone, or with him.

Except … none of that mattered.

Today was the day.

That date written on the wedding invitation. The day he was no longer hers.

"It's too late," Haven said.

Mae laughed softly. "Haven, it is *never* too late."

• • •

Haven had never been a Sunday service, church dress, big hat kind of women. Sure, she believed in God. She had faith in a higher power, and trusted that at the end of someone's days, the good went where they were intended to go, and those who were bad went where they deserved to spend eternity, too.

But organized religion?

Praying every day?

Church on Sundays?

That had never been her thing, or her family's. She was baptized Protestant as a baby, but the last time Haven remembered stepping inside a church was when she was seven, and her only sibling—a baby boy her parents named Caleb—was laid to rest in a small, pale blue casket after dying from SIDs at only fourteen days old.

Her parents never had more children.

They'd never gone back to church, either.

Haven suspected that was because her parents' relationship with God had been severely tested from the death of their son. Up until that moment in her life, she remembered spending every Sunday in church sitting between her parents in a pew. But after that? They spent Sundays *living*.

Because wasn't that what life was for? The living?

Maybe that was why as an adult, Haven had never found herself drawn to church. God was still on the back of her mind, sure. And maybe that was just her personal way of keeping connected to him in the privacy of her own mind. Prayers that no one knew she was saying, and faith that no one could question.

He knew.

Wasn't that what counted?

Haven's awkwardness at standing on the steps of the church could certainly be attributed to her tenuous relationship with organized religion, but that was only a part of it. A lot of it was the fact that she knew the love of her life was about to be married inside this church.

And he was not getting married to her.

She looked no different than any of the other guests rushing up the steps. She was dressed up in the most suitable thing she had been able to pull from one of her suitcases. A pale yellow dress that hugged her curves, and fell just below her knees. Certainly church and wedding appropriate, even for a Catholic ceremony. She used a large similarly colored sun hat that Valeria had left behind when she left to pull off the outfit. Plus, it might keep her face hidden.

Win, win.

If only …

Haven was too late. She didn't need to be told to know it was true. She could tell by the way the last few guests were rushing up the stairs of the church, and the fact that a car was already waiting at the bottom with painted-white tins tied to the bumper.

If the ceremony had not already started, it would soon.

She was too late.

She thought, maybe, she might get there in enough time to see Andino before all of this took place, but it seemed like she hoped for *way* too much. And now she was only left heartbroken all over again.

Turning on the stairs, Haven moved to leave altogether. She didn't need to be there to *see* her future walk away, too. This was more than enough.

"Late too, are you?" came a familiar voice.

Haven's gaze lifted to find a hazel-eyed, grinning Marcello standing just a few steps below hers. Andino's uncle.

Lucian.

"I'm not here for … the wedding," she said lamely.

Lucian nodded. "I don't want to be here for it either, frankly."

Yet, he was.

Like her.

The man tipped his head to the side, and drew a hard puff from the cigarette in his hand. He eyed the cancerous stick with a keen eye. "My wife hates these fucking things, and for the most part, I gave them up years ago. Like a lot of other bad habits. But on days like today, it gets me out of shitty situations that I don't want to be in for at least ten minutes while I have a smoke. Lucky me, huh?"

Haven blinked. "I should go."

"Why?" Lucian asked, glancing back at her. "Because you think he's actually getting married today?"

That lump in her throat was back, and harder than ever. She swore it stuck to her throat like hot, sticky tar. Burning, and refusing to budge no matter how many times she tried to swallow it down.

"Isn't he?" Haven gestured at the car at the bottom of the steps with the words *Just Married* painted on the rear windshield, and then waved the invitation in her hand. "I'm too late, I guess. Not that it would matter. I wasn't what the rest of you wanted for him, anyway."

Lucian smiled softly. "On that, you are *most* wrong. Things always appear one way to those who are on the outside looking in on our life, and for that, we can't apologize. But I assure you that when Andino says *you* are what he wants, then you are what we will give him."

"Has he?"

"What?"

"Said that. Has he?"

Lucian flicked that cigarette down the steps, and climbed the last few stairs to come stand at Haven's side. He offered his arm, and she only stared down at it. "Go ahead and take it. You and I will sit in the back together, and watch just how my nephew decides to tell the world—and the rest of them who haven't figured it out yet—exactly what kind of man he is willing to be, and all the things he wants, Haven."

She still hesitated. "I don't understand."

"I was told you didn't give him the chance to explain. Might that be why you don't know?"

It definitely was.

She was regretting that now.

Haven took Lucian's arm even knowing that it might mean more pain. She took his offer to find out the things she hadn't bothered to ask. Even knowing that it would mean she was likely going to miss her flight, and all over again, upset her entire life and world.

She took his arm because what did she have to lose now?

She'd already lost it all.

Haven just wanted to get it back.

• • •

Sitting in the pew with Lucian beside her, Haven was momentarily distracted by the size of the church. Sure, the place had looked big from the outside, but not *this* big. The vaulted ceilings seemed to go on forever.

There were at least a hundred rows of pews. Maybe *that* was being a bit dramatic, but there was a lot. She could see the altar from her position, but just barely.

Lucian smiled over at her. "I remember that feeling."

"Pardon?"

"The first time I walked into this church as a boy, I was overwhelmed. I was so small, and it was so *big*. Large spaces bothered me as a child for reasons that don't matter right now. And even though the place scared me because of its size, it also ... well, it comforted me. I have found the greatest comfort behind these walls. I may not seem like a God-fearing man, but we all are. Every Marcello has their own unique relationship with God, but especially *this* church."

Haven glanced upward again. "It's your family's church?"

"It is."

Oh.

"I don't really *do* church," Haven admitted. "At least, not since I was a girl."

Lucian chuckled. "No worries. You'll get used to it pretty quickly."

Her brow furrowed at his statement, but he was no longer looking at her. He was glancing down the aisle at something else as though he was entirely unaware that his simple words had made her heart clench in her chest like someone's fist wrapped around it with no warning.

You'll get used to it.

Like it *was* to happen.

No question.

"What do you mean by—"

"Showtime," Lucian interjected with a smooth smile.

A door opened at the back of the church. Haven's gaze swung in that direction as Lucian stood from the pew, and everyone else around them followed suit just as fast. Given Haven had already noticed the fact that the altar was empty but for the waiting priest, she knew who would be coming through those doors.

It still *shocked* her.

Seeing Andino after all this time—dressed in his tux, and with his mother on his arm—was like a punch to her chest. It ached, and took her breath away at the same time. She didn't have time to think on it for long.

Andino and Kim only stayed at the entryway for just long enough to scan the crowd of people standing in the pews before they were moving again. His mother stared straight ahead with a soft smile while Andino's face was a blank slate.

Nothing was there.

No happiness.

Nothing.

It certainly wasn't the face of a man who was happy to be getting married. Why did he look like *that*?

Andino's gaze shifted their way briefly, and landed on Lucian first. The man standing in front of Haven moved slightly. Just enough to make her visible to Andino. She swore the life that had been missing in his gaze was quick to make itself known when he saw her. His lips edged higher at the corners.

A *ghost* of a smile.

That smile was enough to kill her right there on the spot.

It didn't last long, though. Andino and his mother were moving again. Haven had to stand on her tiptoes to watch him walk Kim to her seat before he dropped a kiss on her cheek, too. The moment Andino made it to the altar, the people started to sit again. Haven was pulled back into the pew by Lucian with a chuckle.

"We don't want anyone seeing you here just yet," Lucian said. "That wouldn't be good for us when we're waiting for another show to start."

"What?"

"Just wait for it."

Everyone was sitting when a hush fell over the pews. The doors at the back of the church had been closed again, likely so the rest of the procession could shortly begin.

"Three bridesmaids should be coming through any time now," Lucian said dryly.

No one came.

The doors stayed closed.

Whispers started to move through the pews, but up at the altar, Andino stayed stoic and waiting. His gaze was nailed to the doors, but for a brief moment, they passed to glance her way, too.

It distracted Haven, but that daze was quickly broken when the back doors where thrown open. The man she recognized as Darren Calabrese—the same one who had dropped that fucking invitation off to her a month ago—stormed down the aisle. In the front pews on what Haven considered to be the bride's side, a man stood up.

"Kev Calabrese," Lucian informed. "Darren's brother—Ginevra's, too. You know, the *bride*. Remember his face, he's not as important as he wants to think he is, but he's important enough to cause us problems. Never trust him."

Haven sucked in a fast breath. "Why would I have to worry—"

Lucian glanced her way. "You know exactly why."

Haven went back to staring at Andino. He was staring back at her again.

She supposed she did know.

This wedding was never meant to happen.

He'd only ever wanted her.

"*What?*" she heard Kev roar from the front of the church.

"Showtime," Lucian said, smiling in that sly way of his again. "Do try to blend into the crowd once things pick up, Haven. Andino will find you once he can, I am sure. If not, find his mother or father. They expected this as well."

Expected what, exactly?

"She's gone?" Kev asked loudly. "Where the fuck is she?"

"Gone, Kev."

"*Gone?*"

"Yeah, g—"

"Find her!"

The whispers were getting louder. People from both sides of the aisle were standing and starting to talk instead of whisper in hushed tones. Haven's heartbeat was kicking so loudly, she thought it might start to hurt.

Andino was already stepping down from the altar, and fixing the sleeve of his tux like he didn't have a single care in the world.

There was no missing the grin he wore.

Sly.

Knowing.

Happy.

SEVENTEEN

There was a great sense of satisfaction that came with watching a plan all fall together just as you hoped it would. To watch everyone else around you struggle to understand what just happened, and how to react while you were a calm pillar in a raging storm was … *divine*.

Andino hadn't realized that *this* was how it was going to feel. That it would be this satisfying and amusing at the same time.

The echo of confused voices around him only picked up while he remained still and silent leaning against the wall. His gaze scanned the familiar faces of his family, and those of Ginevra's. They'd been looking for a half an hour now. Searching the church, and surrounding areas. They were unwilling to admit she was actually gone.

He had news for them.

Ginevra was getting closer to the Canadian border with every passing second. With freedom at the tips of her fingers, there was no way in hell that woman was turning back around now. As she shouldn't, he supposed.

He needed her to stay gone.

It had been pandemonium at first when they realized Ginevra was gone. Complete fucking chaos. Now, they were finally starting to calm.

That didn't mean they were happy.

Too bad, so sad.

"Nothing?" Kev asked desperately.

The enforcer shook his head. "Nothing, boss."

"*Nothing at all?*"

"Kev, we're wasting time here," Darren stepped in.

Oh, they were having a right fit, and Andino found it all hilarious. He didn't show it other than the small smile that continued to edge its way over his lips. He couldn't help that. Satisfaction was hard to fucking hide.

And besides …

Well, he supposed a part of him wanted them to know, too. He wanted these fucking snakes from Brooklyn to know exactly what he had done. That *he* was the one who ruined their plots and plans because he could. Because he didn't trust them, he never had, and he was never going to.

There was no way in hell he would bow to them.

Ever.

"Where is Siena, then?" Kev demanded. "She should know! She was supposed to be with her the whole fucking time!"

"She's dealing with Greta and—"

"I don't give a *fuck*. Get her!"

Andino readjusted his stance, and leaned his shoulder against the wall as the Calabrese struggled to find a new angle to which they might use to find Ginevra. It was all rather pointless, he figured. The woman wasn't coming back, and there was no way they were going to be able to find her unless they ripped the truth out of his mouth.

Unlikely.

Marcello people weaved in and out of the panicking Calabrese. Andino mostly paid them no mind because they were only here for him. The one he did care to watch was his uncle—the *boss*.

Only because Dante was watching him.

From the other side of the room, Dante stood similarly to Andino … but without the shit-eating smirk. The boss watched him with that cold, hard stare of his that said *I know what you did*.

How Dante knew was impossible to know. Probably because if the Calabrese were a little clearer headed at the moment, they might understand that there were only a select few people in this church who could actually get Ginevra the hell out of town, *and* had the motive to do so.

Andino, really.

He was the only one with the means and the reason.

Dante kept staring.

Andino stared back, unbothered.

He didn't care if Dante didn't like this. He didn't give a shit what his uncle thought about what he'd done, or why he did it. He didn't even give a fuck about the consequences he might have to face because of all this.

It was time for Dante to really *learn*.

Andino was his own man, and at the end of the day, that's what mattered. He was going to do things his way when it came to this family. He was never going to do what he was told to do just because he was told to do it.

And he would never cower to an enemy.

Not for peace, or power.

"How long before he blows up, do you think?" Andino asked his father. "He looks about ready to, doesn't he?"

Oh, Dante was calm and collected on the outside, sure. But in his eyes? That's where the disbelief, and rage swirled with every passing second.

Gio and Kim had both come to stand on either side of Andino from the moment he stepped off the altar, and left the main section of the church. They didn't leave him—it was their silent way of showing where they stood in all of this, he supposed.

And not necessarily for the benefit of the Calabrese, either.

Gio made a noise under his breath, and passed his brother a look. "He won't do anything here. The last thing any of us needs is for the Calabrese to think we have fractures amongst our own ranks. Dante knows better—that's the one thing you can bet on."

"But the only thing, too," Kim added dryly.

His father nodded, in silent agreement.

"Great," Andino said. "How much longer are we going to have to stand here acting like we give a fuck—"

"Let me go, you asshole!"

Andino's gaze swung in the direction of the familiar, hateful voice. Siena was dragged into the entry of the church by a bull of a man. He kept a tight hold on her elbow until she was almost right in front of Kev. Then, he practically tossed her at her brother.

"Here she is," the man grunted.

Siena huffed, and shot a burning glare over her shoulder. "*Fuck you.*"

"That's quite enough." Kev folded his arms over his shoulder as Siena faced him. "Where is Ginevra?"

"I don't know. Why would I know, Kev?"

"*Where is she?*"

Jesus Christ.

Even Andino bristled at the man's tone. He had to give Siena credit, though. She didn't even *flinch*. If anything, she stood a little bit taller in the face of her brother's rage.

She was subtle, this chick. Her strength was quiet, and small, and sometimes, it seemed like it wasn't even there at all. And yet, he thought she might be the strongest one of them all at the end of the day.

No wonder John loved her.

That was going to come in handy someday.

For now, though …

"*You* were with her all day," Kev snapped at Siena, pointing a beefy finger right in her face. Hell, if he got any closer, then that finger was going to hit her forehead. Siena never even blinked, or backed down. "You were with her right before she was supposed to come down. So, where in the fuck did she go, Siena? Don't mess around with me. Not today."

"I went to the *bathroom*," Siena replied, her jaw tight. "I came out, and she was gone. What do you want me to say? I can't tell you something I don't know."

Damn.

Give credit where it was due, after all.

Siena was one hell of a liar.

Kev let out a harsh noise, and flicked a hand. The enforcer who had come to bring Siena stepped in to take her away. He moved to grab her, but she was quick to slap the man before he could even try.

"Don't fucking touch me again!"

"Siena!" Kev barked.

The woman gave her brother a withering look over her shoulder, fixed the skirt of her dress, and stormed off without another word. The enforcer was quick to follow behind, but he made sure to keep a couple of extra steps between him and her.

It was *funny*.

And boring, too.

Strange how that worked.

"I think it's safe to say that this day is a loss," Dante said, speaking up for the first time as he moved away from the wall, "and that my family would like to go home."

Kev's angry attitude turned on the wrong man, then. "How quick you are to back out of a deal, Dante."

Dante quirked a brow. "What deal, Kev? There is no bride. There is no *deal*."

"There will be a bride!"

His uncle's gaze drifted to him, and then quickly went back to Kev. "For some reason, I doubt that. I think we're done here, Kev."

Dante turned to gesture for his wife to join him, but Kev was already stepping forward. Not a man to back down, Dante stood tall and unmoved when Kev came toe to toe with him. Had that been any other man, Andino figured they would have been quick to make Kev back the hell off.

Not Dante, though.

No, he stood there and *smirked*.

"Do you want something?" Dante asked. "Another wedding that will fall through, maybe? A new way to try and slither your way into our family?"

"We're not finished, Marcello."

Dante glanced Andino's way again. "No, I suspect we're just getting started, Kev."

He was right.

Now was not the time.

It was the shift in the back of the crowd—a flash of blonde hair trying to move further behind the people that took Kev's attention away from Dante. The man's gaze narrowed for a second, before he stepped to the side, and strolled forward.

"*You!*"

Andino finally found what had caught Kev's attention.

Shit.

Haven.

It took all of Andino's willpower not to show the way his heart decided to do a fucking deep dive in his chest every time he looked at her. He didn't even know how to begin to describe the way he felt when he saw her in that church.

But she was here.

She was not gone.

Didn't that mean good things?

He could fix this.

At the idea that Kev might approach Haven, Lucian was quick to slide away from the wall and move through the crowd like a hot knife cutting through butter. His uncle was supposed to stay with Haven, but Andino figured maybe the two had gotten separated at some point. Silently, Lucian moved in beside Haven, and did nothing but fucking *stare* at Kev.

Like he was daring him to come closer.

Haven, on the other hand, glanced between Kev and Andino on the other side of the room. It didn't escape Kev's notice, either.

The man barked out a loud laugh, and spun around. Those icy eyes of his landed on Andino, and he saw the promise of violence staring back at him before Kev even spoke the threats out loud.

"I should have fucking known, Andino," Kev said. "Was it you, then? Did *you* get Ginevra out before she could even walk down the aisle? Was this your plan all along?"

Why lie?

"Yes," Andino said, shrugging one shoulder. "I was never going to marry her. Not for you, and not for fucking anyone else, either. After all you did to me, to my family ... to my best friend, you thought I would *give you something*, Kev? There's your first mistake. I allowed you to have it with this little lesson added on, of course. I won't be as nice the second time around, so try not to make another one."

"You fucking—"

"Insults are for weak men who lack any real ability to challenge their opponent in a better way. Try something else. *Surprise me.*"

Kev's face reddened, and he clenched his fists into tight balls at his side as he came as close to Andino as he had been to Dante earlier. Like Dante had, Andino stayed as still as stone and refused to let the man's size or proximity intimidate him.

Kev was a fucking bully.

Nothing more, and nothing less.

He didn't hold any real kind of weight or power. He couldn't do *shit*. Andino might laugh at the man if this whole thing wasn't so goddamn dull now.

"For *what*?" Kev asked, so close that his hot breath made Andino want to punch the man right in his throat. "What did you do this for, then? Her—*Haven*? A whore your family will never allow you to marry because she'll never be good enough for them? Was that it?"

Okay, so maybe Andino wasn't *quite* like Dante.

He went for the face instead of Kev's throat. His fist came up lightning fast, and slammed into Kev's mouth. He felt the man's teeth split his knuckles before Kev dropped like a rotten sack of potatoes to the ground. The room turned deathly silent as Andino bent down, and grabbed the man's face to force him to look at him.

Bleeding, but still pissed, Kev stared up at Andino. There was a bit too much glee in his eyes. Like maybe he'd just gotten what he wanted.

A reason.

That's all these fucking snakes ever needed. A reason to start a war. A reason to *live*. Shame, really.

Leaning down, Andino murmured in the man's ear, "Put her name in your mouth again, and I will make sure your cock is the last thing you taste when I cut it off and shove it down your fucking throat. I hope we understand each other."

Andino was quick to stand then, and fix his jacket. Kev, on the other hand, didn't move.

"This isn't over," Kev said below him. "Count on that. You're a dead man."

Andino smiled. "Do you think that scares me?"

"It should," Kev murmured.

"It doesn't."

• • •

"What in the hell were you thinking?" Dante asked as he strolled into the office at the large Marcello mansion.

Andino, and his uncle and father, filtered in behind him. Lucian moved to sit on the couch while Giovanni went to his usual perch on the windowsill. Andino, on the other hand, stuffed his hands in his pockets and stayed standing in the middle of the room.

"You ask me that question a lot," Andino noted, "but you never care to actually *hear* the answer. I mean, not if it's an answer you don't like."

Dante stiffened, and his back tensed. Still, he continued pouring a glass of bourbon without facing the room. He did speak, though. "How long were you planning something like this, Andi?"

Well …

"I was never going to marry that woman," Andino replied. "So use that to answer your own question, Dante."

Finally, his uncle turned to face the room. There was no doubt about it—the anger and disappointment written heavily across Dante's brow couldn't be missed. He clutched that glass in his hand like he might throw it at the next person who talked out of turn. Andino swore the older his uncle got, the less tolerable he was to other people's bullshit.

Dante sipped on that glass of bourbon, and stared at Andino all the while. A sharp eye that said his uncle was measuring him as much as he was trying to figure him out. That was the thing about Andino, though.

He was fucking full of surprises.

Dante pointed a finger at Andino, saying, "You purposely disobeyed me again, *nipote*."

"I don't see it like that, no."

"Then how do you fucking see it?"

For the first time, his uncle's mask cracked. The anger lit up his voice, and took it above the level of calm he had been maintaining. But hey, if it was a fight his uncle wanted … Andino was up for that.

He wasn't backing down.

Not on this.

"You preach and go on about family and loyalty and doing what we have to in order to protect this thing of ours," Andino said, "but you forget that those things only work when it is for the betterment of *every* man, and not one man."

Dante took a step forward, and arched a brow. "And you think you are *every* man, Andino?"

"I think I am one man, but I refuse to be an unhappy one, *zio*. I will never be the man who is only the reflection of you because these are the things you chose for me under the guise of *duty*. Not when I could have done it my own way to begin with. I spoke an oath for this life—I did my vows. But it will not take *everything I have*. It is not everything that I am. I will not be a better man for it just because you told me to do it."

That stopped his uncle from coming closer. Dante glanced at him again, reconsidering once more.

"For what, then—the woman? You did this for her?"

Andino shrugged. "Why not? Wars have been started for less, haven't they?"

"Don't sound so flippant. This is not a small thing, Andi. It can't be."

"It is one thing to me. One thing amongst many things."

Dante sighed, and glanced away. "I get the impression that you either don't have the first clue of the uphill battle you're about to face because you wanted something as silly as a woman you knew you couldn't have … or you just don't give a shit."

"More the latter, actually."

His uncle's sharp gaze came back to him. "Is that so? You think you know, then, how you'll lose control of the Commission when they refuse to accept the woman you present to them? You think you understand how it'll stain our name and legacy? You think you *know*? She won't be accepted by outside organizations, Andino. It doesn't matter how *we* treat her, or if we

173

love her. Our actions won't factor into their opinions at all. Is that what you want for her? The constant reminder that she isn't up to *their* standards?"

"She's what I want. I don't give a fuck about them."

"The Commission is *clear* and you know—"

"Who at the Commission will deny me her?" Andino asked, smirking just a bit. "*Me*, when I take over your seat? *John*, when I put him in the seat the Calabrese holds once I bury them? Oh, how about the Donati boss—*Cross*. The man that is so in love with your daughter he wouldn't *dare* consider making a choice that might hurt someone close to her. Maybe Chicago? An organization that has been terrified of another war like the one that decimated them decades ago—unlikely. Who's left?"

"Vegas," his father murmured from the window.

Andino nodded, and gave Dante his attention again "Yes, Vegas. You know, where my other uncle controls. So again, who is going to refuse me now?"

Dante blinked.

Andino smiled. "See what I did there, *zio*? You told me who would take her away, and so I handled it. I always get what I want."

"And you wanted her," Dante murmured.

"I will always want her."

Even if she doesn't want me.

Because that was a real fucking possibility right now.

Dante scrubbed a hand down his jaw, and stared at *anything* but Andino. "You know, I didn't realize you were this manipulative, *nipote*."

"I'm not sure if that's an insult, or not."

"Definitely not, but forgive me for being pissed that you thought to manipulate *me*." Dante leaned back, and sat down on the edge of the large oak desk. He took a second before he spoke again, this time his voice quiet and pensive. "You've essentially started a war for a woman."

"You said that already."

Dante cut him with a look. "What do I tell them now? All the people downstairs who came here because they expected a party after a wedding—a *celebration*, Andino. What do I tell them now? That their whole lives are about to be chaotic and dangerous again because you wanted a *woman*?"

"You tell them that we never cower, and we don't bend. Marcellos take, but we don't give. Not for anyone, and certainly not for the Calabrese. That's what you always used to tell me."

"I wanted peace," Dante murmured. "You think I wanted it for them, but I wanted it for you. So you didn't have to come into this seat with carnage under your feet, Andino. You think it's easy to be this man? This has never been easy."

He didn't expect it to be.

That changed nothing, though.

"I will never make peace with the Calabrese," Andino countered. "Whether today, or tomorrow, or whenever the hell I take over … it doesn't matter. I will not *ever* give them a single inch. They are not even a fraction of what we are, and they shouldn't be allowed to think they are, either."

Dante gave Gio a look from the side. "He's so fucking *difficult.*"

Gio smiled faintly. "I know."

"Where did this come from?"

"Does it matter if he's right, brother?" Gio asked back.

Lucian chuckled from his seat on the couch. "That's a good point."

Dante glanced at Andino again. "Where is the Calabrese woman?"

"Why?"

"Curious. I don't plan to retrieve and return her. Why would I? She deserves better."

"Canada," Andino answered. "She is in Canada with a Guzzi who agreed to look after her for the time being, and once it was safe, return her. I called in a favor."

Dante stiffened, and his gaze cut to Lucian. "Corrado Guzzi? Because I *know* Andino is not the one who is owed a favor by that young man."

Lucian shifted uncomfortably. "What do you want me to say?"

"You *helped* him? You knew what he was up to?"

"Gio isn't the only one in this family who wants to give his son the thing he wants the very most, Dante."

The three brothers took a moment to consider each other silently before Dante's attention came back to Andino once more.

"Do you know what this means, though?" his uncle asked.

"Be specific."

"Our family—the line will end with your boys. The Marcello *name*, Andino. Our legacy will end with your boys, if you even have any. Half Italian from the father's side. Any boys you have—only one can be the boss, and he will be the *last* Marcello boss."

The heavy silence that covered the room almost felt suffocating. Andino didn't have to wonder why, either. He already knew. The idea that their name would end in this criminal world that they had controlled for so long simply because he fell in love and chose a woman that couldn't continue on the line was a lot to absorb.

"There's still John," Andino said, shrugging. Because really, that still did *not* matter to him. *Haven* mattered. And their legacy was always something he was willing to sacrifice for her. He would give up anything for her. "And any sons he might have."

"*John* shouldn't even be a made man if you look into his bloodlines deep enough," Dante grumbled. "His biological grandmother was only *half*

Italian. His mother has less than a fraction of Italian bloodline in her family lineage. And you think his sons could pass the fucking test? *Foolish*."

Lucian cleared his throat, but otherwise, kept quiet.

Andino laughed. "Who is going to be that disrespectful, Dante? Who would be willing to dig into the history of a murdered man and woman just to trace their bloodlines? They killed Lucian and John's bloodline—any man and woman that came from their family are all gone. Who is willing to disrespect the dead to challenge a bloodline? No one, that's who."

Dante glanced up. "You think you have this all figured out, don't you?"

"If we don't evolve, then we fail."

Another sigh echoed.

Finally, Dante asked, "Well, what the fuck do we do now?"

Andino thought the answer to that question was quite simple. "I would like to take Haven downstairs—apparently, she came here with Ma after the church—and introduce her to my family. I would like to see her welcomed, and embraced. Treated with *respect* for no other reason than I love her, and it is what she deserves. That is what I need to happen now."

Dante shook his head. "What did you *do*, Andino?"

Wasn't it obvious?

"What I needed to."

EIGHTEEN

"Haven," her father said. "Did the flight get delayed?"

Haven cringed because *not exactly*. "As far as I know, no, it wasn't delayed. I just won't be able to make it in time. Not today, anyway."

"What?"

"Something came up," Haven said, searching for the right words.

"Oh, the man your mother mentioned?"

Jesus Christ.

"Did she tell you about that?"

She swore she could hear the smile in her father's tone when he said, "She did tell me. She was worried you wouldn't make the right choice."

Haven blinked. "Pardon?"

"In case you're wondering, you made the right choice."

Because she stayed, she realized.

Oh.

"Haven," her father murmured.

"Yeah?"

"I know you're going to feel guilty, and think that you should be here, but please don't do that. *Please don't*. Your mother and I are okay. You have things to handle there, and that's fine. We're still going to be here either way when things settle out."

"I should be there, though," she said.

"You should be *happy*," her father returned. "That's what we want. That's all we've ever wanted, sweetheart."

Well, *fuck*.

How was she supposed to argue with that?

"And on another note," her father said, "about this man."

Haven smiled. "What's that?"

"I expect to meet him. Size him up, scare the shit out of him maybe."

Have laughed under her breath. "If I told you to save your breath, would you listen?"

"Can't. Father's duty. He'll understand."

"Dad—"

"Now, don't you go taking this away from me, Haven. You're all grown up, and this is the *only time* I can do this."

Sure.

She just laughed.

"Although, he must be something I guess, to make you change your plans like this. You always were so stuck in your ways. Nothing could ever change your mind once you decided on something."

He wasn't lying.

"Andino is ..." Haven struggled to find the right words.

"Hmm?"

"Overwhelming."

Yeah, that was as good of a word as any.

Why not?

Her father chuckled. "Yeah, love usually is."

"So, you'll tell Mom that—"

"You will be down to visit as soon as you can," her father interjected. "And that you made the right choice. Yes, I will."

Haven shook her head. "All right, thank you. I love you. Tell her that for me, too."

"Will do, sweetheart. Love you, too."

Once she'd said goodbye to her father and dropped her phone into her bag, she finally noticed the form standing in the doorway. The woman hadn't made a single noise to alert Haven to her presence.

Kim.

"Are you busy?" Andino's mother asked.

Haven shook her head. "No, just filling my dad in on where I was."

Kim nodded, and stepped into the room. "You must be bored in here by yourself. The whole family is just down the hall in the dining room, if you—"

"Maybe not? I ... don't really know anyone, that's all."

And to be honest, Haven wasn't even sure why she was still there. Or rather, what she was waiting *for*. Kim had been the one to approach her at the church, and then practically demanded Haven leave with their family. At the time, she didn't have a reason to refuse, and she really didn't like the way Kev had looked at her like he wished she was dead right where she stood.

Now that she was here ... well, she didn't have the first clue where Andino was, or if she was ready to talk to him. If they did talk, what would he say?

The thought made her heart race.

And *ache*.

"Well, what about me, then?" Kim asked softly.

Haven didn't understand what the woman was asking, but just the way Kim looked at her—so expectant and hopeful—she didn't think she was going to be able to refuse whatever she asked for. Kim seemed sweet, truly. Soft-spoken, and kind. It was hard not to be comfortable when the woman was near.

"What about you?" Haven asked.

"Would you be willing to talk to me for a bit, maybe? I could keep you company."

Haven blinked. "Talk about what?"

"*You.*"

She was feeling really slow on the uptake today.

Kim laughed at Haven's obviously confused expression. "I just feel like … you and me, well we have a lot of catching up to do, Haven. All this time that I could have got to know you, I missed out on. And I would rather not waste more time doing that when you're standing right here."

"Why would you want to get to know me? "

"Because Andino loves you," Kim said simply. "And so, I love you, too. That's how it works."

Huh.

"You seem confused still," the woman pointed out.

Haven shrugged.

What else could she do?

"I guess … this is unexpected. No one cared before. No one was around before, you know?"

"Things are never as simple or as easy as we think they are," Kim explained. "Especially not in this family with the life we live. I think you're going to find a lot of things will be different this time around, and they will adore you just as much as I do and as he does."

Haven gave the woman a look. "You don't even know me, though."

"He's told me enough to know you're amazing, and strong, and everything he wants. So, what difference does the rest make, Haven, when those are the only things that should really matter at the end of the day?"

"That's not the only thing that matters," Haven said sadly, glancing down at her hands. "There's a lot more to think about too."

"Nothing is ever easy," Kim echoed again. "You love him, though, don't you?"

"Does that matter when I also know I can't keep loving someone who keeps hurting me?"

Kim's expression didn't change at all from that soft smile she wore. "Maybe he did all that because that was the only way he could keep you. Have you ever thought about that?"

She did.

Now.

Today.

Kim waved a hand, adding, "But those are things you should talk to my son about. I don't have all those answers. About you, though … I want to know everything."

Haven laughed. "There's not much to tell. Just a normal girl, you know?"

Kim looked her over, but her gaze never felt judgmental or disapproving. "Oh, I think there's a lot to tell about you. He wouldn't love you otherwise. Andino isn't that simple—normal wouldn't interest him. That alone tells me you're something amazing."

Well, then …

How did one reply to that?

• • •

Haven saw him darkening the doorway before his mother did. Andino wasn't looking at anything else but Haven in that second. She could see the wariness in his eyes—like he thought she might bolt, but he was still going to *try* regardless.

God.

She loved him for that, too.

"Ma, care to give me a minute?" Andino asked quietly.

Kim smiled as she found Andino in the doorway. "There you are. And sure, yeah. We were just … chatting."

Andino chuckled. "I'm sure. Telling all my secrets, I imagine."

Giving Haven a wink, Kim stood from the chair and smoothed down the skirt of her dress. She walked across the room, and stopped alongside her son in the doorway. Her hand came up to pat his cheek with an affectionate touch.

"I was most certainly *not* telling your secrets, thank you," Kim said, "and I definitely didn't tell her about the little whale stuffy you kept until you were twelve."

Andino groaned. "*Ma.*"

Kim laughed, and patted his cheek again. "Whoops. I'll see you later."

It was only once Kim was gone that Andino finally turned to Haven again. She couldn't even hide the smile that was stretching her cheeks wide because that was, by far, one of the cutest things she had ever seen.

"I'm sorry," he muttered. "She …"

"Loves you beyond words," Haven said. "She really does."

Andino settled on a nod. "Maybe too much? That's kind of the thing with Italian mothers. They love their boys entirely too much."

"I don't know … I think you love her just as much."

"That's fair." He shoved his hands in his pockets, and leaned against the doorjamb. "You can go, by the way. If you want to, I can call a car for you right now to take you wherever you want to go. That's your call, Haven."

She stood from the chair she'd been sitting in as Kim regaled her with stories of Andino, and his family. "Is that what *you* want?"

Andino gave her a look that heated her up, and yet turned her into stone at the same fucking time. So intense, like fire slipping over her skin and promising love and sin and *forever*. It was all in his eyes. It had always been in his eyes when she cared to look, she thought.

"You know what I want," he said. "You have always known, Haven."

"But is it what you want right now?"

"I want you to stay. I want to take you down the hall, and feed you the best food you're ever going to taste because my aunts and mother helped my grandmother make it. I want you to laugh when they tell you stories about me, and I want them to know you like I do. Because how can they not absolutely love you once they know who you are? That's what I want."

"So, after that, then," Haven whispered, inching closer to him with every word, "what happens?"

Even as she came closer, he remained still. Like he was letting her do what she needed or wanted to do. He wasn't trying to influence her, and she appreciated that. The problem was—this man never needed to do anything to influence her. He just needed to *be*. That was the kind of hold Andino Marcello had on Haven's heart and soul.

Why ignore it?

Why pretend like it didn't exist?

That was impossible.

"What happens if you stay after dinner?" he asked.

She was only a few inches away, now. Less than a foot. If she leaned in close, she would be able to kiss him.

She wanted to.

Badly.

Haven waited …

Andino's green eyes lifted to meet hers, and he smiled in *that* way. The way that made her heart skip beats, and her stomach flip. Like she was the only thing in the world that he cared to see for the rest of his life. She didn't know how he managed to do that.

"If you stay," he murmured, "what happens is that I get to spend the rest of my life explaining why I did what I did, and showing you every single day how much I love you. That you are the first thing I think about in the morning when I open my eyes, and the last thing to grace my mind before I fall asleep. You are in my *dreams*. My fucking blood. There's no getting you out now. I see you everywhere, Haven. Even when you're not here, you're all around me."

Why did she like that so much?

Haven glanced away. "You almost got married today."

"It was never going to happen."

"*Still—*"

"Still nothing," he interrupted softly, finally moving away from the doorway to close the distance between them. Before Haven even understood what had happened, he was right there in front of her, and his lips were seeking hers. The kiss was gentle at first—a soft *hello*, and a gentle *I missed you*. A kiss like he'd never given her before. And yet, it still burned her all over, and turned her world upside down. "I'm sorry that I'm such a selfish fuck, Haven. I'm sorry that I was willing to hurt you, and whoever else I needed to, so that I could keep you. But I'm not sorry that I got what I wanted because that means I get *you*."

His words whispered against her lips like their own soft kiss.

She shivered even as he kissed her again, and drifted the tips of his fingers over her cheeks and jaw. The sliver of a tear escaped the corner of her eye, but he was quick to wipe it away like it hadn't even existed in the first place.

"Is that what they meant?" Haven asked, meeting his gaze. "At the church—when people were talking about what was going to happen now. When they said what you did meant *war?* Is that what it means? Keeping me means war?"

Andino's hands cupped under her jaw, and he tipped her head back, so he could stare into her eyes. "There's a little more to it; more people and reasons than just this ... but it's a big part of it, yes."

"I don't think I'm worth that."

"You're worth the moon and the stars to me, Haven. I would burn this city down if that's what it would take to have you. Don't *ever* underestimate what I am willing to do to make sure you're right where you belong."

"And where is that?"

She knew.

She still wanted him to say it.

"With me. You belong with me."

This man was something else, and Haven didn't know what to do about it. A man so willing to draw blood, and strike out first simply because he could, and he knew what he wanted. That thing just happened to be her. She could see the truth reflecting back in his eyes—nothing and no one was ever going to be worth what she was to him. No one would ever draw his fury and violence out like she could.

May their God save the soul who thought to take Haven from Andino.

May their God have mercy.

This man would have none.

Haven knew that *absolutely*.

"You terrify me, Andino."

He grinned. "Why is that?"

"Because you're never going to let me go."

"But do you want me to?"

Her answer came easy.

So sure.

Whispered, too.

"No, I don't want you to ever let me go."

• • •

Haven could *feel* Andino's eyes on her from down the table. He'd moved from her side to have a conversation with one of his cousin's boyfriends—or husband? Haven wasn't sure if Catherine was married to the man they called Cross, or not. There were *so many* Marcellos, and she was having a hard time keeping up with who was who, and who was married to who or just with so and so.

She loved it.

She did.

But even as she talked along with Catrina—Andino's aunt, and Dante's wife—she could still feel Andino watching her. He'd long since ended the conversation with Cross, but he hadn't come back to join her at the other end of the table.

"I'm sure your mom was looking forward to seeing you, then," Catrina said. "Too bad you missed that flight ... Dante?"

"Hmm, yes, *bella*?"

"Did you know that Haven's mother is sick?"

Dante's gaze turned on her, and then down the table to where his own mother was sitting beside her husband next to the only Irish girl at the table—next to Haven, although she wasn't as Irish as Gabbie Marcello. The girl was married to another one of Andino's cousins. Haven only remembered who she was married to because of the fact she was so vibrantly different from the rest of the Marcellos.

"I did not know that," Dante said, glancing back at Haven. "I'm sorry."

This man—like a lot of the others sitting at the table—was a whole other kind of mystery to Haven. She didn't know what to make of him, and more often than not, when he stared at her ... she wondered if he was trying to figure out her secrets, or just size her up because he could.

He was polite.

Nice.

He was not the same arrogant man who cornered her in her club months ago, and pissed her off without barely trying at all. He was welcoming, and even comfortable to talk to. Yet, at the same time, she didn't know what to make of him.

"Her cancer came back," Haven explained.

"*Merda*," Dante murmured.

"No cussing at the table, Dante!"

Catrina gave Haven a sly grin as Dante shot his mother an apologetic look down the table.

"*Le mie scuse, Ma*," he said, and then when his mother's gaze was turning away he added under his breath to his wife, "She doesn't miss a fucking *click*."

"You know better than to try," Catrina replied, laughing.

Haven smiled.

She couldn't help it.

Dante was quick to go back to their first conversation. "What was that I heard about a missed flight, then?"

"It's nothing."

Catrina shook her head. "*Not* nothing. She was supposed to fly back to Florida this evening ... to stay with her parents." The red-headed woman shrugged one shoulder, and nodded in Andino's direction, adding, "I think that's changed for reasons ... right?"

Haven sighed. "It's a work in progress."

The woman nodded. "It's changed, then."

Dante chuckled at the way Catrina didn't even act like Haven had given a non-answer. His expression softened as he glanced at Haven again. "They must be angry—"

"They're not, actually. They just want me to be happy."

The man looked her over in a whole new way, then, before his daughter down the table caught his attention for a brief moment. "Don't we all? I'm sure they'd still like to see you, though. Especially now."

"I'll figure something out. See if I can get the tickets changed over, or I'll just grab a new flight."

"No need," Dante said quickly. "Tomorrow, there'll be a private jet waiting for you to use as much as you want over the next several months, so you can see your mother as often as you please. I'm sure that would make her smile. And she'll need that with all the treatments, won't she?"

Haven *blinked*. "What?"

Dante smiled slowly. "You heard me, I'm sure."

She had, but still ...

"You don't need to—"

"Do you think Andino won't provide you with the exact same thing? Trust that it's already in his plans, and I have simply saved him money and time as I am the one who owns the jet in this family."

"First of all," Catrina said, "that is *my* jet."

The man leaned over, and kissed the woman on the top of her head. "Yes, Cat, it is your jet. Retract the claws, now."

Catrina smiled, pleased, and then turned on Haven. "But yes, you can take it as often and as much as you would like. Consider it ... a welcoming present."

"A welcoming present," she echoed.

"That's what I said."

"That's an expensive way to welcome someone."

Dante laughed, and gestured at the chandelier hanging over the table. It was the size of a small car, for fuck's sake. Haven hadn't gotten to see very much of the mansion since she arrived, but what she had seen was enough to tell her that the Marcellos were vastly wealthy.

"I think we're financially okay to let you use the jet," Dante said.

"But you don't have to."

"Have to and should are not the same things," he returned, "and if it were my mother, I would move heaven and hell to make sure she was comfortable and happy. Which would absolutely mean having her children there." The man gave her another serious look, adding, "No thanks needed, please."

Haven opened her mouth to do just that anyway—she had the distinct feeling that arguing with Dante was going to get her nowhere fast—but someone else called her name. This time, it was a familiar face.

Catherine, Andino's cousin.

"You want a tour of the place?" Catherine asked.

"Yes, let's do that," the girl next to her said.

Cella, maybe?

There were *a lot* of Marcellos.

Haven looked to Andino, and already found him staring back at her. Of course. He'd not once looked away, and her whole body knew it.

"Have fun," he said, smiling lazily. "I'll find you."

There was something sinful in the way he said that. Something that promised fun and wickedness. It had been far too long since she got a taste of sin from this man.

Haven didn't get to think on it for long.

The women pulled her up from the table, and were already talking about the mansion before Haven could say goodbye. She did manage a quick glance over her shoulder, though.

Andino watched her leave, too.

NINETEEN

"Thank you."

Dante peered down the table at Andino, and silence blanketed the room. Andino was acutely away of the eyes of their remaining family members turning on him and his uncle. He'd wondered, after the things he did and the shit he said in the office earlier, how this night would shake out for Haven.

But he especially wondered about his uncle, and how Dante might treat her. Oh, sure, he expected his uncle to be nothing less than respectful. That was just who the Marcellos were. That didn't mean Dante would actually make an effort to ensure Haven was comfortable, and *entirely* welcomed into their folds.

That had been a toss up.

Dante surprised him.

"For what, *nipote*?" Dante asked.

"What you just did for her. She didn't want to accept it; she isn't the type. You didn't have to do that at all, so yes, thank you."

Dante lifted one shoulder, and reached for his glass of cognac. "Do make sure you are on quite a few of those trips with her. I am sure her parents would like to meet the man who has effectively changed all of her plans, huh?"

Smooth.

Andino chuckled. "I planned on it."

"Good."

Dante's attention was taken away when Catrina leaned closer to her husband to whisper something in his ear. He nodded, and kissed her cheek before she stood from the table and excused herself from the room.

Gio came to sit beside Andino, smiling in that way of his. So fucking cocky—even at his age—and proud. "She did okay, though, didn't she?"

"Who, Haven?"

"Who else, son?"

Andino smirked. "She did okay with everybody, yeah."

To say the least.

The Marcellos could be overwhelming. They were not, by any fucking means, a small family. Unless someone grew up under everyone's feet, it was ridiculously easy to get confused about just who everyone was.

Haven, on the other hand, barely acted like it fazed her at all. If she had been the least bit confused or overwhelmed, she didn't show it. And

Andino had been watching just in case she needed him to step in and save her from something awkward. She hadn't needed him to do that at all, clearly.

But ...

Well, he had enjoyed watching her. A little too much maybe. The woman could dominate a room when she was in it, and she probably didn't even realize she was doing exactly that. Her laughter drew attention, and smiles. When she talked, people turned to listen even if she wasn't talking directly to them.

It was ... enthralling. Sure, that seemed like a good enough word. After all, she'd enthralled him from the very beginning.

Andino loved watching Haven. He planned on doing exactly that for the rest of his fucking life. Nothing less would be acceptable.

"My wife adores her," Dante said, bringing Andino's attention to the table. "*Loves* her already."

Andino raised a brow in question.

Dante chuckled at the sight. "I can tell, if you were wondering. You know your aunt, Andi. She doesn't even *try* to pretend when she could do without a person."

That was true.

Catrina was just about the only Marcello in their family that did not subscribe to the normal politeness of society like the rest of them did when it came to new people. She could be incredibly cold, and intimidating. Especially to other women.

And yet, she hadn't been like that to Haven at all.

It was also not lost on Andino that ... in a way ... Haven would be the woman taking over Catrina's position in their family. Eventually.

Sure, his aunt had her own thing as a successful Queen Pin sitting alongside her equally dangerous husband. But she was also—next to his grandmother—the matriarch of the Marcellos as the boss's wife.

Dante smiled at Andino's sudden quietness. "I suggest you allow my wife to spend as much time as she possibly can with Haven. It will make that transition easier, believe me. Haven may be naturally able to handle a room, but that doesn't mean she wouldn't benefit from having an influence, if you get my drift."

He'd never thought of that before. All over again, he found a great need to be grateful for the way his uncle was making a conscious effort to do whatever he needed in order for Haven to be comfortable and welcomed.

Even after all he'd done ...

"I'm a bit of a shit, aren't I?" Andino asked.

Beside him, his father laughed. As did the rest of the people at the table. He was more curious about the amused smile his uncle wore.

"You are *you*, Andino," Dante replied, "and I no longer care to make you into someone else. Why should I? You're doing fine being exactly who and what you are, Andino. Even if you are a bit of a shit."

• • •

"Oh, my God, you're *awful*."

"But you love it."

Andino pushed Haven back on the bed in one of the *many* spare bedrooms in this particular wing of the mansion. The skirt of her dress was shoved up over her hips, and he caught sight of pale lace between the heaven that was her thighs. He couldn't help but lean in closer to get a taste of her pussy and that lace at the same time. She was tart, and hot, and *sweet*. It made his mouth water with the need for more. She laughed as he pulled back just enough to yank those damn panties down her legs.

"Pretty sure this was not supposed to be a part of the tour!"

"But do you want me to stop?"

Haven tensed on the bed, whispering, "Please don't."

He chuckled, and went back to his task. Nothing pleased him more.

This hadn't been a part of the tour, but when he went looking for her and realized that he had a chance ... Andino took it. All it required was a look at his cousins, and the women scattered to leave him alone with Haven.

A minute later, and he had her on a bed.

Perfect.

No one was going to come looking for them. And even if they did, they safely had a while before they would be found. Andino was going to make good use of that time. He had a lot of missing days to make up for.

"*Fuck*," Haven whined. "*Andino.*"

Her back arched high off the bed when he finally got his mouth on her bare pussy. She was waxed again—smooth under his lips and tongue. It allowed him to taste the flavor of her arousal but so much more, too. The salt on her skin, and the way her blood rushed to the surface when he sucked her sweet little clit between his lips hard. As much as he wanted to keep his attention focused on the throbbing bud, he moved down to get another good taste of her.

Her hands thrusted into his hair, and threaded along the strands. He didn't even mind the sting of her fingernails scraping along his scalp. That only made him harder. And as it was, his dick was painfully fucking hard and trying to punch a hole through his goddamn jeans.

Just to get some relief, he pumped his hips against the curve of her leg while he took his time enjoying the spread between her thighs. A pretty pink pussy, and all its offerings.

Hot.

Wet.

So ready.

"Yes … God, yes, eat that pussy."

He loved her like this.

Wild, unbidden, and so fucking wanton.

He loved the way she looked underneath him. All the colorful art on her thighs gleaming from her perspiration, and dampness. He'd messed up those curls of hers, but who fucking cared?

She looked good anyway.

Haven came hard, and *fast*. Shaking all over, and heating up again. He was shoving his pants down before she'd even stopped calling his name, and he kissed a path from her pussy up to her throat as she helped him remove that dress.

It only took a shift of her body with his, and one of his arms grabbing her around the waist to pull her closer, and he was thrusting inside her cunt. The place he wanted to be the very most.

It'd been *way too long*.

"Fuck, yeah," he grunted against her throat. Haven's legs wrapped around him like a vise—tight, and unwilling to let him go. It kept his cock so goddamn deep in her that he couldn't breath. She squeezed him like a glove—all those soft, wet muscles inside her pussy driving him wild with each aftershock of her orgasm. He kissed her neck, taking a taste of her skin there, too. And then her mouth. "Fucking give it to me—give it all to me, Haven."

He shifted back on the bed, and took her with him before threading his fingers through her soft hair. Sitting up with his legs flat to the mattress, and hers wrapped around him, all she could do was rock her hips back and forth to get what she wanted from him.

It was still delirious.

Still *amazing*.

"Missed you," she whispered, her head falling back as he kissed her chin and throat. "God, I missed you."

"*Love you.*"

"So much, Andino."

"Would you do this all over again?" she asked. "If it meant you got the same thing in the end, or would you do it differently? Would you choose another trail? Make Snaps walk his old route? What would you do?"

"You already know the answer to that, Haven."

Her blue eyes darkened. "Yeah, I guess I do."

He didn't know how long they stayed like that. Soft loving, and relearning. Gentle touches, and whispered kisses.

It wasn't fucking.

It was something else entirely.

And then her hand came up to press against his chest. She pushed him back on the bed, and rode him until she came a second time—wild and shaking all over again. She climbed off him just long enough to get on her knees, and suck him clean. And then she bent over the bed, and let him gag her with his tie as he fucked her hard enough to make her throat raw from screaming his name into the silk.

He loved this woman.

He loved her *crazy*.

And she was right.

Andino would do this all over again. He'd lie, and hurt, and ruin everything for everyone if it meant this moment right here was the same.

He'd do it again.

And he regretted nothing.

· · ·

Siena slipped into the backseat of the car with a hat pulled down over her eyes, and her head down. She didn't even notice the woman sitting in the front seat until Andino cleared his throat. Siena's eyes widened, and he had to laugh.

"Oh, Haven."

Haven beamed. "Sorry to crash your party."

Siena's gaze drifted between Haven and Andino. "It's okay."

"Ready to see John?"

The woman in the backseat relaxed instantly. "Beyond ready."

Andino nodded his head in Haven's direction. "Do you think he'll mind that I brought someone else along to meet him?"

Siena laughed. "Well …"

Haven shot him a worried look. Andino grinned, and gave her a wink to calm her down. She knew how important John was to him, and the only thing he really wanted now was for the last person in his family who hadn't gotten the chance to actually meet this woman properly to do exactly that.

And hopefully, adore her, too.

Haven deserved nothing less.

"I think he'll be okay," Siena said. "But surprises, you know."

Andino made a noise in the back of his throat. "Yeah, I know. Any good news for me?"

Siena met his gaze in the rearview. He wasn't sure if she would be willing to talk about her brothers, and the fact she was feeding Andino information about the Calabrese family, so they could move forward with ending them for good with Haven sitting right there or not. He wouldn't mind either way. He'd understand if she didn't.

The woman surprised him. All the women in his life seemed to enjoy doing that for some fucking reason. He was getting used to it now.

"Kev called a meeting with the Capos last night," she said, "and it looks like the streets are going to get very tense again."

Andino's jaw ticked, but Haven's hand coming up to stroke his cheek calmed him instantly. The tension was still there, and so was his irritation about the fucking Calabrese, but it wasn't nearly as bad.

He just needed her to help.

That was all.

"How tense?" Andino asked.

"They're planning on starting to remove any Marcello presence in their territory, to begin with. They'll go from there, and see how the Marcellos answer back."

Andino would have to give his Brooklyn Capo a heads up on that, then.

"So, basically they're going to provoke us into violence," Haven murmured.

Andino couldn't help but look over at his girl, and smile. Even if what she said was nothing to smile about, he couldn't fucking help it.

"What?" she asked.

"You said us."

Because she was.

His.

One of them.

It still stunned him sometimes. Oh, sure, he knew he still had a lot to make up for yet. But fuck him, because he was willing to do all that for her. He was going to put in all the work. Whatever she needed from him, he was there to do.

He was hers.

Haven rolled her pretty blue eyes like he was being silly. "Was I wrong, though? That's what they're doing, right?"

"No, you were right. That's exactly what they're going to do."

Siena made a noise in the backseat. "Because they think whatever happens then will be justified to other families."

"Yes," Andino agreed.

"Have you told John, yet?"

Andino looked in the rearview mirror again. "Told him what?"

"Your plans for him—to take over the Calabrese side of things. Have you told him that?"

He tensed in the seat, but Haven's hand was quick to find his thigh, and squeeze. Life was about to change in a lot of ways for all of them. All because he had decided to start the ball rolling on something, and the damn thing wasn't going to stop anytime soon.

That was fine.

He was ready.

A boss had to be.

"I haven't told him, and no one is going to mention it to him until the time is right," Andino said pointedly.

Siena nodded. "Something like that could really upset his—"

"I can't hold his hand and watch his back forever, Siena. That's not my job now. Remember?"

The woman glanced down. "I know. It's mine."

"Yeah, so let's worry about that later."

Because later was coming all too soon …

• • •

"Just give me a second with him first?" Andino asked.

Siena nodded, but he could see in her eyes that *she* wanted to be the one to greet John first. The woman really did love his cousin, and after this was all said and done, Andino was going to make damn sure Siena and John were able to be with each other.

It was what they deserved.

"This place is beautiful," Haven said.

Andino smiled over his shoulder at her. "Doesn't look like a psychiatric ward, huh?"

"Not at all."

"Good, it shouldn't," Andino said. "People who struggle with mental health don't need to feel like they're being shut off from the rest of society like there's something wrong with them when they need a chance to reset, and figure shit out."

Haven nodded. "You're right."

He would have continued that conversation, but something else caught his eye. John coming out of the entrance of Clearview Oaks Facility. Despite being two steps ahead of Siena and Haven, John's gaze went to the woman behind Andino first even as he approached his cousin.

Not surprising.

Siena wasn't the only one who was ensnared in this thing they called love, apparently. Funny how that worked.

"John, my man," Andino said, opening his arms to embrace his cousin. "You're looking good."

John hugged him back with a firm squeeze, and even patted his back, but his cousin was still a little distracted in starting at someone else.

"You could say hi, you know," Andino joked. "And I brought Haven along to meet you properly. It's about time you meet the woman I plan on marrying."

John blinked, and glanced at his cousin. "What?"

Andino laughed—not even the slightest put off by John's distraction. Sure, he hadn't seen John in far too long, but he would wait a little longer for a conversation as long as John was happy. And right then ... he looked happier than ever.

"Shit, you didn't hear a word I just said, huh?" Andino asked.

John glanced at Siena again. "Not really, no. Sorry, man."

Andino slapped John lightly on the cheek and chuckled. "Nah, it's okay. You've got a good reason to be off your game today. I guess they didn't fill you in on who I was bringing along to visit, or what?"

"Leonard has his odd ways," John muttered.

Still distracted as hell.

Andino found it funny.

"Sure, sure."

"It's good, though."

He knew his cousin didn't typically like surprises, but he figured this was a good one given he brought Siena along.

"Anyway," Andino said, gesturing at the woman he'd brought along for him—*Haven*. "I said, I hope you don't mind that I brought someone else to properly meet you. I mean, I know this place is supposed to be sacred for you, and all. Focusing on you, but I might not get another time to do this before you come home."

His cousin quieted as he glanced at Haven, and took her presence in for what seemed like the first time. It wasn't like John could *miss* Haven, but you know ... Siena was there.

"You don't mind, do you?" Andino asked again.

John smiled, and shook his head. "No, man. Of course, not."

"Good. I want you to meet the girl I'm going to marry, you know." Andino shrugged, and shifted from foot to foot. "Properly fucking meet her, John. Not hear things about her from someone else, or see her in passing. Actually meet her *with* me. Take some time to sit down and have a real conversation with her. I talk about you all the time, and she's a little out of the loop about me and you. Kind of a big fucking deal to me, and everything."

John cocked a brow, and glanced at his cousin like he was seeing him all over again for the first time. Andino almost laughed out loud. "Seriously?"

Andino nodded. "Yeah, man."

"I thought ..." John trailed off like he was considering his words before settling on saying, "I mean, the family didn't have a high opinion of her a few months ago, and all. I thought they had made it clear she wasn't acceptable, or some shit. You kind of gave me the impression you didn't know what the hell you were doing about them, her, or the rest."

True.

Nothing John said was a lie.

Andino still had the same answer for that as he always would, now. "It's not about them."

It took his cousin a second, but John was John. He was quick to roll with the punches when it came to Andino—it's just how they were. John laughed, and clapped Andino on the shoulder before pulling him in for another one-armed hug. Andino laughed, then, too, and gave his cousin a nod.

Their silent way of chatting.

John seemed a hell of a lot more relaxed in those moments, and Andino was grateful. He knew this place was supposed to be good for John. Something to let him focus on himself, and getting to a better place. Andino wasn't supposed to bring outside stressors and problems into these grounds. He'd worried bringing Haven here might do exactly that as John really didn't know the woman, and all of that.

It seemed Andino worried for nothing.

Thankfully.

"Give me some time with Siena," John said quietly, pulling away from Andino's embrace. "It's been too long."

Andino nodded, and stepped away. "You got it, John."

John only needed to hold out his hand without saying anything for Siena to dart away from Haven's side. Once the two were face to face again, it seemed like Andino and Haven disappeared to them.

Andino didn't mind.

For now, anyway.

John and Siena headed down the walkway, and Andino moved to stand next to Haven's side. Wrapping an arm tight around her waist, he pulled his girl in close, and kissed the top of her head. She tipped her head back, and smiled sweetly up at him.

"We'll have to give them some time," Andino said. "Or he'll never forgive me."

Haven shrugged. "That's okay. It sucks when you love someone, but can't be with them. I don't blame them for wanting to have five minutes."

Andino smiled. "Yeah, me either."

Turning her around in his arms, Andino dropped a quick kiss to Haven's grinning lips. She used the pad of her thumb to wipe away the small lipstick stain left behind on his lips. Not that he gave a damn about it.

"And I love you," he told her. "Entirely, Haven. More than anything in my life. I love *you*. I will spend the rest of my life telling you that as often as you will allow me to. I hope you know that."

Because someone had almost made sure he wouldn't be able to tell her. So, Andino was going to make damn sure she never questioned how he felt about her, and *them*. He was never going to let her feel anything less than the most important thing in his life from this point forward.

No matter what.

Her gaze softened. "Good because I expect it."

"*Demand it*, woman."

She smiled slyly. "Noted. What was that you said to John, anyway? He kind of looked at me funny."

Andino chuckled. "Did he?"

"I mean … a little."

"I think I shocked him a bit, that's all."

"By bringing me here, you mean?"

"No," Andino murmured, slipping a hand into his pocket to bring out an item he'd been keeping hidden. Haven glanced down between them just as he started to lower down on one knee, and he offered the velvet box in his hand like a prize for her to take. "Because I told him that I wanted him to meet the woman I intend to marry."

Haven blinked, and her pretty pink lips fell open as she whispered, "Oh."

"I know it's a strange time, and maybe this isn't the best place. That's the thing, though—I don't give a damn about any of that. The only thing I care about is you. Look at all the things I did just to have you, and keep you, Haven. I'm so tired of waiting. I don't want to wait to do what I should have done from the start."

"And what is that?" she asked.

Andino smiled crookedly. "Vow to love you … forever. To always put you first, and to make sure you never feel like an afterthought in my life. How could you be an afterthought when you're the first thing on my mind in the morning, and the last thing at night? I will give you the world if you ask me for it, I promise. I will give you everything … if you just marry me."

She pressed her lips together, and glanced away. Andino didn't miss the wetness clouding her eyes, though, even if she did try to hide the tears. "And you'll keep those vows?"

"Until you no longer want me to."

"I will always want you to, Andino."

"Say yes," he murmured.

Haven looked back at him, but he was already standing because he knew her answer before it could slip from her lips. How could she refuse him—she loved him. Every horrible, good, and gray part of him that scared her, loved her, and wanted her forever.

Andino had hurt her, and he'd done things that he knew he would spend the rest of his life making up for. He was willing to do that, though. He was willing to grovel every morning, and crawl through broken glass just to please this woman as long as she was waiting there at the end for him, and she still wanted him.

He would do all of that for her.

She'd brought out the very worst and the utter best of who he was, who he could be, and who he would be. He would not be half the man he could be in ten years if this woman was not standing by his side.

And she knew all of this.

All those parts of him …

They were hers.

Softly, she whispered, "Yes."

EPILOGUE

"Let him have his moment, okay?"

Andino glanced over at her as they came to a stop at the front door of a quaint Florida beach house. "Pardon?"

"My dad," she said, laughing a bit. "Just … he might try to size you up, or something. Let him have his moment. I know he won't actually scare you, but would it hurt to let him think it did?"

He raised a brow at her, and Haven wanted to laugh at the amusement dancing in his eyes. "But this does scare me. I don't have to fucking *pretend*."

That was not the reply she had been expecting from him.

"Why would this scare you?"

"Meeting your parents at the same time we're going to tell them we're getting married in a couple of weeks?" Andino made an anxious noise, and shoved his hands in his pockets. "Also, if you missed the memo, I didn't have relationships. I don't know how to do the whole *meet the parents* thing, Haven."

"Awe," she cooed, reaching up to pat his cheek. His facial hair tickled her fingertips. He was due for a shave, but she loved the feeling of it between her thighs first thing in the morning. He knew it, too, so he'd been holding off. "Poor you."

"Stop that," he murmured.

"But it's *cute*."

"Keep doing that, Haven, and I will tan your ass later."

She winked. "Promise?"

Andino groaned, and stared up at the sky. "Stop it, woman. I don't need a fucking hard on when—"

"Are you two just going to eye fuck each other out on the porch, or come inside?"

Haven laughed at the way the color drained from Andino's face at the male voice filtering out from the opened window. Apparently, her parents had been listening the whole time if the laughter coming from inside the house was any indication.

"Jesus Christ," Andino mumbled under his breath.

A wild, anxious gleam lit up his gaze as it turned on her. She could tell he was silently asking her what the fuck to do, but she didn't know what to do for him. Her parents were pretty laid back, all things considered.

And still, even after all their years, very much in love.

Haven often stayed in hotels when she visited simply *because* of how in love her parents still were. She'd gotten woken up by their antics one too many times over the years, and as an adult, she just didn't need to be hearing it anymore.

"Well?" her father called again. "I hear we have something to talk about. I did just hear marriage, didn't I?"

"Neil! Stop it," Mae hissed. "I would like to talk to them before you run them off."

"I'm not gonna run them off, woman."

"Keep thinking that."

Andino was still looking at her in that way.

Haven only laughed, and shrugged. "Don't worry. It's going to be great."

How could it not be?

After all, she loved him. And so, they would love him, too.

The front door swung open, and Haven's father loomed in the doorway. *Loomed* was an appropriate word considering her Irish and German father stood at eye level with Andino, and in size, filled up the whole doorway. Much like Andino did standing on the other side.

"Andino, is it?" Neil asked, cocking a brow.

Behind her father, Mae lingered close. Her mother beamed—all tiny and sprite-like with her painting smock on, and her wild curls pulled high into a messy bun. At least this time around, the chemo wasn't taking huge chunks of her mother's beautiful strawberry blonde hair. Medical advancements were miracles, really.

"Oh, move, Neil," Mae muttered, pushing her much larger husband out of the way. Her mother bounced out the doorway, and gave her daughter a hug first before doing the exact same thing to a still quiet Andino. Mae pulled back, and gave him a look. "You are handsome."

Haven grinned.

Andino *blushed*, and cleared his throat. "Thank you."

"He is, isn't he?" Her mother glanced back at her husband. "Isn't he?"

"Mae," Neil started to say, "I am not going to—"

"What, he is!" Mae smiled widely again. "I hope you like steak."

"Love it," Andino said.

"Good. You can help Neil cook. I paint—I don't cook."

Andino's laughter filled the front yard. "I can absolutely do that."

Her mother gave Haven a look. "And he cooks, too. I approve."

Neil only laughed.

Because really, what else could they do?

Yeah, it was going to be great.

It couldn't be anything less.

• • •

The movement around Haven's still form seemed chaotic, and while she knew this was a *big* day ... these women, and even her, had every single reason to rush, all she could do in that moment was stand there and *watch*.

How long had she wondered ...

How often had she asked ...

Haven never thought—after everything that happened—this day would be possible for her and Andino.

Their *wedding* day.

So, maybe her still daze could be excused because this was all a little surreal for her. Oh, she was happy. *So happy*. She wanted Andino more than anything else in her life—hadn't she proven that time and time again?

It was only Andino's mother stepping in Haven's line of vision that broke her daydreaming. Kim wore a soft smile—as proud of a mother as she could be. The woman really was sweet, and wonderful.

All the Marcellos were, really.

They were just ... protective.

Careful.

A little too cautious about those they allowed inside their family, and what the consequences might be when they did allow someone as close as Haven now was with them. And she understood, too.

They had something to keep safe.

This life.

Their love.

All of it.

She didn't blame them for the hesitance they might have felt about her, or the warnings they'd repeated again and again. None of it had been *personal* ... not when business and family was on the line, too.

Haven knew this now because she was one of them.

Or she would be.

Soon.

And once that little fact had become officially decided—although Andino hadn't really given anyone a choice in the way he handled his business to get what he wanted—the rest of the Marcellos were quick to do what they needed to do for Haven. *Anything and everything*—she was pretty sure if she asked, they would try to give her the world.

She had a family.

A *beautiful* family.

She also had a second one, now.

"Did you decide?" Kim asked. "Birdcage, or traditional for the veil? Jordyn brought both."

Across the room, the woman in question held up both options for Haven to decide.

"What do you think?" Haven asked. "I like both."

"If we were in a church," Kim said, glancing over her shoulder at her sister-in-law, "then I would say traditional. But we're not in church, and the birdcage *would* fit your dress better. But that's my opinion. This is your day. And you can have whatever in the hell you want."

"Yes, she can," Catrina called as she slipped between the rooms. "And you should choose the birdcage!"

Haven laughed. "Birdcage, then."

Kim nodded. "Sounds good. We should start getting you ready beyond …" Her future mother-in-law waved a finger at Haven. "This. You can't walk down the aisle in a robe."

True.

Although, Haven didn't think Andino would care *how* she came down the aisle to meet him, or what she looked like as long as she did it. He would be there to meet her at the end, of that, she had no doubt.

There was no need for cold feet.

Not today.

"Let me grab your dress," Kim said.

"Thanks," Haven replied, smiling.

At least her makeup and hair was done—one less thing to worry about. A quick check of the clock on the bedroom wall told her they were getting dangerously close to the time the wedding was supposed to start.

From the moment she woke up that morning in the Marcello mansion, no one stopped moving. That's sort of what happened when you only had a month to plan a wedding, and there was a mafia war raging on the streets outside of their safe homes. Everything had to be planned down to the finest of details—nothing could be left to chance.

Even their safety—given how violent and dangerous the streets were right now with the Calabrese family on their rampage—was taken into account every step of the way for this day. In fact, while they were safe inside the Marcello mansion, and would be until the dinner and reception later that night in a Manhattan hotel, there was an enforcer posted at the doorway of Haven's room.

None of the women questioned his presence. He barely said a thing, and they didn't even acknowledge him. Not that he seemed to mind—he was there to do a job, and very little else.

He was not the first guard she noticed today.

Or the second.

Apparently, there was a small army of them.

Nothing left to chance.

"Has anyone heard from my mom or dad?" Haven asked.

Stillness and silence responded back to Haven's question. The wedding had been last minute, and despite her mother's cancer recurring, her father *promised* to be there. His flight should have left the night before. An early morning flight that would allow him to get in early. Her mother couldn't come—fucking *chemo*—but she promised to take lots of pictures for her, and call her right after the ceremony.

Her parents barely batted an eye about the fact she was marrying a man they only met on a couple of occasions when Andino was able to fly down to Florida with her. They never questioned her beyond, *are you happy?* And when she said yes, they were all too willing to congratulate her.

It's why she loved her parents.

She wanted them here.

"I can grab your phone," Catherine, Andino's cousin, said, "and you could call your dad?"

"Thanks, that'd be great."

Catherine quickly left the room while Jordyn closed the door right after. With a bit of privacy from the guard, it allowed Haven to slip into her dress when Kim pulled the mermaid-style, lace-covered gown from the thick garment bag. How she had managed to find a dress this beautiful with it's detailed bodice and elbow-length, sheer sleeves in such a short amount of time ... never mind the fact it fit her like a glove *without* any tailoring ... she would never know.

Luck, probably.

Or the universe was giving her another sign.

This day was meant to happen. Andino had always meant to be *hers*. Haven couldn't wait to keep him. *Forever.*

Kim was just finishing doing up the last of the small buttons on the back of Haven's dress when Catherine entered the room again. She knew just by the look on the woman's face that ... something was up.

"What is it?" Haven asked.

Catherine flashed Haven's phone. "There's a couple missed calls from your dad. Voicemails, too."

Of course.

Because her dad still didn't understand the concept of *texting*. Hated it, really. It amused Haven to no end, but not today.

"Let me see," she said, holding her hand out.

Catherine was quick to hand the phone over. Haven wasted no time unlocking the screen, and dialing the voicemail. She listened to her father explain that he needed her to call him as soon as she possibly could.

Haven's heart sunk a little lower.

She should have kept her phone on her—someone else took it away because *no distractions*. This day was supposed to be for her and Andino, and nothing else mattered.

Her father picked up on the second ring with an instant, "I am so sorry, baby."

Haven blinked, aware that everyone in the room was watching her all of the sudden. She didn't mind attention, usually, but she had a feeling whatever her father was apologizing for wasn't going to leave her very *happy*.

"For what?" Haven asked.

In the background of the call, she could hear muffled voices complaining, and getting louder with every passing second.

"The plane had an engine issue as we were taxing out to the runway," her father explained. "They couldn't get another one on standby. I won't be taking off for another hour or more. I'm not going to—"

"Make it in time," Haven whispered.

She wasn't really the kind of woman who cried, and yet, the sharp realization that *neither* of her parents would be there on her wedding day was the heaviest weight sitting on her chest all of the sudden. She felt the telltale prickle behind her eyes that said tears were threatening to fall.

She didn't want her father to know that, though.

"I'll be there in time for the dinner, at least," he said. "I am sorry. I wanted to be there. Your mom, too."

"I know, Daddy. It's okay."

"It's *not*," he muttered thickly. "I'm supposed to walk you down the aisle. That's what father's do. That's what I *wanted* to do, Haven. You only get married once."

She laughed, but it sounded weak. "Maybe we'll do this again, then, in a few years just so you can walk me down the aisle."

"I didn't mean—"

"I know. Please don't feel bad, okay?"

"All right. Still will, though."

No doubt.

Across from her, Kim mouthed, "Get the new flight time."

Haven repeated the question to her father, and once he rattled off the approximate time, she gave it to Kim. She turned her back then to the other women so that she could privately say goodbye to her father. She still had to finish getting ready, after all. This day was going to go forward whether he was there or not, even though she *wanted* him there so badly.

"I'll see you tonight, Daddy," Haven said. "I love you."

"Love you, too. Try to call your mom."

"I will."

Haven hung up the phone, but kept her head lowered even as she turned to face the room again. She really just needed a second or two in order to get her sadness under control. This was still her wedding day.

"I'm sorry," Kim murmured.

Haven shook her head. "Things happen, right?"

It wasn't like they could control everything.

No matter how powerful they were.

"Yeah, but we still want someone there, too. That doesn't change no matter what."

"True. I really wanted at least one of them here. I know I could walk myself down the aisle—I just *wanted* him to do it for me."

"I have an idea," Catrina said out of the blue, smiling slyly. "Give me five minutes."

The red-headed woman didn't give anyone the opportunity to ask her anything before she was gone from the room. Kim and Jordyn, on the other hand, distracted Haven with putting the finishing touches on her look including another layer of lipstick, and placing the birdcage veil. Kim was just clasping the rope of diamonds—a gift from Andino's grandparents—around Haven's throat when an unexpected form graced the bedroom doorway.

Dante Marcello had an ... imposing way about him. Even on his good days when the man was in a pleasant mood, it was sometimes hard to tell. Right then, however, he smiled when Haven's gaze met his. Behind him, Catrina gave her a wink and a nod.

"Would you give us the room?" Dante asked.

Kim shot Haven a reassuring smile before she slipped out of the room with Jordyn close on her heels. Dante waited until the women were out of his sight before he stepped inside, and closed the door behind him. Haven wasn't the type to get *nervous*, really, but Dante had that effect on people.

Up until recently, he hadn't exactly been fond of her.

"First things first," Dante said, his smiling softening as he looked her over, "you look beautiful."

"Thank you."

"I'm sure I'm not the first to tell you that today, and you can rest assured I won't be the last. Second—I need to apologize."

Haven's head snapped up, and her eyes widened. "For what?"

"For not giving you a chance at first."

"Oh."

Dante chuckled under his breath. "They call me a traditionalist—my brothers, I mean. They say in our life, I am the one who is still stuck trying to keep everything as it always was, and I don't like change."

"Are they wrong?"

"Not at all."

Haven smiled; she couldn't help it. "It's okay."

"It isn't," Dante returned. "Time moves forward, and the rest of us—mostly *me*—needs to get in line. The person who comes after me can't be expected to *be* me, or do everything as I would. That's not how we continue to thrive in our life."

Andino, he meant.

Haven understood.

"And I hope you're ready, too," Dante added, "for everything that's about to change in your life. It's not easy to be this man you're staring at—it's harder to be the wife of a man like this, Haven."

She nodded. "I know."

"Do you?"

She knew enough to know she wanted it.

Wanted Andino.

"Yes. I've never been more ready."

Dante grinned. "Good. Now, I have a … well, let's call it a wedding gift, of sorts, for you."

"You didn't have—"

"I do. We all do. Your friend … Valeria Gomez."

Haven blinked. "What about her?"

"About a month ago, Andino asked me to use some of my contacts—I have the very best given how long I have been around, and who my wife is—to find your friend, or whatever information I could pull."

Why did her chest feel so tight?

Why was she scared to ask … "Did you find her?"

"We believe so," Dante murmured. "In Mexico, it seems. When she up and left from your place, did you notice anything strange? Someone following you or her? Did she mention—"

"No."

"And your place was—"

"Fine," Haven said quietly. "Nothing was out of place. A couple of her bags were gone. She left a lot of her stuff, and Maria's."

"She didn't have very much to begin with, did she?"

"More Maria."

Dante cleared his throat. "But what she had, I assume, would be important to her?"

Haven nodded. "She left her mom's necklace behind. A picture of her sister."

"And she wouldn't have left those, you think?"

"Probably not."

"I have every reason to believe Valeria was taken by force, but in such a way that it would look to *you* like she decided to take off again."

God, she didn't want to *ask*.

"By the cartel?"

"The Gomez cartel," Dante confirmed. "She's married to the son who runs the majority of the operation—Andino said you had that information."

"She never told me that, though," Haven admitted. "She never told me anything about why she ran from Mexico."

"Because she probably didn't want to be married to him."

That prickling feeling behind her eyes was back. The tears were threatening to fall again. Dante didn't miss it.

"Haven," he said gently, "we know, and so that allows us to do something now. Or call someone who can do something for your friend. This is something for another day. And we will get to it, I promise. Today, though, is all for you."

"Soon?"

"As soon as we find the right man to retrieve her safely."

What else could she say?

The only thing that felt appropriate was simply, "Thank you."

Dante waved a hand. "It's a little thing, that's all."

Haven didn't think it was so *little* ... nor would it be easy, or safe. She didn't know a lot about cartels, but what she knew was enough to tell her this wouldn't be easy at all.

For Val, though ...

Well, it might be worth it.

"Also, my wife mentioned something," Dante said, bringing Haven's attention back to him for a moment. "Your father is stuck somewhere, huh?"

"Engine problems."

Dante frowned. "I'm sorry."

"Shit happens."

"At the worst possible times."

That made her laugh. "Right?"

Because where was the lie?

"I was hoping," Dante continued, "that you might give *me* the honor of walking you down the aisle. I want to welcome you into our family, Haven, and make it very clear that this is where you belong to anyone who might be wondering where I stand. And what better way than to be the one who walks you to your future?"

Haven stared at the man, quiet and still. "Really?"

"Really. *If* you would allow me to. It would be the greatest honor for me to do this for you, Haven."

Well, then ...

"Okay," she said.

• • •

Dante peered around the grand hallway that led into the main ballroom. All the sheer tulle hanging from the ceiling only accentuated the vaulted aspect. Soft lavenders and pale pinks melted together in all the decorations.

It was beautiful.

"They really came together for this, didn't they?" he asked. "Our wives certainly know how to decorate this place."

Haven agreed. "It's something else."

"As long as you like it."

"I do."

And she was so grateful.

The music changed in the ballroom—the muffled noise filtered out beneath the cracks of the closed door. Haven took a deep breath, and relaxed. It was almost time.

Dante smiled down at her. "Ready?"

"You don't even have to ask."

"Thought I should give you one last chance to escape the Marcello craziness. It's only fair."

"Nowhere I would rather be."

Dante squeezed her hand that was tucked into his elbow. "Well, then let's get you married, Haven. By the way, your father's plane landed twenty minutes early, and with the way my man drives ... he will get here in lots of time to see you before we move to the reception."

The doors opened in front of them as relief swept through Haven. "Tell him not to drive *too* fast. My mom needs someone, too."

Dante chuckled. "Not to worry—as of tomorrow, your mother will have the very best doctors working on her case, and there won't be a single thing she has to fret over except *getting better*. And she will get better, Haven."

Haven stared straight ahead even as Dante's words filtered into her mind, and the people stood from their chairs. With a gentle tug of his arm, Dante moved them forward one slow step. She barely even realized how quickly they walked the aisle, and that she smiled the whole way.

Because once she laid eyes on Andino, nothing else really mattered. Once she saw him waiting there just like he promised ... everything else faded away.

As it should be.

Tall, dark, and handsome. Three-piece suit, as always.

Her entire life was waiting.

He was standing *right there*.

Andino had a hand out for her to take the second she was close enough to do just that. Heat shot through her palm when her skin connected with his. An electric sensation that passed through her soul, and touched her very heart. Soft, and sure, yet his grip was firm, and possessive. She answered that back by tightening her own hold on him.

"Thank you," he said to his uncle.

Dante nodded. "Always, *nipote*."

Dante left her side, then, and while the priest said something … she was too busy staring at Andino. He was looking back, too.

"I love you," she whispered.

Andino smiled. "*Ti amo. Sempre.* That's my vow to you—*forever*, Haven. I will love you forever."

She knew it was true.

This ending of theirs—this happily ever after—was not really the end. Not all endings were tied in a perfect little bow. Not everything could be easily summed up when their story was one with many roads yet to go. There was more yet to come for them.

More love.

More life.

More *everything*.

This ending was their beginning. They were just getting started, and life had so much more to offer and teach them.

And she couldn't wait to learn.

A NOTE!

Thank you so much to all the people who helped me to get this book to the end, and to everyone who cheered for Andino and Haven to get their true HEA. This book was very much about the journey, in a way, considering a great deal of my readers already knew Andino and Haven had their HEA moment—sort of—at the end of one of John's books in his duet. So yes, this was all about finding out the way they got to that point. And I hope it was a good trip for you all.

Thank you to my editor, Eli, for your hard word, as always. You make the words shine. To my cover artist, Mignon, for making the covers beautiful. To my proofreaders, Tracy, Mia, and Felicia, as well as my PA, Tori, who keeps the pages and fans engaged while I put all my energy where it needs to be the most—making the words go.

Sasha, thanks for loving these two. For all those conversations. For making me laugh. For the edits. For being wonderful. Never forget you're wonderful.

London, for being my favorite. What else needs to be said?

To the readers … you already have my words, and my love. You've got it all.

To my hubby … thanks, babe. Just, thank you.

Until next time, loves.

—BK

ABOUT THE AUTHOR

Bethany-Kris is a Canadian author, lover of much, and mother to four young sons, one cat, and three dogs. A small town in Eastern Canada where she was born and raised is where she has always called home. With her boys under her feet, a snuggling cat, barking dogs, and a spouse calling over his shoulder, she is nearly always writing something ... when she can find the time.

Find Bethany-Kris at:
www.bethanykris.com
www.bethanykris.blogspot.com
www.facebook.com/bethanykriswrites
www.twitter.com/bethanykris
www.instagram.com/bethany.kris
www.pinterest.com/bethanykris

Sign up to Bethany-Kris's New Release Newsletter here:
http://eepurl.com/bf9lzD.

OTHER BOOKS

Andino + Haven
Duty
Vow

John + Siena

Loyalty
Disgrace

Cross + Catherine

Always
Revere
Unruly
The Companion
Naz & Roz

Guzzi Duet

Unraveled, Book One
Entangled, Book Two

DeLuca Duet

Waste of Worth: Part One
Worth of Waste: Part Two

Standalone Titles

Effortless
Inflict
Cozen
Captivated
Dishonored

VOW

Donati Bloodlines

Thin Lies
Thin Lines
Thin Lives
Behind the Bloodlines
The Complete Trilogy

Filthy Marcellos

Antony
Lucian
Giovanni
Dante
Legacy
A Very Marcello Christmas
The Complete Collection

Seasons of Betrayal

Where the Sun Hides
Where the Snow Falls
Where the Wind Whispers
Seasons: The Complete Seasons of Betrayal Series

Gun Moll Trilogy

Gun Moll
Gangster Moll
Madame Moll

The Chicago War

Deathless & Divided
Reckless & Ruined
Scarless & Sacred
Breathless & Bloodstained
The Complete Series

The Russian Guns

The Arrangement
The Life
The Score
Demyan & Ana
Shattered
The Jersey Vignettes

Find more on Bethany-Kris's website at www.bethanykris.com.